This book is a work of fic
and dialog are products of
any resemblance to actua
dead, is coincidental.

Copyright © 2014 Tickety Boo Press Ltd
Cover Art by Aty S Behsam
Book Design by Gary Compton
Edited by J Scott-Marryat
Minister for Ghosts by Tim James and Gary Compton

Malevolence is the first book in *Tales From Beyond the Veil*
Ghost Story Series.

ISBN 978-0-9929077-3-0

Check out our other books at www.ticketyboopress.co.uk

Novels

Goblin Moon by Teresa Edgerton
Abendau's Child by Jo Zebedee
Oracle by Susan Boulton
Endeavour by Ralph Kern

Anthologies

Malevolence - Tales From Behind the Veil
After Midnight by Joseph Rubas
Biblia Loncrofta by Simon Marshall-Jones

MALEVOLENCE – TALES FROM BEYOND THE VEIL

INTRODUCTION

by Simon Marshall-Jones

A nthologies can be awkward beasts at the best of times, for editor and reader alike. But writing introductions for them can be even more so, especially if the person asked to write said piece finds the collection only so-so. BUT, I am glad to say that this isn't the case here, as the quality throughout *Malevolence Tales From Behind the Veil* is top-notch and consistently so. And that is testament to the fine job that J Scott-Marryatt and Gary Compton have done with this anthology and also to the writers whose stories appear in it.

Editing an anthology isn't as easy as it looks, especially if you want to wow your potential audience across the board. I know – I've edited one or two myself for my own independent publishing concern, Spectral Press. I learnt a great deal from editing them and selecting the stories: yes, personal taste does enter into it to a certain extent, but it has to be balanced with the knowledge that you are not aiming the anthology at readers with the same tastes as you possess. A production of this nature requires discernment, as genre in this instance is a broad church, as a natural consequence of which it encompasses many different instantiations and definitions of it: you can never please everyone, that's a given, but nevertheless one has to attempt to include as wide a spectrum of styles, tones, themes, and treatments as possible, without diluting the quality.

That last word, *quality*, has to be the watchword for every anthologist, or potential anthologist. In this age of digital publishing and the democratisation of technology (once reserved solely for the High Priests of Techno-Wizardry), wherein anybody who so wishes to get something published regardless of literary merit can do so, it is ever more incumbent on those who take publishing seriously to embrace the meaning and tenor of that word to the fullest. And, I am more than happy to report, Tickety Boo Press' team has discharged their duties admirably in that respect.

So, what can you, the reader, expect from this fine volume? In the opinion of this writer, a great deal more than the usual. Here we have vengeful ghosts, curses, the consequences of hubris, a sad farewell, the shades of the malign, hauntings, searches for redemption, an uncanny detective duo, kinky spirits, and descents into madness, but with pleasing twists on these themes. The lyrical, the elegiac, and the haunting turn of phrase can be found in these pages, as well as prose which beguiles as it entertains. Some will have you barrelling along on a wave of adrenaline, some will sweep you up on an emotional tidal wave, and others will have you meditating on the complexities of life (and death). But all the stories have two things in common: each one will stay with you after you put the book down, and that you will want to reread them again and again. Better yet, each tale is carefully and thoughtfully crafted because, when all is said and done, that is what writing is: a craft, to be as finely honed as the potter's skills or the woodworker's eye for creating beauty and balance with the tools at hand. Every writer in this book is a craftsman or craftswoman – let there be no doubt about that.

Light the fire in the grate, put a candle on the table by your favourite armchair, then pour yourself a glass of wine or port, sit down and settle until comfortable, and finally open the book to let this selection of stories send shivers running deliciously up and down the spine.

Enjoy!

MINISTER FOR GHOSTS

My name is Isambard Roxton-Smythe and sadly I have to report that I am speaking to you from beyond the veil. Please do not be frightened or feel sorry for me, I am truly having a wonderful time, continuing my work investigating the supernatural.

My passing into this world was quick and unexpected. I was enjoying afternoon tea with some delightful homemade scones covered with generous helpings of strawberry jam, when a rather annoying interruption to my particularly pleasant afternoon occurred.

I died.

I had been very lucky on the Earth plane and had enjoyed a long and wonderful life as an exorcist working for the Church. On my retirement I was approached by Queen Victoria and asked to head her newly-formed Ghost Ministry.

Her Majesty's private secretary had reported to her many infestations of evil, apparitions of the unexplained, manifestations of the undead walking through the corridors of her palaces and numerous instances of funny goings on in the royal residences across her kingdom. Of course, it goes without saying that I jumped at the chance of expunging all manner of supernatural incursions from the royal households.

My work started, and I worked at the ministry in a physical sense for many a happy year until my sad demise. Death was a shock but after my spirit moved across the veil, I have to report that I was quite pleasantly surprised that my transition would be a continuation of my rather splendid life and my work would continue in eradicating evil.

The higher powers in the spirit world tasked me to seek out and employ spiritual vessels on the earth plane; sensitive human beings with a part of their consciousness still rooted in the astral plane. They would be channelled and inspired to bring these tales to you and by doing so my work for the good of mankind would continue.

In this first account: Christopher J Milne had linked with the spirit of Lucy in sleep state, a young girl who had the smile of an angel; a wicked sense of humour but died in tragic and unconventional circumstances. I hope you take heed from the lessons needed to be learned.

Christopher, a New Zealander, now resides in either New Zealand, the United Kingdom or Spain. I have my eye on him as a rising star in my ministry.

LUCY

by Christopher J Milne

The worst thing was that even I didn't know who'd killed me. I was in the police station with Dad, and I'd seen him arguing with the nice police lady at the desk. I had to leave when he got upset. And I mean really upset. I couldn't blame him, though, and I guess neither could the police officer. After all, it'd been a week and they still hadn't found out who'd done it.

I obviously wasn't much use either. Not that I would have been, even if I wasn't... well... dead.

I didn't really remember anything before the cremation, anyway. I mean, I remembered things two weeks ago. Like that stupid Maths test, and when me and Dad had bacon and eggs for breakfast in the caravan. But after that, the next thing I knew I was watching smoke curl up from the chimney of the crematorium. Well, watching me curl up from the chimney, I guess. Somehow I knew the smoke was me, and that I was dead. Of course the whole floating-twenty-metres-in-the-air-thing kind of gave it away.

Everyone seemed really upset, of course. All my friends from school were there, and Dad. His messy grey hair was actually brushed, and his bald patch was even more obvious because of it. He had on that same old, grey suit he wore whenever he was going to something serious, but it looked like it was getting a bit tight over his belly now.

I watched all my friends crying and hugging each other. The strange thing was, I didn't really feel sad then. It had happened, I was dead, and now I just felt, kind of empty. There were a few adults there as well and I recognised Mr Deans, my Arts teacher. He shook Dad's hand and I heard bits of his words.

"... such a lovely little girl... Really didn't deserve this, and neither do you..."

Then I kind of expected to... I don't know, go to heaven or something. At least then I could see Mum, because I knew she'd be waiting for me. But I didn't go anywhere. So I figured there must be something left for me to do here, like in the movies. Or maybe there wasn't any heaven after all. No, I reckoned there must be something to do. That made more sense.

So I followed Dad. I followed him as he got in that old heap of a green Vauxhall he loved, and I watched as he wiped his eyes and blew into his hanky. Then, somehow, I kept up as he drove like a crazy person through town to the police station. And now I watched as he left.

Dad still looked really upset. He stared at the police station for a while before getting in his car. This time he drove slowly. Well, slowly for him. Like, well almost like he was driving and thinking at the same time. It was easy for me to follow him. I was getting the hang of this whole floating thing now.

Dad drove out of town and turned down a tiny country lane. Just down the lane there was a police car, almost hidden in the hedge. A nice-looking constable in a bright yellow jacket stood behind the car. As we got close I could see a rusty old iron gate in a gap in the hedge

As Dad pulled in behind the police car, I got chills. Bad chills. I didn't like this place. It felt... angry. I watched Dad talk to the policeman. I was hoping he would make Dad leave, because I really didn't like being

4

here. And I didn't want to see what was on the other side of that hedge. But the constable let Dad climb over the gate. I heard him call out to Dad as I drifted over.

"Just don't touch anything Gerry, or the Sarge'll have my arse. I shouldn't even be lettin' you over there but, well..."

As the policeman's voice seemed to die in his throat, I recognised him. It was Ted Catcher; his mum lived three houses down from us.

When I saw the Police tape on the other side of the hedge, the chills got worse. I felt even more anger and pain, and something else too. Now I felt sadness... and fear. But not mine, someone else's. And then I knew where we were. This was where little Elsie Woodcott was found. I recognised it from the picture in the paper. No wonder it felt so bad; she got murdered too. I remembered seeing the picture of her, all blonde pigtails and toothy smile, and thinking how sad it was such a beautiful little girl got killed. Of course, she was 8, and I was only 12, so really me getting killed wasn't much better.

I wondered what Dad was doing here. He stood, motionless, at the edge of the tape, looking down at the bottom of the hedge. My stomach started to twist. Clouds covered the sun and it got cold and dark. Then I saw the bloodstains on the grass. I guess it hadn't rained since they found her. I really wanted to throw up. This place felt evil, and it was making me scared.

Dad stood there, staring at the blood. He looked back to the gate and then crouched down to look closer. That was when it clicked. He was trying to figure it out. Of course. The cops weren't doing anything so he was going to do it himself. That was my Dad after all. If something wasn't getting done, he'd just "jolly well do it himself". And he must have guessed that the same person that killed Elsie also killed me.

So that must be what I was here for. To help. I dropped down to where he crouched and touched his shoulder.

I'll help you Dad

Dad shivered and looked up, and I could tell he was scared. But then he looked straight through me and seemed to calm down. Still, he shivered again as he stood up. He glanced around and pulled his suit jacket tight around his body, as if he could feel the cold chill too. With a last look down at the blood, he turned and almost ran back along the fence. I followed, but lost control of the whole floating thing in my hurry. I felt myself getting dragged down towards the hedge and then something jerked me sideways into it. I fell face-first as if someone had pushed me. I would have got a face full of thorns if... if I had a face. But instead I just passed through the hedge to the ground. I closed my eyes as my stomach twisted and turned again, then slowly opened them as it settled. It was dark in the hedge and full of shadows. That's when I saw it. A clue!

It was a small blue bow. Like something a little girl would wear in her pigtails. How could the Police have missed it? Of course, they couldn't fall through a bush like I just had. Still, it was a clue. I grabbed at it, but I had as much chance of picking up a bow as I did of feeling thorns on my face.

I pulled myself out of the hedge to see Dad jumping over the gate. I got to him as he opened his car door.

Dad! There's a bow! In the hedge!

Dad's head whipped around, fear in his eyes again. He stared wildly at the sky, then his eyes slowly focussed. With another shiver, he swallowed and then got into his battered old Vauxhall.

Dad! The bow!

But it was no good. He couldn't hear me. Not really. The green car backed up and then Dad gunned the engine, spinning the wheels on the grass before sliding around in a squeal of tyres and speeding off back up the lane.

***

Dad finally stopped the car in front of our caravan. He had been driving around for ages, and it was getting dark now. I shivered, even though I wasn't cold. I felt dizzy, which was strange. I wouldn't have thought you could get dizzy when you were dead. That sick feeling in my stomach was back too. But much worse. And I was starting to hurt. My wrists and my neck burned, and I felt like I had been in a tumble drier. My body felt sore all over. I had felt bad in Elsie's field, but this was a hundred times worse.

Dad got out of the car and stood, leaning on the roof, staring at our old caravan. He looked down the long, line of other caravans; all quiet and dark. It was late October after all. Not really holiday season anymore.

A sharp pain hit me in the stomach. I let out a cry and Dad glanced up, that look of fear in his face again. I watched as he closed the car door and slowly walked up to the caravan. As he entered, the sick feeling in my stomach and the dizziness got worse. I wanted to throw up, but I stopped myself. Not that I probably could have thrown up, anyway.

Then I realised why I felt so bad. This was where I had died. As soon as I thought it, I knew it was true. But, this was our caravan. Mine and Dad's. And Mum's when she was still alive. How could I have died here? Unless....
I looked at our old caravan as the lights inside blinked on, and I saw Dad's shadow inside. Pain shot through my stomach like a knife and I gasped. A nasty thought entered my mind. No! That couldn't be right!

The pain bit into my stomach and everything went blurry. I was having trouble breathing, and when everything settled down I realised I wasn't in front of the caravan any more. I was in the woods behind the caravan park. Now the bad feeling was so intense I wanted to cry. I felt alone. More alone than I've ever been. I could smell blood. I knew it was mine. I could just see a heap of heavy rope lying at the base of the big oak tree in front of me. My stomach tossed and turned and I felt so sick and sore that I did start to cry.

This was it. This was where I had actually stopped breathing. I could feel it. So I cried. I cried for what felt like a long time. Until the pain in my stomach eased and the burning around my throat and wrists died. It was properly dark now and I could almost feel the darkness on my skin. As my tears stopped I felt myself being drawn back to the caravan, and I didn't resist. I felt so sad now that I was actually numb.

I could see Dad in the caravan. I stopped outside. I didn't want to go in, I didn't want to see him. If I stayed outside then maybe it wouldn't be true. It couldn't be true, could it? Not Dad.... Not my Dad.... I started to cry again.

Then, out of the corner of my eye I saw a flicker of... something. It had come from another caravan towards the other end of the park. I was sure of it. The moon had come out now and there was enough light to see the path that ran down past the other caravans. Something moved. I hardly saw it, but it was there. A dark shadow that ran across the moonlit path. And then I felt it. Something bad, something evil was in this park. Real bad. The pain stabbed my stomach again and I gasped. I thought I saw the shadow again. But this time closer. Who was it? I didn't know, but I knew they were bad news.

I rushed in through the wall of the caravan to see Dad standing in front of the old yellow bench in the kitchen. He had his little box of keepsakes in front of him. Full of the funny little things we collected on the beach or in the woods. I could see his eyes were full of tears.

Dad!

He looked up in alarm, searching the caravan for the sound. Which meant I must have made a sound. I tried again.

Dad! You have to get out of here!

Dad looked around frantically but he didn't move.

"Come on Gerry, get a hold of yourself," he muttered.

8

There's something bad out there Dad, you have to go!

Dad looked around again. This time straight at me. But he didn't see me. And he didn't seem that scared any more either. His lips twitched into what looked like a faint, sad smile.

"You're going mad," he said to himself quietly.

This wasn't working! I knew the shadow I had seen outside was still there. I could feel the evilness in the caravan park. And it was close. It could only be one thing. It must be the person who killed me. It couldn't be anything else. And Dad couldn't hear me! I felt so annoyed with him that it made me angry. Why couldn't he hear me? I opened my mouth and screamed as loud as I could.

Dad!

The mirror behind Dad cracked right down the middle as I screamed, and Dad jumped in alarm. He had heard that all right I thought, a strange happiness flowing over me.

"Lucy?" he cried, asking the impossible question. "Lucy?"

I felt stronger now so I yelled at him again.

Dad! Get out! It's not safe!

I guess I was still angry and as I yelled, a cup fell off the small shelf above the sink, crashing and shattering on the yellow bench.

"Lucy?" Dad wailed. He was truly frightened now. Good. Maybe that would save him.

Go!

He leapt back and started to cry. Now he was finally listening to me. He stumbled to the door and flung it open, almost falling out onto the paving stones.

I watched as he ran to his car door. He was really scared now, and that's what I wanted. That will make him run. I could feel the badness around us now. It was even stronger than before. He had to get out.

Dad stopped at the car door. He looked down at his hands and then started to fumble about in his pockets. Then

9

he looked back at the caravan. What on earth was he doing? He needed to go!

Dad! Go!

Dad shrieked in true terror and backed away from the car.

"Leave me alone!"

No, Dad, get in the car. Go!

Dad shrieked again, like a girl, and then turned and ran.

No!

He was running into the woods! I knew that was a really bad idea. My killer was out here somewhere. Because I knew that's what the shadow must have been. He was around here somewhere. And now Dad was disappearing into the woods, crying like a baby. That was where my murderer felt most at home!

Dad! Stop!

Why didn't he listen? Sometimes he could be so stupid! I got angry again as I chased him into the woods. As I followed him, the pains returned.

Dad was heading straight for where I died, and I couldn't stop him! My neck and wrists hurt so bad now, like a million Chinese burns. And my stomach was really sick again. But mostly I was angry. Really angry with Dad for being so stupid. Then he disappeared in front of me. Where had he gone? I panicked, and then realised I wasn't actually angry with Dad at all. I was angry with the man who'd killed me. The man who had ended my life and hurt me. And that thought made me so furious that my mind turned black. And I don't mean black like without anything. I mean dark. Dark like the bottom of a really deep well. But not empty. Full of... darkness, somehow. And I could feel the shadows again. Because now there were more than one of them in the woods.

And then I saw Dad. At the base of my oak tree. On his knees. Crying. Crying real bad, his shoulders shaking so hard it looked like he was going to fall over. I wanted to feel sad for him, but now I couldn't. The only thing inside me was darkness. But even through that I could feel the evil presence in the woods. Dad wasn't safe. All I could feel in this horrible place was pain and anger. I could feel the dark shadows closing in. My chest felt tight, like I couldn't breathe.

So I cried with Dad. I closed my eyes and wailed my heart out. The pain in my body eased and the darkness lifted a little. Then I realised that Dad had stopped crying. I opened my eyes to see him staring up at me. Or most probably through me. A terrible sadness was in his eyes. Or fear. I couldn't tell which.

"Lucy?" Dad croaked, barely able to get the words out. "Lucy?"

Dad looked down at the untidy heap of bloody rope in front of him. He picked it up and as he did, something fell from his hand and fluttered to the ground. In the moonlight that made it through the trees, I could see what it was. A small bow. Like something a little girl would wear in her pigtails.

The darkness rushed in and pain hit me everywhere. My wrists and neck felt like they were on fire. My body was so sore all over and that deep knifing pain hit me in my stomach again. And worst of all were the horrible sharp pains that stabbed down between my legs. And then I remembered. I remembered everything. And the pain became so intense I thought I was going to pass out. The shadows descended and the darkness took over. And suddenly I wasn't alone. There were others there with me. I could feel them. I could feel them all. And I could feel their pain and their anger. They became me, and I became them. I screamed. And they screamed with me.

I screamed with the pain that now rushed through my body. I screamed at his betrayal. But most of all I screamed with a deep, raw anger. I was angry like I had never been angry before. As if the darkness inside me was flowing out like water. And I could feel that the anger was not just mine. We screamed – no we howled – with fury and hatred.

11

And he knew. He heard. And his eyes filled with such terror. Terror that, a minute ago, would have made me feel sorry for him. But now all his fear did was make the horrible pain fade a bit.

He ran. He ran away from us. Too scared to face it, to face what he knew he had done, the coward ran. But I ran faster. We howled and I ran. And the darkness inside me gave me strength. And it gave me form. I wasn't floating any more. My footsteps pounded on the path behind him.

He shrieked in terror and darted off the path, crashing through the undergrowth. But I followed him. And then I – no, we – were on him and around him. My cold arms enveloped him and held him and we screamed in his ear. He shrieked again and tumbled to the ground. I pulled back and watched as he struggled to his hands and knees and tried to crawl away.

I stopped screaming then. I leant forward and silently ran cold, lifeless fingers down the back of his sweaty neck. He squealed like a pig and tried to scramble away but his arms didn't work and he fell flat on his face. He turned back to me on his knees, holding out his hands, pleading.

"Please, Lucy!" he cried, his dirty, pitiful face grey like a corpse. "I'm sorry! Lucy!"

But there was no pity in our hearts for him. Only hatred and darkness. Darkness that I now knew belonged to him. His futile pleading did bring us some pleasure though. I smiled at the horrible killer in front of me and took a step forward. He shrieked once more as the leaves on the forest floor moved around my unseen feet.

And then he was off again. Running in a blind panic, bashing off trees and through bushes, zigging and zagging. But he wasn't going to get away. This was our time now. So I followed. I knew where he was going. Drawn back like a moth to his dirty, horrible flame.

When he got there I pushed him again. I felt his foot catch in a root and he fell forward with a cry of pain. The sound of his suffering dulled our pain. And the muffled cry when he saw the bloody rope and crumpled blue bow in front of him dulled it even more.

I leant forward and whispered cold words in his ear. Cold words in six different voices.

Do it.

As we spoke I recognised one of the voices. It was my mother's.

The horrible pig squealed again with unfamiliar terror and tried to stand. His leg gave way and with another pathetic squeal he crumpled back to the floor, looking up with abject horror in his eyes. His terror filled us with delicious warmth and I closed my eyes as it eased the pain further.

"Lucy..." His voice was quiet and broken, full of pain, fear and probably regret. But it was too late for that. The sound of his loathsome voice filled us with pain and darkness again. We did not want to hear his pleading, only to feel his terror and his pain.

Do it!

We hissed at him and he heard. He picked up the dirty rope and fingered the rough strands. As he looked up at the all too familiar branches of the old oak tree, I knew he was beaten. The anticipation was now almost too much for us to bear.

He paused there for a long time, and when he looked back to where we stood, there was defiance in his eyes.

"No," he said quietly. "You're dead Lucy. You can't hurt me." He looked around the clearing and his voice got stronger. "This is all your fault anyway. You should have just done what I wanted. You're just like your mother." He struggled to his feet, leaning against the trunk of the dark oak tree. I watched, speechless, as colour returned to his face and he smiled. A wicked, horrible smile that made my insides shrivel and the pain inside me burn. I gasped. He could feel my hesitation and his awful smile got wider.

13

Then the darkness of the others engulfed me and my hesitation was forgotten. They screamed. We screamed together, like I have never screamed before. Everything that he did to us, all the pain, betrayal, and disgusting things, all of them were in a howl that knocked him clean off his feet. The vile man in front of us fell to the ground again. Right into the leaves that were stained with my blood.

He lay there silent for a second, and then he noticed. And it was his turn to scream. There was blood on his trousers. My blood. The bloodstains from the leaves crept over his legs and up to his waist, soaking his trousers. The blood kept rising and soaked his shirt too. All that blood of mine that had seeped away into the earth returned and flowed slowly up over his neck. Frantically he tried to wipe it away, screaming, all defiance gone from his deathly white face. But it was no use. I didn't really know what was happening, or how it was happening, but the blood kept flowing. And his pathetic attempts to stop it only made us feel good, and the blood flow faster.

My blood flowed over his chin and then entered his mouth. The horrible murderer spluttered, choked and retched as his mouth and then his throat filled with the blood of his dead daughter. A wonderful gurgling sound made it though the blood. Then he coughed and a fine red mist sprayed in the moonlight, falling silently into the pool of blood he now lay in.

He thrashed around now, in absolute panic. Oh, how good it felt to watch that. The rope was flung from his side in a red, splattering arc and then his hand hit something in the grass. Somehow he spat out the blood in his mouth and rose to his knees, the all too familiar knife he had picked up slashing defensively in front of him. His eyes were wild and my blood dripped from his chin. He waved the knife in my direction but we only laughed. He flinched at the harsh sound of our laughter.

14

Do it.

We said it one last time, barely more than a whisper. But it was a whisper that contained all the pain, anger and darkness that was inside us. His eyes clouded and his head dropped.

"Lucy... I... I'm..." Was all he managed to get out, then he turned his head up to the night sky, gripped the knife tightly, and drew it savagely across his throat. For a second his blood spurted out violently, and then it slowed and pulsed down his neck, mixing with mine.

And then he fell forward, dead. The darkness inside me lifted immediately. The shadows melted away and I was alone again. The rope burns on my wrist and the pain inside me faded as well. So did my anger. As the shadows disappeared into the night I heard my Mother's voice faintly on the breeze.

Sleep now, sweet Lucy.

I tried to follow Mum's voice, but suddenly I felt really stiff. And really tired. As I stumbled through the trees, away from Dad's body and towards Mum, I closed my eyes. A golden warmth wrapped around me, and I could feel Mum there too. Happiness overcame me and I felt at peace.

MINISTER FOR GHOSTS

Well I have to say that story pricked the hairs on the back of my neck. Lucy and her mother are being looked after by loved ones in the spirit world and they are fine but I have to report her father is not fine. Indeed, he is anything but fine and is currently enjoying the company of Satan and his soldiers of debauchery; and will do for a few hundred years before we decide to release him. Lessons have to be learned to enable his spirit to evolve.

So on to my next account - the complexity of the world of spirit. Mother Nature has created some truly wonderful things. The sea is one of them and is the source of livelihood for the great men and women who harvest the crops of the ocean and sail upon it. Where does it end?

I can report that it does not finish in the physical world; it carries on past the veil of life and death and beyond. The sea exists in many dimensions and a journey upon it can take you to many planes of existence.

My next vessel to channel the insights into this rather wonderful world is Jo Zebedee, a management consultant, who lives in a seaside town in Northern Ireland with her husband, two children, two fish and a dog and a cat. She was a perfect choice to bring you this tale. A splendid lady and truly wonderful mother and wife.

Sometimes the sea is not always what it seems. Its calm and friendliness can change in the blink of an eye and can be the darkness that pervades a tale of torment and suffering.

SILVER THREADS OF CORALLINE

by Jo Zebedee

Boats of glass and transferred ink; useless anywhere other than on Krista's crusted sea's surface. Below, silverfish follow the cut chasms; beneath them lives something older, colder.

Slane sits on the long prow of *Silver-threads*, the fastest and sharpest coralline harvester. His sharp eyes scan the horizon's colours, looking for their elusive shift. He sits for three years, long enough for the prow to etch into his skin, and only sees it once, when it is far away and they get there after the coralline is stripped. Only a few silver fish are left, dying in the open wake of water and ink, a silvered-red bloodbath. Then, Slane pulls his feet onto the prow before the sea-spirits rise and claim him as their own.

Now, in the blazing sun, a bead of sweat runs from his brow and he lifts his hand to wipe it. His chains clank and he winces as the manacles drag at his salt-raw wrists. He scans the horizon: he needs only to find one harvest with his sharp, sharp eyes to win his freedom. He sits still, taking no notice of the agony of his bent-stooped back or the pain behind his eyes from the beating sun. He just watches and prays to be freed before he's sacrificed to the depths as another failed Caster.

***

18

I don't know how he is not mad -- I don't *know* that he is not mad. His eyes cast ceaselessly, barely squinting. His skin is burned and burned again, peeling white, and tanned beneath. His feet hang down, inches above the crusted surf. I clank my pail onto his sleeping dais, making sure to avoid my skirts. He doesn't turn – he is more a part of the silvered sea and its threaded promise than he is of our world.

Sea-caster; a privileged childhood on the South Islands developed his reading eyes. No one told him his value would be met by the highest bidder, or that he'd spend his days chained to a needled prow, his nights curled in a tiny dais, sleeping whilst the Sea-listeners took his place, alert to the night-kelpie. My chest hitches - did anyone tell him the ship's future lies with him? We needed to find coralline a year ago, it's why we all survive on salted silverfish, and why we mount extra watchers at night, bent over his sleeping nest, ready to repel the thieving spirits. I shift my tongue against my sharp tooth and it moves. A month, I guess, until it falls and tinkles against the glass deck as my last did. It bounced off the side to be taken by the sea. Now, the spirits know me and call me, mournful and sweet and chilling.

"Sea-caster," I say.

He turns with his desperate eyes and salt-dried lips bleeding. His missing teeth don't tinkle as they fall, they drop straight through the threads. He's more than named; he's halfway to the other world, more spirit than man. He's so thin, his bones are like needles. He doesn't speak - he stopped once he learned his shrieks and pleas bought no mercy – but turns his head away so I can't drown in his seeking, shifting eyes. "Food. The meister says you mun eat all or he'll whup both you and I."

He turns back and reaches his hand forward, stretching until he grasps the bucket from me. Even as he swallows the silvered mush, gagging on the guts and bones, his eyes watch for his freedom.

***

19

The horizon shivers in front of Slane's eyes, turning from orange to purple, shimmering past green. He blinks; he's imagined it before only to be fooled by the light. Blinks again. It *is* coralline. His breath catches as he remembers his orders. He's not to yell - they don't trust his voice – so he lifts his wrist, crying as his skin tears, and clutches the heavy bell rope which bites into his hands. He clings to it, half-unbalancing, sick with fear, sick with opportunity, sick from fish guts. He swings the bell, cutting the still air. It rings in time with the waves that slap between the crust and boat, a rhythm of hope, until he hears booted feet behind him. He points, just off to the right. Light-blind eyes follow his finger, give directions. The coralline's near. More boats converge, their ink-trails' colours marking each one, but further out. His eyes blur with tears, his finger shakes. A hand falls on his burned shoulder, making him cry out.

"Aye, lad, we see it there."

The ship turns in a circle, cutting the salted crust, its ink marking the patch as theirs. They draw over the coralline and the light hits Slane's eyes with the most vibrant colours he's ever seen, the haze he'd been promised as a boy. This is his end, when the sea-spirits will claim him as their own. He shivers, both scared and relieved it will be over. Soon, his hands will fade, his body will become one with the sea, and he'll wait for the next Caster to find his shifting power and capture it for their own. He holds his breath, watches the air shift before him, blinding him.

The ship beaches itself on the coralline, lifting from the water. The centre of the glass splits in two, the boat-hooks are lowered to rip coralline from the sea bed and haul it through the gap in silver strands, one after the other, coiling it into skeins. The remaining crew line the decks, holding the other ships at bay with glass-slicing harpoons. The boat's filled; the strands have ended, and the hull is closed as the sea rushes to re-claim the coralline reef.

Slane's breath catches. He balances on the prow.

Tears fall over twenty-year-old skin, withered to sixty. He lets go of the bell, clutches the bow, closing out the sounds behind him, and starts to scan the horizon. It's black. All around him is black. The colour haze has stolen his vision. Now, he sits, fear surging through him, and waits for the spirits to take him.

***

The Captain approaches Slane, a jangling key in hand. The caster backs along the prow, but Captain pulls his chains so that the manacles can be opened. They fall from red-raw wrists. Slane's mouth moves in a croaked plea.

We watch, the whole crew, some decent and dropping their gaze as the Captain starts at Slane, forcing him towards the crusted sea. Slane stumbles onto one knee but, unseeing, can't avoid the boot that catches him and knocks him into the sea. The spirits race below the glass bottom, sensing him. The sea churns behind, a living tide of despair. Faces grow in the salt-crust, old, bearded and thin. A first sailor screams and falls, hands clutching empty air. Not fallen; taken. The precious coralline glistens and we hold firm, even as more of our crew fall to the demanding spirits, some clutching their treasure with them, as if it would keep them safe. The captain gives the order, the ship turns from the reef and starts for the open sea.

Slane flashes past the side of the boat, his face an ecstasy of pain. The spirits are close to him, moments away.

I reach, hands out, and catch his red-raw wrist. I pull him in; man to my girl, he's all bone and no weight. I grab my share of the coralline booty - two skeins, hauled by myself, wealth enough for three year's living. "I mun buy him."

The crew laugh when they cast me aside. The island stretches for miles, sand untouched. Just me and Slane. I turn to his once bright eyes -- now dead -- and he reaches for me, feeling my face.

21

"Free," he whispers, his voice croaked and wondering.

I smile; we are, the future's bought and ours, the spirits denied. I hug him to me. The deep is denied - the spirits can't take me, nor steal him from me. I throw my head back and laugh at the fallen fools who clutched their treasure to their death, not strong enough to stay on the boat and resist the spirit's pull.

I challenge the spirits to leave the sea and take *my* treasure, standing firm beside me. A rescued sea-caster for myself. A son, perhaps, to bear his father's eyes. I clench my fists by my side; my son will never face the coralline-search that will destroy him, but live a treasured life, here on our own South Island. I paid for him to do so.

MINISTER FOR GHOSTS

What a splendid tale. Thank you Jo Zebedee. Watch out for me coming to you in your dreams as I have another tale for you to tell.

In the physical world, nature can act like a recorder. The trees, the sea, the rocks, the mountains; all have stories to tell. In this next account, years of living have been absorbed into the stones of an old mining village in Wales.

The story is told by my next vessel, Bob Lock: a wise man and deep thinker from the Valleys unlocks this heart-warming story. The words and emotions bleed out from the stones and take you to a place where boys were turned into men. Sadly though, the weight of the years ended in being too much of a heavy burden on this old man's shoulders.

Enjoy.

IN THE STONES

By Bob Lock

The town glowers down on me, I feel its eyes. Dark hollows of lightless windows, like the eyeless sockets of empty skulls, follow my creeping passage with a wariness that is palpable. I have no right to be here, both the town and I know it, not at this time of night and not at my age. In an instant Psalms 90:10 springs to mind - *The days of our years are three score years and ten; and if by reason of strength they be four score years yet is their strength labour and sorrow, for it is soon cut off, and we fly away* – and I smile as the memory of old Reverend Richards preaching those words from the chapel pulpit return to me as if it was only last Sunday. I've beaten that sum by another dozen or so years, but the spring within this old clock has wound down fast and furiously, especially in the last few months. I *feel* time ending. Treacle, ebbing from an upended tin. Soon it will be empty and the clock will tick no more. All tomorrows left as they are. Unobtainable - at least for me.

The moon flits through a gap in the clouds and the ebon streets turn to silver, but beyond her reach the darkness deepens and I peer hopefully into the gloom for faces I knew. Am I being childish to think they'll peer back? Yet my faith, if somewhat antiquated and sorely tested, makes me believe they *may* be there. However, though I wait, sit on the cold hard slab of slate outside The Gwalia

Stores, they will not show themselves. The coal-blackened boys, trousers stiff with dust, tied off at the knees, boots clanking down cobbles, voices hoarse with labour and the deadly, sooty powder promising pneumoconiosis or massive fibrosis. Yet those same voices, once lubricated with ale at the inn, are all too happy to challenge even the angels with their singing. Stubbornly they remain hidden. I listen for them now, a gruff laugh, the scratch of a match before the flare and then the glow of a Woodbine cigarette to be followed by the hack of a lung-despoiling cough. But only an owl's call, the wind's whisper and the soft scrape of an unlatched window teases my hearing. Perhaps it *is* later than I thought.

My knees creak and my back pops and clicks as I stand. There, in the plate-glass window of The Gwalia Stores, is the reflection of a ghost. An ancient ghost. A bent ghost. A ghost that fishes in its pockets for the battered tobacco tin: the papers the matches, the makings. Gnarled fingers roll – as they've always done – to make a few more cigarettes. A few to add to the countless already made in my lifetime. The thin white cylinder scars the night with its presence. I sigh and strike a match. They said *this* would kill me. They said wrong. I'm still here. Just about. The ghost in the window is superimposed over the counter with its display of Bovril, Coleman's Mustard, pots and pans, the little cabinet with John Players, Woodbines and Capstan Full Strength cigarettes. The ghost pulls deeply on his own tobacco tube and the black and silver night turns an angry red for a moment. I turn my back on him; the street offers me a sleek river of argent. Do I follow it upwards? Shall I navigate past the dour chapel? Risk admonishment by its glowering façade? Or is it time to drift downstream, go with the flow, finish fighting the current that I've fought against my whole life? Time seems a worthy opponent when you are young, to swim against the tide as natural a state as to swim with it. Only when time becomes a precious commodity do you treasure it more. Then you rail against its passing as it narrows, increases in velocity in a desperate rush for the fall into oblivion. I leave the stone-mullioned windows of St.Teilo's church upstream and let the old road wash me home.

Eighty three years old. Too old to be sneaking through deserted Welsh streets like the last thief on the planet. Too old to be returning to your place of birth. No one will be there to greet you. Unless the walls of where you were born turn their sleepy eyes your way and in their thousand year blink, see, and remember you. I do not have the ten centuries spare to find out, and upon reaching the white-washed building with its crown of thatch, I push open the oak door and, out of habit, duck beneath the low lintel. When I left this place I stood tall. I return to it bowed. It feels right, almost a genuflection of thanks to the solidness of stone which cocooned my childhood until it was time to leave before the coal mine took more than its due. Another match, another cigarette and the glow shows the coal-dust filled scars across the back of my hands like crude tattoos.

'If I'd stayed there would be even *more* of them across my lungs too.' I inform the house quietly and the wind moans its reply. I stroke a hand across the walls and feel the huge boulders, dragged from ancient glaciers. I smell the earthy tang of wood and coal smoke ingrained in their permanence. There, at the fire-side, would sit my mother surrounded by huge pots. The kettle – whose blackness put even the night sky to shame – bubbled and gurgled with hot water in anticipation of my father's return from work.

'*Evening, mother...*' he'd say, carefully placing his work-clothes on the settle by the door.

'*Evening, father...*' she'd reply and fill the tin bath.

'*Evening son...*' his second greeting, and then my reply.

'*Evening, dada...*'

I sit by that empty fireplace now, in Mam's spot and

listen carefully; even their voices seem ingrained into the house's very fabrication. As solid as the stones. As everlasting as the stars.

Delilah plays in my pocket along with a subtle vibration to inform me of an incoming call. It's almost 1.30am and I wonder who'd be up so late, and more to the point, how did they know *I'd* be up? I flip it open. It's my grand-daughter. I should have guessed.

'Grandad?' Strange to hear her young voice in this ancient place. And what had been, for a little time 1937 for me, once again spools forward seventy something years to today.

'Yes, what're you doing up so late, Gwen?' I ask, knowing quite well what the answer will be.

'Looking for *you*, Grandad,' she sighs; I hear the relief in her voice. 'Where are you?'

'Well, you've found me; just as well I wasn't asleep eh?' I ask. 'I'm *home*.'

There's a moment of silence.

'You can't be! Mam was contacted by the nursing home, and they said you were missing. She's gone down there because you wouldn't answer your 'phone.'

'I didn't say the *nursing* home, Gwen, I said *home* and I didn't take your Mum's call because I knew she'd only nag me and not listen to what I had to say.'

Again there's a moment's pause as she digests my words. 'You don't mean *Carreg Fawr?*' She asks, using the Welsh name for my old cottage *Boulder*. I smile to myself in the darkness.

'Aye, cariad, *Carreg Fawr*, place of my birth, and...' I don't continue.

'Gramps, I don't believe you've gone and done that.'

I laugh then, risking a bout of coughing which will probably have me on my knees. Who would have thought I'd have lasted this long with lungs ruined by the coal? Even getting away from the mine at an early age

27

hadn't been enough. But the cigarettes had to have played their part too – however much I ignored the fact. 'The bones might be old, Gwen, but my soul thinks it still belongs to a twelve year old.'

'How did you get in?' she asks.

'Climbed the bloody fence of course,' I reply.

'Gramps, you've *climbed* over the security fence to get into St.Fagan's Welsh Museum of Life?' It's a statement more than a question. I needn't reply, but I do.

'Took me longer than I thought,' I shrug ruefully, 'but I did it. If they hadn't torn down the whole village and brought it here it might have been easier.'

'I don't think so, Gramps,' she answers and I hear a smile in her voice then. 'The village would have been under the reservoir for twenty or more years. Not even Super-gramps could have got around *that* problem.'

I nod in the darkness. 'Don't be so sure; I can hold my breath for two hours, you know?'

She laughs at that and I wait quietly for her next question which I know she is leading up to. 'When are you coming back?'

There it is. Now for the hard bit. I sigh.

'Gwen, cariad. I *won't* be coming back.'

The timbre of her voice changes and I know tears are not far away, 'Gramps. Don't do anything silly. Let me come get you.'

'Silly? You know me better than that.' I pause and think for a moment. 'Remember the elephant graveyard?' I ask, recalling a film we once watched together.

'Yes, it made me cry.'

I smile sadly.

'Me too. But somehow the elephants *knew* when it was their time. Something pulled them back to that place. Something pulled me back here. I'm not going to do anything silly, Gwen. I haven't any need to; it's just the time, that's all, time...'

28

'I don't understand...'

'Neither do I, Gwen, dear. But now I'm here it *feels* right, this is where I should be. There's a letter explaining everything to your mother. Tell her it's what *I* wanted; it's where *I* wanted to be. Now whenever you come here I'll be here with you. In the stones. In the beams. In the heart of *Carreg Fawr*.'

'I'll miss you, Grandad...' Gwen's voice breaks, and for a moment I want to climb the fence and return to her side, but I hear *them* then. The singing. The tramp of boot on cobblestone, and I hear the winding down of the old spring, the last ticking of the tired clock.

'I'll always be here, Gwen,' I answer softly and glance out of the window. Far up the darkened street dance a line of small lights. 'I have to go now, dearest. It's time.'

'Bye, Gramps, I love you...' her voice sounds a million miles away, the light from the mobile barely a glimmer in the encompassing blackness.

'Bye, Gwen, I love you too...' I answer and close the 'phone as the soft lilting voices filter through the thick walls. The boys from the mine are here at last. The quiet night air becomes calmer still as their voices raise the hairs on the back of my neck with their rendition of *Calon Lan*.

Calon lan yn llawn daioni
Tecach yw na'r lili dlos
Dim ond calon lan all ganu
Canu'r dydd a chanu'r nos

A pure heart full of goodness
Is fairer than the lily of the field
Only the pure heart can sing
Songs day and night

I catch a glimpse of myself, an old man, huddled near the fireside. And I realise it is only a shell, a vessel with all its contents consumed, each bitter or sweet moment swallowed by time, uncaring of its flavour. I stride out of the door with a spring in my step and my voice becomes one with the many, encouraged by the nods and smiles. I link arms with Catrin, my wife, my Mam and Dad, long-lost family and friends and then we raise our faces to the heavens and our voices to the stars...

MINISTER FOR GHOSTS

ndeed, that was an inspiring story by one of my more experienced vessels. Thank you, Bob.

My next lesson explores a partnership with a difference. It can be many things, personal, professional, between a man and his loyal dog or a marriage between worlds. When a person passes, the spirit world opens up a vortex of light to allow the essence of the newly departed to move on. Sometimes they refuse to walk into it because of their loved ones still living in the physical world.

Thaddeus White recounts this dilemma in a thrilling, fast-paced tale, that gives you all you could ask for and more. White is one of my, shall I say, more peculiar spirit-vessels. His interest for loud, powerful Formula One cars is balanced with his work as a representative of the Ghost Ministry. I like him, though. I like him a lot.

SAXON & KHAN

by Thaddeus White

Khan ignored the ghostly harbinger of doom in the corner of the office and lit up his cigar. "Those things will be the death of you," Saxon warned.

"Death of you! Death of you!" Gandhi, their budgerigar, agreed enthusiastically.

Khan scowled at the bird. Except for himself, Gandhi was the only one who could see Saxon since his fatality. The bird had picked up the annoying habit of echoing whatever the ghost said.

"Don't worry yourself," Khan said. "The way things are going I won't be able to afford them much longer."

Private investigators had gotten something of a bad name in recent years, given the various scandals involving the media and business. It hadn't helped matters when Khan's partner had been brutally murdered, leaving Khan trying to restore the business with nobody living to watch his back.

The office had always seemed slightly small for the two of them. The desk and surrounding chairs occupied most of it, and before Saxon's untimely demise the two men had constantly been bumping into one another. A strategically placed folder hid the deep gouge that scarred the desk's surface, a memento from whoever had killed Saxon. The investigator had slowly bled to death after being attacked from behind, and soaked the carpet in so much blood his partner had been forced to replace it. Khan hadn't had the heart to throw away Saxon's lurid purple scarf, which was still on the coat-stand in the corner.

The brass carriage clock on the mantelpiece ticked noisily. Khan glanced at his wristwatch and then the family heirloom, which had managed to lose 15 minutes despite being wound up yesterday.

"The business will recover," Saxon said as his partner opened the clock face.

Khan puffed on his cigar, wound up the clock and closed it again. "Let's hope so."

"And in the meantime you could have another crack at finding out who killed me," Saxon suggested.

Khan unlocked his top drawer and took out the black folder that contained all the details of Saxon's murder. The pair of them had been through it more than once already, but Saxon was convinced they had missed something. He had been working on several cases: a missing Lithuanian called Dmitri Vodolya; Mrs Bentham, whose husband was certain she was having an affair with the milkman; and Mr Crestchurch, who believed his son had returned to drug addiction. Before Khan could open the folder a quiet tap on the door demanded his attention.

"Come in, Marjorie," he called.

Neither Khan nor Saxon had any idea how old Marjorie was. Her hair was so perfect and grey it could've been carved from granite, and her dress sense was that of a Victorian governess. During the London riots of 2011 a juvenile delinquent had attempted to mug the secretary, only to get clobbered by her sizeable handbag.

Marjorie walked in holding a china cup of tea in one hand and a plate of sandwiches and chocolate biscuits in the other. She set them down and smiled at Khan.

"I thought you should have something to eat and drink," she said. "I know you miss Mr Saxon terribly, but you must keep your strength up."

"Thank you, Marjorie," Saxon said.

"Thank you, Marjorie," Gandhi echoed.

The secretary frowned at the bird. "I wonder about that budgerigar. Sometimes he seems almost as clever as a human."

Khan sipped his tea. As usual, she had waited a few minutes before bringing it in so that he could drink it straightaway. "Thanks, Marjorie. And for the flowers you got for Saxon's grave. I know it would mean a lot to him."

She gave him another matronly smile, and then left his office, closing the door behind her.

"That woman's a godsend," Saxon said.

"A godsend! A godsend!" Gandhi concurred.

Khan nodded, his mouth full of delicious chocolate biscuits. It was very strange to see Saxon. His partner had been killed several weeks ago, and had first appeared to Khan during the funeral. Saxon, aside from being very slightly transparent, looked identical to his living self. Khan had imagined that it was simply his mind playing tricks on him. Gandhi's habit of repeating his words and the ghost passing some rigorous tests had persuaded Khan that Saxon was real, albeit dead.

Khan had just about polished off the biscuits when the telephone sprung to life and Marjorie's voice announced an unexpected arrival.

"Mr Khan, there's a woman here to see you, a Mrs Sarah Greene. She doesn't have an appointment, but was hoping to speak to you. Could you spare a moment?"

Khan stubbed out his cigar, and brushed the biscuit crumbs from his suit and waistcoat.

"I have a minute or two spare. Please show her in."

Marjorie showed Sarah Greene into the office and then closed the door. Mrs Greene looked nervous, and to be getting the first few wisps of grey hair herself. Her nose protruded beyond the point of beauty and the features of her face were consumed by fat.

"Good afternoon, Mrs Greene," Khan greeted her warmly as she sat down. "How can I help you?"

34

"Thank you for seeing me, Mr Khan. It's... well, it's my husband. I'm worried he might be having an affair."

"Understandable," Saxon muttered.

"Understandable! Understandable!" Gandhi squawked.

"Shut up, Gandhi!" Khan snapped. The bird fell silent, and Saxon laughed. "What makes you think that?"

Mrs Greene fidgeted in her chair, and brushed a stray lock of brown hair behind her ear. "He's been spending a lot of time away from home lately. Says it's the job, and he keeps getting lumbered with overtime. If you could just follow him, see where he goes and... who he meets." She sighed. "I hope I'm just worrying about nothing, but I've got to know."

Khan nodded. "That's no problem, Mrs Greene. If you provide me with his details, I'll see about following him this very day. How long do you want him to be followed?"

Mrs Greene took a moment or two to answer. "I think a week should be enough. Thank you, Mr Khan." She pulled a small folder from her handbag and placed it on the desk.

Khan opened the folder and scanned the contents. She had included contact details, the address of her husband's workplace, and photographs of both her husband and his car.

She stood up to leave, and he opened the door for her. "Not at all, Mrs Greene. You can rely upon my discretion. I'll begin working on this case today."

He waited until Mrs Greene left, then relit his cigar. "Finally, some good news."

Saxon raised an eyebrow. "Sounds like a pretty tedious case to me. Perhaps you should concentrate on trying to find out who killed me?"

Khan shook his head. "You know I'll investigate that when I can, but right now I need to make some money. If things don't pick up, the business will fold. I can't investigate anything from the Job Centre. Maybe I should look into getting a new partner."

"You have a partner," Saxon objected.

"I meant a partner whose abilities stretch beyond fiddling with electrical equipment and tricking budgerigars into being obnoxious." Khan exhaled a cloud of cigar smoke. "Look, you know I trust you. But this can be a rough business, and I could use someone who can watch my back when the going gets tough."

Saxon shrugged. "Yeah, I know." The ghost glanced at Khan's watch. "It's only 3pm. If Mr Greene's workplace is near then you should be able to tail him on the way home from work."

***

Khan's car was beautiful. A Morgan Roadster, in Connaught green. It was polished like a mirror and turned heads everywhere it went. Unfortunately, that also meant his car was about as inconspicuous as clown shoes and a top hat. So, instead of waiting for Mr Greene to emerge from the swanky skyscraper in London's financial district in his Morgan he was sat in Saxon's old Vauxhall Vectra. Grey, second-hand, and the dreariest driving experience this side of a Lada, it did have the redeeming quality of being absolutely everyday and easily forgettable.

Khan listened to the radio and had his binoculars focused on the entrance to the building. He'd found the husband's car, a yellow Porsche Boxster, in the car park, and had both the motor and the entrance in his line of sight.

The cost of the capital had forced him to make do with a shoebox of an office, but in the financial heart of London it was a different world. A landscape of glass and steel spires, temples to capitalism and profit, soared into the sky.

"Hannibal," Saxon said. "Seven across."

Khan lowered his binoculars and looked away from the building just long enough to fill in the crossword entry on behalf of his partner. Crosswords weren't his cup of tea, but it was one of the small pleasures Saxon could enjoy as a ghost.

Coldplay came on the radio, and before Chris

36

Martin could utter a single high-pitched word Saxon waved his hand and the station shifted. It had taken the ghost only a few days to work out how to affect basic electrical equipment. Sadly, he couldn't do anything as finessed as typing, but changing radio stations and even setting off car alarms were well within his powers. The deceased detective flicked through a few more stations until he found one playing Seven Seas of Rhye.

"You know, it's ok to listen to music that isn't thirty years old," Khan said.

Three more crossword clues later, Mr Greene emerged. At a distance, even with binoculars, Khan was unsure if it was him until he climbed into the Boxster.

"Can't be doing all that well if he can't afford the 911," Saxon observed.

"Could be worse. He could have a Vectra."

He waited until the Porsche left the car park, and then set off in pursuit. Like cholesterol choking the arteries of the obese, London's roads were clogged with cars. They had no choice but to stay close to their target, and even that was difficult in rush hour. Eventually Greene left the financial district and headed west, towards the M4. Once on the motorway Khan settled back some distance from the Boxster.

"Could be a mistress in Cornwall," Saxon suggested.

Khan checked his watch. "It's half past five. Bloody long way to drive, have his wicked way with her, and then drive back. And he's turning off now."

They were somewhere between Reading and Swindon, and Greene had left the motorway to head further south. Khan stuck with him, closing the gap enough to ensure he didn't lose Greene. The Porsche turned off again, this time onto a minor country road, barely wide enough for one car to pass another. After struggling up a steep hill, Khan lost him.

"Bloody hell," he said, stopping the Vectra at a T-junction. There was no sign of anything on the road, in either direction.

"Is that a pub?" Saxon asked, gesturing at a thatched building a mile down the road.

"Could be. Worth a look, at least," Khan said.

He drove down the road and navigated into the narrow entrance to the car park. A dry stone wall encircled the few dozen spaces, one of which was occupied by the Boxster. There was neither driver nor passenger in the Porsche. Golden lettering on a black background depicted the pub's name: The Red Lion.

Khan's stomach rumbled. "Shame I can't go in for some pork scratchings and a packet of crisps. Better safe than sorry, though. If I'm tailing him for days it's better to stay out of sight."

Saxon sighed. "There's no justice. I exercised, ate healthily, never drank, never smoked, and yet I ended up dead whilst you're still alive, and always getting crumbs all over my car seat."

"Maybe you died of boredom?"

Saxon glared, and a shiver ran down Khan's spine.

"Right, time to see what Greene's been up to," Saxon said. "I shan't be long. Well, unless his mistress is very pretty."

The ghost stood up and strolled away, passing through the Vectra's roof and door like a man walking through mist. Khan wished his friend weren't dead, but it undoubtedly had certain advantages when it came to spying on unsavoury sorts.

Khan got out of the car, locked it and wandered away from the Vectra. Beneath an oak tree that shaded half the car park, he took a seat on a bench and lit up his cigar. It felt good to enjoy the fresh air of an English evening and the mellow aroma of his cigar smoke. Given Mr Greene was probably hammering the bedsprings he anticipated a pretty lengthy wait. Should the errant husband be rather quicker than expected, the Boxster was in plain sight and it wouldn't take a minute to get back in his, or rather Saxon's, car.

"Put your hands up, and get to your feet. Slowly," a man with a deep voice and a French accent said from behind him.

The safety of a gun clicked off, and Khan felt the cold metal of the barrel pressing into the back of his neck.

Khan swore, but obediently stood up. He raised his hands and kept them up when the gunman walked in front of him. The man's thin-lipped mouth interrupted the brown beard that covered his face, and he wore a black suit and tie. Perfect attire for attending a funeral, Khan thought to himself.

"We are going for a little ride," the Frenchman informed Khan. He jerked his gun in the direction of the Vectra.

Khan, cigar still in his mouth, asked, "Mind if I ditch the cigar?"

The gunman gave a Gallic shrug, and Khan took one last drag before removing the cigar with his right hand and tossing it at the Frenchman's face. Khan stepped forward and seized his enemy's wrist, ramming his knee into the gunman's stomach. A swift twist of the wrist prised the weapon free.

"I don't know who the hell you think I am, but you just made a serious mistake," Khan said, levelling the gun at its erstwhile owner and reaching into his inside pocket for his phone.

The Frenchman smiled. "Au contraire."

Pain exploded at the back of Khan's head and darkness swallowed the world.

***

When he awoke, pain stabbed at the back of his skull. He tried to feel the injury and see if it was bloody, but found that his hands had been bound behind his back. Even more alarmingly, he could not see a thing.

"You're in the back of the Vectra," Saxon explained, "wearing a hood. There's a Frenchman sat next to you, and a cockney's driving. And, unlike you, he's not abusing the gearbox."

Despite the situation, Khan laughed.

"Laugh while you can," the Frenchman sneered.

"Mr Greene wasn't meeting a lady friend," Saxon confided. "He had a pint and then got a call from his boyfriend telling him he'd be half an hour late. It's lucky I overheard and headed back, otherwise I would've missed these punks bundling you into the Vectra."

As the dying light of the sun gave way to night Saxon told him the Vectra was being driven deeper and deeper into the countryside. The southern landscape was entering twilight, and occasional smatterings of light were the only sign that anyone lived in the rural world at all. It was a long way from the constant blazing lights that illuminated London in the dead of night.

There was an unholy silence. More than once Khan tried to engage the kidnappers in conversation, to try and learn something of where he was going, but the two criminals would not tolerate any idle chatter. Saxon was his eyes for the journey into the unknown. Eventually the Vectra entered a little village of thatched cottages and tiny, winding roads. The car trundled through the village until it came to a large stone house encircled by black iron railings.

"When we leave the car," the Frenchman said, "I'm going to lead you inside the house. Make a move and I'll put a bullet in you." He heard his door being opened and someone firmly grasped him by the arm. Gravel crunched beneath his shoes and creaking hinges told him the front door had been opened. The thug escorting him failed to mention the small step inside, and he stumbled forward. He felt a draught as the door was closed behind him, and heard the lock turning. A room or two away a television burbled.

"We've got some stairs ahead," the Frenchman warned Khan.

Khan managed to avoid stumbling until he reached the landing and was surprised by the absence of a step. His guide turned him to the left and then stopped. There was the sound of a door opening, a grinding noise and then something heavy struck the floor near his feet.

"There are stairs to the loft immediately to your right. Climb," the brute barked.

Khan slowly placed his foot on the first step. "You know, I'd be able to do this more quickly if you untied my hands," he suggested, his words muffled by the hood.

The thug shoved his gun into Khan's back. "We've got plenty of time."

"Try leaning forward," Saxon suggested. "They're pretty steep, but you should be ok."

After much struggling Khan eventually reached the loft. Somebody pushed him to the ground and he landed roughly on his backside.

"Good evening, Mr Khan," another man greeted him. He had an English accent, and an upper-class one at that. It was the civilised, elegant sort of voice that could have belonged to a pleasant fellow at a dinner party.

"Have we met?" Khan asked, racking his brains for who the kidnapper's master could be. He'd made enemies during the course of his investigations, but nobody who'd be willing to commit kidnapping.

The man laughed. "You and me? No. I did have a brief encounter with your late partner, Mr Saxon, however. He got a little too close to my... business interests."

Khan cast his mind back to the black folder in his desk drawer. "Dmitri Vodolya?" he guessed.

"Indeed. But since Mr Saxon's untimely demise, nobody has been poking their nose into my affairs. There's just one loose end I need to tie up." He took a few steps towards Khan and tore off his hood. He blinked in the sudden light, but the criminal's face was silhouetted by the light behind him. "I'm afraid, Mr Khan, that the time has come to reunite you with your late partner. After struggling with the trauma of losing your friend, the world will understand your suicide. Give my regards to—"

A burglar alarm burst into life and shrieked unceasingly. It drowned out the villain's voice at first, but then Khan's ears adjusted to the blaring alarm.

"Bloody hell," the man swore. He walked over to the hatch, and the wooden steps to the loft groaned as the criminal climbed down them. The loft seemed utterly empty.

"Khan!" Saxon said. "I managed to set the burglar alarm off."

"That's great. Can you see anything around that I can use to get my hands free? If I wander around like this I won't get far."

There was an odd sort of quiet, as Saxon said nothing and the burglar alarm continued to screech.

"No..." Saxon's voice trailed off. "Wait a minute. I can try to break the bulb. No idea if it'll work, but it's worth a shot. Maybe you'd be able to use a shard to slice through the rope."

"Quickly, Saxon."

His partner didn't say anything. Khan could hear raised but muffled voices, which he guessed were coming from the ground floor. Evidently the criminal scum were having problems solving whatever Saxon had managed to do to the alarm.

The energy saving bulb flickered, then glowed brightly before exploding into shards of glass and plunging the loft into darkness.

"That was hard," Saxon said, his voice barely a whisper. Khan watched in confusion as his friend became more transparent than usual.

"Good work. Where's the biggest shard?" he asked.

Saxon didn't reply, and faded from sight entirely.

"Saxon?"

Bereft of an answer, he felt around on the rough wooden floorboards. Slicing pain announced he had found a piece of glass sharp enough. It was a struggle to grasp it and cut through the rope binding his wrists, but the promise of joining Saxon in the afterlife if he failed spurred him on. By the time he had cut through the rope his wrists were slippery with blood and he was losing the feeling in his left hand.

The alarm stopped, the house was suddenly very quiet.

42

"Shit."

Khan stood up and was about to run for the loft hatch when an unfamiliar man climbed up. His features were shrouded by shadow, but he appeared quite thin, and even taller than Khan's six feet. He was unarmed, but didn't seem concerned by Khan's freedom.

"Impressive. But the alarm has been turned off and you aren't going anywhere."

Khan threw a punch at his head, but the stranger sidestepped and whipped his boot into Khan's stomach. Before he could step back the criminal thrust his knee into Khan's face and sent him sprawling. Spots of light danced before his eyes, and he looked around for some kind of weapon. Saxon had been right; there was nothing in the loft, except the hatch and three large windows.

A moonlit shadow fell across him. He staggered to his feet, but his assailant was quicker and kicked him to the floor again.

"I was just going to put a bullet in your brain, Mr Khan. But that alarm has given me a headache, and I think I'll take it out on you."

Khan's fingers wrapped around a jagged shard of glass. He threw a feint, and as his enemy moved to avoid the fake blow he stabbed the glass into his thigh. The razor-sharp shard plunged deeply into soft flesh. Khan twisted the blood-soaked glass and then ripped it free, eliciting a scream of pain from the thug. Before he could recover himself Khan charged and pushed him through one of the loft windows. The murderer snatched hold of Khan's shirt and the pair tumbled out of the loft together.

The ground rushed towards Khan, but the criminal was beneath him and broke his fall. The murderer landed on the iron railings, Khan's weight driving his body onto the spikes. Khan fell roughly and hit the gravel hard. He tried to stand up but pain shot through his right leg and he slumped back to the ground. All feeling had fled his left hand, which had been torn to shreds by the glass. His vision was dimming when an agonised groan reached him. He raised his head. Saxon's killer had fared worse. Gravel was not a great safety net, but Khan muttered a prayer of thanks that he hadn't landed on the cast iron railings that encircled the house. The murderous, malevolent bastard was impaled on a dozen of the iron points. Saxon's killer retched violently, and a cloud of bloody mist erupted from his mouth. The points piercing the body glistened red in the moonlight, and he moved no more.

"Khan!" Saxon said. "Bursting that bulb exhausted me. Are you alright?"

The ghost appeared more insubstantial than usual, and Khan had to strain his eyes to make him out.

"Bloody terrific. You should see the other guy," he murmured, nodding towards the criminal.

Saxon smiled, and then looked at the impaled body. Slowly, the smile fell from his face and he gazed in horror at the corpse.

"He's... dead," Saxon said.

Khan snorted with laughter. "Very observant. The vicious bastard had it coming."

"No, you don't understand," Saxon replied, a thread of urgency running through his voice. "He's a ghost."

Khan looked at the corpse. Standing beside the motionless body was the translucent ghost of the killer. The dead murderer strode towards Saxon and wrapped his hand around the investigator's throat. Saxon tried to prise his fingers loose, but the killer was far stronger.

"Saxon!" Khan shouted.

The killer actually looked at Khan and smiled. Saxon took advantage of the distraction to punch his assailant in the shoulder. Saxon was released and staggered away from his attacker.

"I'll kill you slowly this time, Mr Saxon," the well-spoken murderer promised.

A smoking red hand thrust from the gravel and sunk its claws into the killer's calf. Tendrils of smoke curled around his leg, and he screamed in agony. The killer tried to pull himself free, but a second clawed hand rose from the ground and seized his other leg. The two hands slowly, inexorably pulled the malicious spectre down. His smoking legs burst into ethereal flames, cobalt blue fire that raced up his legs and wreathed his body. Screams for help elicited none from Saxon or Khan, who watched in fearful astonishment as he was dragged through the earth to whatever fate claimed the malevolent dead. His final shriek was devoured by silence as the demonic hands pulled him down, and he disappeared.

"Are you alright?" Khan asked.

Saxon, looking even paler than usual, nodded. "Bloody terrific. You should see the other guy."

Minister for Ghosts

ometimes someone seeking fame and wealth might believe that no matter what, the end justifies the means. Off course as you should know by your own moral compass, this is not the case. Irish writer John J Brady, who I have watched develop as a Doctor of Psychiatry, and caster of concrete gnomes, delivers this short shocking lesson where, as you will find, the end is probably more shocking than the protagonist could have wished for. But it is justice, nevertheless.

STILL MOTION

by John Brady

erry clicked the mouse and the still motion sequence ran one more time. The child, his belly swollen with malnutrition. *Famine*. The teenager with his stump in the air, his forearm hacked off by paramilitaries. *War*. The old man, skinny and listless from dysentery. *Pestilence*. And the girl: a close-up of her dead face, eyes staring at nothing. *Death*.

The Four Horsemen would be his best exhibition yet, and hopefully the most lucrative. The product of six months in war-torn Africa, it had almost cost him his life on more than one occasion, but it had all been worth it.

And yet ... the sequence wasn't right. These shots were to form part of a still motion slideshow at the front of the gallery. It would be the punters' first glimpse of his exhibition and it had to be perfect. Something was wrong with the shot of the girl. It was her eyes. They were dead -- he knew that -- but still, something shone out of them, a sort of defiance.

She'd certainly been defiant at the time, he remembered. She'd fought the two men like a lioness, which was probably why they'd made their fun last so long before shooting her. Hiding in the bushes, he'd cradled his handgun against his chest, just in case he needed it. Anticipation had brought him out in a sweat, until they'd left and he could creep into the village to take the shot. It was

47

risky, but at the time he'd been certain a photo of the dead girl could make him a household name.

Now he wasn't so sure. Everybody else said it was a fantastic photo, a critique of the futility of war and all that rubbish. Some even cried. But that defiance ... it sent a quiver of uneasiness down his spine. No, that wasn't what he was looking for. He needed *victims*, not people who fought back. He replaced the photo of the girl with one of a dead mother and baby from another village, and sighed in satisfaction. *That* was the one.

***

"Well?"

"We got orders by the bucketload," Victor said as he dimmed the gallery's lights.

Terry grinned. Three hours schmoozing and glad-handing the city's wealthy elite had been well spent. People's appetite for vicarious misery knew no bounds. It was only the first night; by the end of the fortnight he could be set up for the year. "I think this calls for a celebration," he said.

Victor smiled. "There's a good pub just around the corner." He locked the door and pulled down the shutter over the entrance.

Terry looked at the screen in the window again. The slideshow had done its job, as it would for the rest of the exhibition, displaying the best of *The Four Horsemen*, twenty four hours a day.

"Coming?" Victor asked.

"In a minute." He saw his own reflection, backlit by a burning tank.

"I'll keep you a seat." Victor ambled away, whistling.

The familiar images sped by; the hungry child, the one-armed boy, the sick man, the woman, the -- what? They were gone, the woman and child. Instead, the dead girl stared back at him, her image fixed on the screen. Her eyes peered into his, and for a moment it was as if he saw his own soul, exposed to the world: as black as the pictures he took; as diseased as the old man; as starved as the child; as dead as the girl.

He staggered back and the car struck him, throwing him up into the air. He landed head-first on the footpath with a sickening crunch. He lay paralysed, facing the gallery; helpless and alone.

The last thing he saw before darkness took him was the girl's face. She was smiling.

***

"All right, mate?"

Terry squinted up at Gav's silhouette, wincing as the movement sent a stab of pain through his arm. "I'll live."

He pressed his hand over the field dressing, as if that would actually help. Maybe he could get some more painkillers off the Doc later – he'd already run out of his own the day before, a consequence of taking double doses morning, noon and night, because *she wouldn't bloody well leave him alone!*

"I'll leave you to it then," Gav said, slinging his rifle over his shoulder. He moved off to trawl through the bodies, looking for whatever weapons or ammo took his fancy.

Terry shifted on his crate and turned towards the village. The aid lorries had nearly been unloaded, ready to move on to the next outpost. The villagers should be happy at least, unlike the rebels who'd tried to hijack them. They probably hadn't expected the convoy to be escorted, but they'd got what they deserved. Not without fighting back, though, and he'd been lucky only his arm had taken a bullet. Just one more pain, to add to all the rest.

"Look what I found!" Gav held up a handgun. Terry pretended to know what was so special about it, and gave him a thumbs-up.

Time to move on. He picked up his own rifle and struggled to his feet. As he hobbled to the Land Rover, one of the village elders was shaking the Doc's hand.

Another little bit of good, another attempt to atone –

No, not again! She was staring at him from a doorway, her dead eyes as accusing as ever.

He ran, ignoring the pains, but by the time he reached the hut she was gone. He pushed the straw-matted door aside and darted in. An old, toothless woman looked up from a table, her wide eyes afraid.

"Where is she?" he shouted, his breath ragged.

The woman waved her hand. She didn't know. He looked about frantically, checking every corner of the hut, but no-one else was there. There never was, not when he just wanted to say sorry.

"What is it?" Gav stood in the doorway, rifle in hand and ready for action.

"Nothing." Conscious of the old woman, Terry ushered him out and towards the Land Rover. He eased himself in, grimacing at the familiar ache in his leg. His hand shook and he gripped the door handle tight so the others wouldn't see. Damn, he needed those painkillers. He'd take as many as he needed.

When would she leave him alone? Even as he asked himself the question, he knew the answer. *Whenever the next bullet finishes me.*

MINISTER FOR GHOSTS

Where do I start with my next vessel? Jeff Richards grew up in a house without a television, which forced him to read, which he did, prolifically. His great, great grandmother, wrote several books about spiritualism so clearly reading and writing ran in the family.

I heard about Jeff's talents as a writer and more importantly his psychic awareness and my interest was well and truly pricked. I watched him, closely; probably as close as I have watched anyone. Like most young men he believed he was indestructible and drove his motorbike, recklessly. I worried terribly about him, as did his loved ones. I hoped he would live long enough to become a vessel in my ministry.

My worst nightmares were confirmed one sunny day, many years ago when to my horror; he rode his bike on the open road – fast and furious - and without a care in the world. I was close to him, just back from his shoulder when a car-contraption pulled out in front of us. I had to think quickly. I linked with the spirit-world and summoned up enough energy from the surroundings to allow me to manifest a physical tug at his hand, which squeezed the accelerator.

Thankfully, his speed decreased sufficiently enough for him to avoid certain death. Of course, there were consequences and he suffered multiple fractures to his right arm. He still shows everyone the scars to this day.

I am glad to report that he has calmed down with age and now works for the Ghost Ministry. He now eloquently brings you this next lesson in life.

I will let you decide about this small village in Dog Valley, which carries many secrets, some much darker than others and whether the saying, "You reap what you sow," carries any validity.

DOG VALLEY

by Jeff Richards

ama stabled his horse at the nearest village and walked. By the time he reached *The Traveller's Rest* his kerchief was tied around his nose and mouth, soaked with oil of cloves. He tried breathing only through his nostrils, concerned he'd vomit if he opened his mouth. The stench had worsened, the closer he got. The inn's signpost had been changed to *The Fool's Rest*, with crudely-painted brushwork. The remains of a few buildings stood alongside it – some crumbled brickwork, mostly captured by weeds and long grass which bound it tightly, squeezing the existence from it. Beams lay here and there, rotted through, ready to yield to one small nudge of wind and collapse into dust.

It was a miracle the inn still stood. The roof sagged, pushed down, and the leaning walls reminded Yama of giant nutcrackers, ready to fold inwards and crush everything. Wooden steps up to the main door looked as if a decent weight would snap them through. A spark would have turned the inn into a decent bonfire in no time. Yama felt the eyes on him as he approached the inn. He knew what they'd see: a tall man, no more than mid-twenties, lean and burnt from travelling in the wind and sun, with a good sword at his hip, and saddlebags over his shoulder. The door opened before he reached it, and his hand twitched to his blade as a man stood there.

Yama thought him about forty-five, maybe fifty. His face was weathered, with craggy lines, and his eyes were sunken. A good shave would have taken years off his face. Yama wondered how he could stand the smell.

"What do you want?" the man demanded. "You'd better get in here before you throw up on your boots."

The man stepped aside with a jerky movement, dragging one leg. Yama hesitated and then hurried up the steps, tensing for the snap of the wood, trying to tread close to the supports. The man's mouth turned up in what could have been a smile or a sneer, and he closed the door.

A wide serving bar stood in front of an open door, with two beer barrels mounted on a rack. Five tables, each surrounded by wooden chairs, were scattered around haphazardly. Large candles stood on every table, unlit. Dust cloaked everything except one table and a chair, near a stone fireplace. Smudged footprints carpeted the floor, and Yama could see nobody had been up the stairs. Cobwebs hung in all the corners. The smell in here was not much better than outside.

"Sit down," the man said. "For three stripes I'll light the candle – gives off a powerful scent, and burns some of the stench from the air."

Yama made his way to the clean table and draped his saddlebags over the back of a dusty chair. He reached in his pocket, found a twenty and flicked the coin to the man, who caught it deftly enough.

"Light them all," Yama said.

The man grunted and leaned on a walking stick as he limped to the fire. He lit a taper from the flames and used it to set the candles burning. Yama waited until all five candles were alight before he removed the kerchief. He used it to wipe dust from another chair and sat in it. The man stomped to the clean chair and fell into it, the wood creaking alarmingly under the sudden weight. The candles gave off a strong scent of pine and eucalyptus, and the relief was very welcome.

"Well, what do you want?" asked the man. "Here to win a wager? Two days and nights is the record, that was twelve years back. It's going to cost you – I have to pay triple prices to have supplies hauled up here."

"I'm going into the valley," Yama said, and the man stared at him.

"Good luck to you," he said, harshly. "You don't look stupid, but I don't see many sensible people up here. Thirty eight fools tried it, by my reckoning, and thirty three of them never came back. Why'd you stop here?"

"I heard of a man who endured purgatory every day of his life, and thought I'd listen to his tale."

"What makes you think I'll tell it?"

Yama reached into his saddlebag and drew out a leather purse. He untied the drawstring and brought out a gold liefling. He placed it on the table, and then drew another, lining them up together.

"These are yours if you tell me the truth."

The man stared at the coins.

"Take your money and get out of here," he said.

He reached out to snuff the candle and Yama moved quicker, grabbing his wrist.

"I paid for those," Yama said. "They burn until I say so."

The man glared at Yama and he stared back for a moment, then released his grip.

"I told the truth twenty five years ago," the man said angrily, rubbing his wrist. "Magistrate didn't want to believe me, because they'd have had to go into the valley to investigate. I've been dubbed the biggest liar this side of the mountains, and yet fools and gamblers come up here to make a name for themselves, when they don't know shit."

"I'm neither a fool nor a gambler," Yama said. "And I'm sorry to have troubled you."

He stood and hoisted his saddlebags across his shoulder, then walked to the door and shook out his kerchief.

"You get in the valley, you tell them Paulus Smit greets them," the man said, sarcastically.

A peculiar stillness took Yama, and he stood stone-like for a few seconds. He looked back at the man.

"You're Paulus Smit?"

"What of it?"

"You were there when it happened."

"How d'you know that?" Paulus demanded, his knuckles white as he gripped his stick. "Damn Magistrate never wrote a word down, said I was wrong in the head. How d'you know?"

Yama stared at him for long moments, then walked back and looked down at him.

"Paulus, I'm going into the valley. Maybe I'll die trying to get in, like the others, but maybe I'll live. You telling the truth might make the difference."

"Who are you?"

"A man seeking the truth. My name is Yama."

"Yama? What kind of damn-fool name is that?"

Yama shrugged, waited a few seconds and then half-turned away.

"Sit down," Paulus said, sighing. "I'll tell you what I know, and the gods take you after that."

***

Dog Valley was reckoned to be one of the safest regions in the whole kingdom. Anyone who passed through was made welcome, and traders used to come here first, after the winter snows cleared. Prosperity and safety, all because of the big mountain dogs the villagers tamed hundreds of years back. Legend has it Redbeard Hinton wrestled a pack of 'em, until they were all beat, and they followed him faithfully after that.

But you want the truth, and the truth is, nobody knows why the dogs and the people in the valley became guardians to one another, but they did. Shelter and warmth in the winter for the dogs, and protection throughout the year for the valley folk. I never saw it, but the elders say the dogs tore two intruders to pieces, when they drew swords and tried to rob a home.

Some of the dogs stood the size of a small pony, and yet they were the gentlest animals you ever could meet. So long as you lived in the valley, that is. They reserved their love for the folk here. They'd watch over the little ones, hunt with the adults and be company for the elderly - sit with them until they died and bring comfort to their passing. You could always tell when someone died, because the dogs would set up a howling. Not for long, you understand, just enough of a lament to tell the gods a spirit was coming their way. I reckon there were over three hundred of them scattered across the Valley when I was a boy, but there could have been more.

I was twenty when the trouble started - barely a man back then, hoping to be betrothed soon, and looking to build my own cabin for a home. Maisie Turner and me had been courting - well, almost courting, if you count holding hands and taking long walks. The Elders approved - I'd heard cracks about keeping up the population, but I didn't see anyone else contributing in that area any time soon. But if I'd known what was ahead, I'd have signed up with the army and left Dog Valley there and then.

Regrettably, I ain't gifted with second sight, and evil arrived one night in late summer. I've had enough years to wonder if the village invited it along, but that's dogshit, pure and simple. In the end, everyone there took the punishment, but that's the way of things, ain't it? The menfolk may have deserved some punishment, but not the women. But a forest fire will take anyone in its path - good or bad, it don't discriminate. What happened fanned the flames, in a way of speaking, and everyone standing on its trail paid for it.

It began with the baby crying in the night. I woke in darkness to the sound of it, and after a minute or so the baby shut up, just like that, and I put my head back on the pillow. The dogs started howling a moment later, and they didn't shut up. I got into my breeches and stumbled outside, along with just about everyone. Torches were lit and shouting and jostling were the order of the night until Mayor Brent Thornbury took charge.

"Quiet!" he yelled, striding out from his house, a burning torch held aloft. He'd dragged on breeches and shirt and he'd had the sense to draw on his boots, unlike the rest of us. His wife and daughter stood in the doorway behind him, in their nightclothes, clutching each other.

At that precise moment all the dogs shut up. The hairs on my neck and arms rose, and I couldn't contain the shiver.

"What's happened?" demanded Mayor Thornbury. "Who's died?"

We looked round, but nobody was missing

"Someone must have died," the Mayor said. "Check every house."

Father said we should search our house, even though we all stood there in the road, and of course we found nothing. We put on warmer clothes and boots and went back outside to where Thornbury waited. More and more villagers reported back. Nobody had died. Nothing was found.

Elder Whistler suggested the dogs had gone to deal with intruders, and we waited for their calls, to show us where. But no calls came. Eventually, Mayor Thornbury told us all to go back to bed, and meet in the village hall next day.

That morning the village hall was packed, and the elders and the mayor waited until we were all inside.

"We believe one of the older dogs died last night, and the others greeted his death by howling," Mayor Thornbury said. "We think they've learned to grieve for their own, in the same way they do for us."

There was a momentary silence, and muted conversations started all over. Then Maisie raised her hand, and everything changed. The Mayor pointed to her.

"I recognise Rosemary Turner," he said, and the noise died immediately.

She stood, and fussed with a pleat in her dress as she spoke.

"I heard a baby crying last night," she said, in a voice that wrung my heart. I thought she'd burst into tears. "Just before the dogs started howling."

"A baby?" Mayor Thornbury asked, frowning. "Are you sure? There are no babies in this village, Maisie. Pittock's youngest is three, going on four. Dawie, was she crying last night?"

Dawie Pittock stood.

"No sir, she was distressed at the howling, but she's a good girl."

"Can't have been a baby," Mayor Thornbury said, shaking his head.

"I heard it, too," came another voice, and we all swivelled to see.

"I recognise William Kentnish," said the Mayor, sarcastically.

William coloured up, and mumbled an apology. Maisie sat down and William stayed on his feet.

"It was crying fit to burst," he said. "Then it stopped, sudden... and the dogs started howling."

Another seven people stood and told the same tale, and I was one of 'em. When I thought about it later, I realised we all lived close, but nobody'd had a baby, because nobody was pregnant. There was a lot of debate, and in the end the conclusion most people took home was that a trader's wagon must have passed through in the dark, and their baby crying alerted the dogs, who took off after them.

It would've remained a mystery, only the very next night I woke to a baby crying, bawling its lungs out, and the dogs set up howling again. This time, everybody heard the baby crying, because it continued for nigh on two hours. We searched every scrap of ground, but we were chasing Jack o' the mist. The sounds came from everywhere and nowhere – when you thought you were close, the crying would erupt from another spot, and you'd rush there. Rennie Cooper and Lee Smith collided in the dark chasing the same sound from different directions. Nothing was found.

And the next night the dogs didn't sleep on the porches, like they'd always done. My favourite had been one I'd called whitepatch because of the colouring over his eye, and though you never said you owned 'em, I always thought of him as my dog. We'd grown up together, and it hurt something fierce when he deserted me. Gradually, over the coming days they withdrew further – one growled at Mayor Thornbury and the Elders when they tried to approach it, teeth bared, and they'd beat a fast retreat, fearing it would attack.

Every night the crying and the howling went on and on. It could be anytime – the late evening, midnight, the early morning – it was random and all the more frightening because of it. We burned torches all night, so many torches it was bright as daylight outside, and still the crying started and stopped. Shadows spread under people's eyes, and chores were left off because people fell asleep in the daytime. Children clung to their mothers, refusing to leave their sides, and wouldn't sleep in their own rooms.

The Crindles left within a week and the Courtneys, the Farwells and the Pittocks followed them pretty soon after. Two men sent their families away to visit relatives in the city and toiled their fields alone. Tempers flared, arguments broke out over nothing and life was becoming intolerable. My father wanted to send mother away, but she wouldn't go.

The Mayor called a closed meeting of all the men. Unfortunately for me, I'd passed into adulthood only a week previously, so I attended.

We sat in the village hall with all the shutters closed, and trusted men guarded the outside, so no women could approach. I sat beside my father, and drew comfort when he slipped his arm around my shoulder. The air was thick with fear, and Mayor Thornbury bid us gather in a circle.

"I recognise the men of Dog Valley," he said, and we returned the greeting.

"We have owned this valley for centuries," he said.

"Toiled it, farmed it, hunted it, and above all, respected it. The dogs recognise us as the true inheritors of the land, and have been our faithful companions as long as we can remember. Now they draw back. A restless spirit threatens us all, and it seems we are powerless. Twenty eight of our community have left, and I fear more of you will go soon. I would go with you, if I could. But I will not give up the life I love without doing everything humanly possible to rid us of this evil."

There were murmurs that could have been agreement from the gathered men.

"What can we do?" he asked. "We can leave Dog Valley, and make our lives in another place. But who's to say this restless spirit won't follow us? If you gave up the valley, and woke in the night to find the spirit screaming in your ear, could you live with that? I'd sooner die."

More murmurs. Stronger.

"Can you remain here without going mad?" he asked, and looked round at us. "I don't know how much more I can take. Unless we do something, this valley will soon be empty. Desolate."

Silence spread through the room, as each man considered this.

"There is something we can do," he said into that silence, and looked at each man in turn, measuring us. "It will be hard - harder than anything we've ever done - but if we do this together, as one, we can remove the spirit that haunts us, and go back to the lives we had before. You've all remained here, living this nightmare because you want - nay, need - the life we had. Our families are wilting, and we *must* do something. We must be united, to carry it through."

He let us absorb this, and I saw hope blossom on many faces.

"How, Mayor Thornbury?" asked Gord Atkins, and Thornbury didn't rebuke him for speaking without his permission.

"The baby seeks its mother," he said, and let a long pause drag on before speaking again. "We must provide a mother for it."

I didn't grasp what he meant, but the silence that greeted this was cold and deadly. My father's hand gripped my shoulder hard, and then I understood. Shock was clear on every face, each man taking in the awful thought. But not one man, myself included, leapt to his feet and condemned it for the evil it was.

The silence stretched on, and nobody wanted to be the first to speak.

"Who?" a shaky voice finally asked.

"Does every man here agree we must do this?" Mayor Thornbury asked. "It must be undisputed, that we all play our part."

A long silence followed and I wanted to say no, I swear I did. I waited for my father to stand and reject the wickedness we considered, but he stayed where he was. I was a coward. I sat beside him and did nothing.

Thornbury got to his feet and walked around our circle, taking a sworn oath of secrecy from each man. I could barely look him in the eye, but I gave the oath, like all the others.

***

Scurrying interrupted Paulus – claws scratching on floorboards, and Yama saw two rats scuttle into a nook below the fireplace. He heard the same sounds on the floorboards above his head.

"You've got rats, Paulus," he said.

A grim smile twisted Paulus's face.

"Everything's entitled to some life, I don't hold with killing 'em," he said. "You might want to prepare yourself."

"What for?"

The dreadful sound cut through the air like a surgeon's knife, acid-cold, and paralysing. A high-pitched, keening wail that pierced the building, seeming to vibrate its essence forcibly outwards, as the scream of a baby echoed from the walls. It went on and on, unearthly, not drawing breath, and the temperature in the room plunged. Paulus threw a large log onto the fire, and sparks cascaded up the chimney. He clambered to his feet, grabbing his stick.

"We'll need some brandy," he said, and hobbled to the bar.

Yama tried to breathe normally, but his chest felt constricted, as though he was bound in canvas. He watched as Paulus reached over and pulled up an earthenware jug, corked, and fished out two beakers. Yama tore himself from the icy dread that had encased him, and left footprints in the dust as he hurried to help, taking the beakers and returning to the table. Paulus splashed a good measure into both as soon as he sat, and pushed one across to Yama. The drink burned down his throat, and blessed warmth spread through his chest and stomach. Paulus refilled it.

"How do you stand it?" Yama asked.

"You can get used to anything," Paulus said, shrugging. "Especially when you deserve it."

***

When we got home, father instructed my mother to start packing whatever belongings she could fit into our wagon, without arousing the attention of our neighbours. She was to do it slowly, over a day or so, because we were leaving Dog Valley. She didn't ask what happened in the meeting, and we didn't tell her. But next morning, Mayor Thornbury arrived at our door with Bryn Oswald, Rennie Cooper and Karl Breuchner, and 'invited' my mother to stay with his wife and daughter for the next few nights, since she was the village herbalist. Elise, his daughter was poorly, and not sleeping, even during the day. Perhaps mother's close attention could help? There was nothing we could do.

It happened five days later. Word had spread among traders about our troubles, and there were less coming through, but eventually, what Thornbury needed arrived – a small family, with a nursing mother, and we left on horseback as they traded in the square. My father was being held at sword point, and Thornbury's punishment of our disloyalty in trying to leave, was to make sure I was deeply involved.

I prayed the dogs would leap from the bushes and stop us, but there wasn't one to be seen when we halted the wagon deep in the valley, just as the sun set. Looking like footpads, the men dragged the traders from their wagon, and cudgelled all but one. The nursing mother had the baby wrenched from her arms and a heavy blanket thrown over her. The men stood, uncertain, and the baby began to cry.

"I'll take it," I said and the child was thrust at me. I rocked it gently, and it soothed.

"Deal with it," hissed Bryn Oswald and my heart stopped. It fell to me to place the woman's baby in the river, but the mother would never be found – 'lost in the waters somewhere', they'd say. I stumbled down the slope, sick at heart as the men watched in the gloom from above. Pushing through the shrubbery I waded into the river, and held the bundle underwater, then released it, to let the current carry it away.

When I got back, soaked and shivering, I watched as the men drove the traders' wagon from the road above the river. The horses screamed in terror as whip and iron drove them over the edge, and then the weight of the wagon toppled them, dragging them, twisting them in the traces as the wagon smashed down the slope, turning over and over. Legs shattered as they fell and I clapped my hands over my ears to block the awful sounds of their suffering. The wagon and horses hit the stony riverbank, and the grinding crash drowned out everything. The trader's possessions scattered all over, as the wagon broke in pieces and I saw the body of a young man crushed between timbers.

The baby's mother was locked inside Mayor Thornbury's cold store. There were no windows, just a panel that could be opened in the thick oak door. She could scream all day and never be heard. There was no way out.

When the spirit baby cried, Thornbury opened the panel and told the woman it was her baby crying, and she tried to go to it. She screamed and raved and beat upon the door, clawing at the opening. He closed the panel when the spirit baby stopped crying. He told us at the meeting her desire to go to the dead baby would be increased every night, and when she died, she'd take it up, and the village would be free of it. Each night the evil was repeated and each night the woman screamed and pleaded.

On the fourth night, my father came to me as I lay waiting for the inevitable. He wore a sword and carried a heavy cudgel.

"Paulus, we have to act," he said. "I'll get your mother out, you must release the woman."

He handed me the cudgel and it weighed heavy in my hand. A reassuring heaviness, and I hoped Mayor Thornbury sat guarding the cold store. But Bryn Oswald was there, and I waited until the dogs began their howling; it covered the sound of my approach and I hit him hard, and dragged his insensible body behind the store. Then I hurried to the door, slid the bolts open and carefully opened it.

"Hello?" I whispered.

I heard short panting sighs. They ceased and the breath caught in my own throat.

"Why are you doing this?" her whisper came. Slurred, like a drunken man. "My baby..."

She lay sprawled in the corner, and closed her eyes at the light from the torches. Her mouth was cracked, her lips split. Black shadows circled her sunken eyes, her hair was matted and she'd pulled clumps out in her raving. Dried blood encrusted her hands, fingernails torn out where she'd scrabbled at the door – and I couldn't imagine the mortal anguish we'd inflicted on her. She wore a black dress with purple flowers embroidered, and it was soiled through.

I slid down and put my arm around her, drawing her head onto my shoulder and told her the truth. She listened and her breath quickened when I spoke of her child. My tears fell on her face, but I didn't ask for forgiveness – I didn't deserve it.

"I'm getting you out," I said.

"Too late," she whispered.

Her voice was fading as she spoke her curse, preventing us from leaving the valley and preventing any person from entering. The smell of evil would always be upon us, and no child would be born in the valley. The dogs would ensure her curse was kept. She gave a last, long sigh and her head fell forward as she died. The mist thickened, and the dogs came out of the haze, into the village, growling and threatening. Then her spirit came towards me holding a baby wrapped in cloth, and I felt, rather than heard her voice.

'Leave now, or suffer their fate.'

I wanted to run to my parents to get them out, but the dogs blocked my way. They growled when I tried to get round them, but I was desperate. I lunged and one sunk his teeth in my thigh, behind the knee. They drove me out of the valley, and I collapsed. The howling started right after, worse than it had ever been. Fear drove me to crawl away, to drag myself by my hands when my leg gave out. Old Lambert, who owned this inn in those days, found me and nursed me back to health.

Her curse sealed the valley, and it's stayed that way for twenty-five years. Not many can stand it here; nobody has ever come out, and the dogs will tear you apart if you try to get in. Some of the people still live, you can see the smoke from their chimneys when it's cold.

***

"That truthful enough for you?" Paulus demanded.

66

Yama stared at him for a few seconds. The wailing had stopped at some point during the telling, and he hadn't been aware of it. He drained his beaker.

"Why do you stay?"

Paulus swallowed hard and he couldn't look Yama in the eye. He struggled to speak.

"Because I could have prevented it, and didn't," he croaked. "I deserve their punishment, and this is the closest I can get to it."

"I don't believe that's true, or the woman would have trapped you in the village."

"Don't you think it's worse, being here, not knowing?" Paulus said, his voice breaking. "Knowing my parents suffer, when they were good people?"

"There's more to say. Come, tell me, and I shall be on my way."

Paulus stared at Yama.

"Damn you," Paulus said.

***

The first time the crying and the howling started, people clung to each other for comfort, but in the nights that followed, I was alone with my fears. I lay by myself, hands over my ears, and tried to block the sounds. About four or five nights after it all started, I heard my name whispered urgently, from outside. Maisie Turner stood there, trembling, and I opened my shutters, helping her to climb in.

"What is it?"

Tears flowed down her face and I wrapped my arms around her. We lay on top of my bed and she wept silently. When the howling stopped, she fell asleep against me and I slept, too. Funny how fear can drive you together quicker than love. I'm not saying I loved Maisie right then, but we needed the comfort of each other, and it helped us both.

She returned each night and slipped away before dawn. We didn't do anything more than hold each other, and kiss now and then, but not in a way that stirred desire.

67

It was the day after the men's meeting that Maisie told me her secret, and I told her mine. I knew what she said was true, while praying it wasn't. On the very first night, before the crying started, she'd been down to the privy at the bottom of their garden. Mayor Thornbury's house bordered her own and she heard moans and groaning, and couldn't work out where it was coming from. Later on, she was in her bedroom when she heard a long shuddering wail, which was followed by the cries of a baby.

Maisie said she was rooted to the spot, but heard the door in Mayor Thornbury's house crash open. The mayor ran down the garden and pulled open the door to the cold store, and the crying of the baby could be heard in the clear night. He stood for a moment and then reached down. The crying stopped immediately, and Maisie held her breath, terrified of what had happened. When the howling started straight after, she knew the baby had died, and the mayor had killed it.

She watched as Mayor Thornbury gathered up his daughter in his arms and scurried back to the house, locking the cold store. The following day, she plucked up the courage to stand up and say she'd heard a baby crying, and listened to Thornbury's lies in response, but didn't have the courage to denounce him.

When the mayor outlined his plan to the men, the only person I told was Maisie. I took the baby down to the river as Maisie waited, hidden in the shrubbery. I handed it over, exchanging it for the bundle of cloths. She fled into the night when we left and I never saw her again.

I'm sorry for many things in my life, but the one that will haunt me to the grave, is why we didn't say anything. Midwife Elstone would have examined Elise and seen the truth at once. We both knew our mayor was a liar and a murderer, but we should have done something. If we'd spoken up, none of it would've happened. We were too scared to speak up. I can't hate myself any more than I do.

***

"That's why I sit here and share their punishment," Paulus said after a long silence."If I had the courage I'd walk into the valley and let the dogs finish me off."

"Come with me, then," Yama said. "End your miserable life and start a new one."

Paulus glared at Yama with hard eyes.

"What do you want?" Paulus asked, harshly.

"To *see* the truth, Paulus. Not just to hear it, though I thank you for your honesty."

Yama pushed the two gold lieflings across the table towards Paulus, and stood up.

"When I return, I'll be as honest with you, Paulus Smit."

Yama held out his hand and Paulus hesitated for a moment and then shook it. Yama smiled and turned and walked towards the door.

"Wait."

Yama looked back at him.

"I'll come with you. Let me see to the candles."

Paulus snuffed the candles and Yama put his kerchief back in place as he waited.

Yama walked at a pace Paulus could manage, and they reached the rim of the valley quite soon. The stench was almost unbearable - sulphurous rot mixed with pigshit, Yama decided, and was glad he'd taken the brandy earlier, it settled his stomach a little.

The trees were darker down there; close-set, impenetrable, and it was impossible to see if there were any dwellings because of the mist that veiled the valley. Yama stopped, opened the collar of his shirt, and pulled a locket free, then drew his sword. He cut back brambles, hazel branches and stinging nettles, careless of the effect on the blade, and they made slow progress. After some time Yama stopped, and removed the kerchief.

"The dogs will come soon," he said, "and I hope they'll admit us."

"You hope?" snorted Paulus.

"Can't live without hope," Yama said.

He stepped forward and the air changed, cooling.

"Stay there," Yama warned him, as Paulus moved towards him.

The dogs seemed to emerge from the earth itself, gliding out of the undergrowth, stalking Yama. He knelt on the earth, opened his arms wide and the dogs approached him. They stood at the height of Yama's head, and he stared at the largest, which advanced closer. The dog halted barely six inches away from Yama, sniffing. It sniffed at Yama's open shirt, then backed away. As one, the dogs faded back into the brushwood. Yama touched the locket.

"What is that?" Paulus asked, as Yama stood up.

"Something my mother gave me. You might want to prepare yourself."

"What for?"

The air chilled further, and thickened somehow. Wind swirled impossibly around them, circling them, lifting their hair, pulling at their clothes. Then the air distorted, misting, and they saw an opening, terrifying to look upon. A mass, like a huge globe made of shimmering glass, swept towards them up the slope. The bushes and undergrowth bent and swayed with its passing, and shapes could be seen inside it. Paulus clutched his stick to steady himself and a moan escaped him. Then the shimmer faded to nothing, the air stilled, and a dark-haired woman stood before them. She wore a black dress, with purple embroidered flowers across it. She carried a baby wrapped in white cloth in the crook of her arm.

"Hello, mother," Yama said.

She reached out with her free hand and cupped his face. He took her hand and kissed it tenderly, holding it against his lips. A tear escaped her eye, and rolled down her cheek. Yama reached out and caught it on the tip of a finger, and it wet his lips as he kissed it.

"My son."

The words vibrated in the air, and Yama smiled. She turned her eyes on Paulus and he shrank back.

"Paulus Smit," she said. "It has been many years since we met."

"I'm so sorry," Paulus mumbled, and tears welled up in his eyes. "I'm so sorry."

"You have paid the coin of regret," she said. "I do not forget that my son lives because of you. Others will pay today."

She stepped towards him and he flinched back.

"I will do you no harm, Paulus," she said. "Hold a child for the second time in your life, and play your part. His name is Ben."

She settled the baby in Paulus's arm, and then waved her hand. The path opened, as though it had never been choked with weeds and plants. The air cleared, and the smell of woodsmoke reached them. Baked clay showed through meagre grass. The mist drew back, and some of the chill left the air. The woman shimmered and disappeared.

"How is this possible?" Paulus whispered.

"It doesn't matter," Yama said. "Today all things pass, that should pass, and all that should remain, will."

Paulus stared at him, incomprehension written on his face.

"Maisie remembers you to this day," Yama said. "She thought you were trapped with the others, and regretted you could never be a father to me."

Paulus stared at him. "Where is she?"

"In Meister's Bay, a year's travel from here. She's very happy."

"Did she... did she tell you everything?"

"Yes. Now we must go."

They walked down the slope and into the village. The baby lay silent in Paulus's arm, and he leaned heavily on his stick, as they went down. Yama steadied him over difficult ground and at last they entered what was left of the village. Ramshackle log buildings had toppled and ivy spread over them, like a green blanket. Here and there stores of firewood showed the homes were still used, and

71

one porch had two empty chairs sitting on it. A pale face showed at a window, pulled quickly back as they passed.

Paulus stopped, disbelief on his face.

"What is it?" Yama asked.

"There were four houses here," he said, indicating with his stick. "Where've they gone?"

Overgrown weeds and brambles covered a wide area, as though they'd always been there.

"They probably burned them for fuel in the winter."

"The store was there, how can it—"

He broke off, shaking his head, and they walked on. Nearer the square, the buildings were better kept, and shouts went up. But not one person approached them. They reached the village hall, and two chairs awaited them in front of arranged benches. Their footsteps echoed on the wooden floor and they sat down. The baby murmured and Paulus rocked it gently.

"So, all the time you asked me, you knew?"

"Only once I heard your name."

"Bastard," Paulus said. "What now?"

"You must recognise them, as they enter."

They heard muted voices and a woman appeared in the open door. Paulus stood.

"I recognise Yolanda Burswith," he said loudly, and she took a step inside. Paulus saw another person behind her.

"I recognise Andrew Burswith."

Yolanda tugged him by the arm, into the hall. They shuffled in, and sat on the bench nearest the door, ill at ease.

"I recognise Gord Atkins."

More villagers entered, and the benches at the back of the hall filled. Shabby, patched clothes and scuffed boots were worn by most of the villagers. Threadbare blankets were wrapped around many shoulders. Paulus had difficulty recognising some of them and they had to give him their names. More villagers entered; fearful and hesitant, but an air of expectancy rose.

"I recognise... Rebecca Smit," he said, and couldn't

continue until Yama squeezed his arm. "I recognise Thomas Smit."

His mother wore a blue dress with a patchwork shawl. White hair was tied back in a plait, and her face was wrinkled, though her eyes still shone dark brown. His father stooped a little, and wore a hunting jacket that hung from thin shoulders, with patched breeches. A long grey beard hung down to his chest, obscuring the lower half of his face. His parents peered at him as they walked slowly to a bench near the front, and Yama had to nudge him again, as others had entered the hall.

"I recognise Joseph Turner."

The hall was less than a third full when the last group of people entered together - a woman and five men, accompanying an elderly man with very white hair.

"I recognise Bryn Oswald," Paulus said in a tight voice.

He recognised the other men: Karl Breuchner, Rennie Cooper, Lee Smith, and Janni Orson, and they took a bench near the front, leaving the woman and the old man standing. Paulus took a deep breath

"I recognise Elise Thornbury."

The silence drew itself out as the man waited beside her, holding her arm. He wore his chain of office, as though it counted for something, even now.

"I do not recognise Brent Thornbury." Paulus said. "You may not speak, unless invited by me."

Elise and her father walked in total silence to the five men and sat alongside them. Paulus took his seat as they did, and Yama stood. Every eye turned to him.

"Today is judgement day," he said. "None of you may leave this hall."

Bryn Oswald leapt to his feet and strode to the door, pulling it open. He almost fell as he skidded back. Outside, the dogs waited. The hall was surrounded by them, and they set up a growling that vibrated through the building. Bryn let go of the door and staggered back to his seat, his face ashen.

"Today you may take back a life of peace, or you may die in torment," Yama said. "The dogs will choose which." He turned to Paulus. "Give the child to his mother."

Paulus stood and looked down at Elise, and she moaned, clutching at her father. A storm of murmurs filled the hall as he walked towards Elise, and gently placed the baby in her arms.

"This is your son," Paulus said. "His name is Ben."

Elise held the baby close and wept deep racking sobs that shook her body. Brent Thornbury did nothing to comfort her, and Paulus took his seat again.

"Elise, you may leave," Yama said. "Thomas and Rebecca, will you help her?"

Paulus's parents tentatively approached Elise, and she stood. Rebecca put an arm around her waist and Thomas walked ahead of them and opened the door. The dogs drew back and allowed them to leave. A sigh went through the hall.

"The child has found his true mother," Yama said. "The curse will be lifted if the child's father will come forward."

No movement, no sign from any of them. Then a hand went up.

"I recognise Gord Atkins," Yama said.

"Mayhap the father has perished, already?"

"I think not."

There was another long silence and then Thornbury's hand went up. Yama turned to Paulus. He stared at Thornbury full of hate, but finally nodded.

"I recognise Brent Thornbury," Yama said.

"I know who the father was, and he's dead," Thornbury said.

"Do you swear so?"

"I do."

"If this is true, the day may yet end happily," Yama said. "But for an oath in the valleys to be proved, it requires Goodmen to attest the truth of it. Do you have those?"

There was a moment's hesitation, and then Bryn

74

Oswald held his hand up, quickly followed by Rennie Cooper, Lee Smith, and Karl Breuchner. After a moment's silence Janni Orson raised his hand.

"Name the father," Yama said to Thornbury.

"Godfrey Ward."

"Do you men give your solemn oath and attest to the truth of Brent Thornbury naming Godfrey Ward as father of Elise Thornbury's child?" Yama asked.

"We do," they chorused.

Yama's eyes glittered as he looked at them.

"Shame on you."

A percussion, like a strong gust of wind, slammed into the roof of the hall and the beams creaked. Startled cries broke out as darkness descended, blinding everyone. The temperature in the hall plunged, benches tipped, screams rang out and panicked villagers fell to the floor, tripping over each other in terror.

Then light blazed, and a dark-haired woman stood in the centre of the room, clad in a black dress. Radiance coalesced around her, coiling through her dress, illuminating purple flowers that decorated it. She looked down at Thornbury, sprawled on the floor.

"The time is nigh for me to take you," she said, and Thornbury's eyes almost burst from his head. "Come."

She held out her hand and he scrambled back, terrified, his boot-heels slipping on the floor as he tried to get away. He fetched up against the wall and she took hold of his shoulder, pulling him to his feet. An opening formed behind him, a long tunnel where dark shapes writhed and twisted, and he screamed as she turned him to it.

"No! Please!"

She pushed him and he fell into the tunnel. Black tendrils reached for him, enfolding him, passing him down the channel, and his screams grew terrible as he was swept away. Abruptly, the tunnel closed and the wall restored itself. She turned to the five men, who cowered away from her. Rennie Cooper fell to his knees, hands raised, beseeching.

"You must pay for the deaths of my family," she said. "Your actions brought punishment on the village, and all these here have suffered because of you. Three of you will die – a life for a life – and the others will live with their shame for the rest of their days. The dogs will choose."

Rennie slumped down, weeping, and she looked down at him disdainfully.

"Weep, as I wept. Scream as I screamed, but your torment will be short, and well-deserved."

She turned to the villagers, and they drew back, fearful.

"The goodness that some of you possess gives Dog Valley a final chance. The dogs will remain for a year, guarding you as they once did, and if Ben Thornbury is raised with love of all, if you cherish him as your own, they will remain. My curse is lifted."

She turned her back to them and enfolded Yama in her arms, and he kissed her. After some seconds, and reluctant to let go, Yama stepped away from her.

"I will wait for you at the end of path, my son. Live a good life, and be happy."

"I will, mother. Thank you."

Something moved in the air, she blazed with light, and when it faded she was gone.

"You may try to leave now," Yama said, and nodded to Paulus.

They walked past the villagers and opened the door. The dogs waited, but allowed them passage. Paulus almost fell as he stumbled towards his parents, and Yama left them weeping in each others' arms.

Yama waited with Elise as the villagers pushed their way through the dogs. Eventually, only five men remained inside. When Karl Breuchner tried to leave, the dogs snarled and he fled back inside.

"You should all go to your homes," Yama said to the villagers. "Justice will be bloody."

"I'll stay and witness," Paulus said, and his parents stood beside him. Three more villagers waited, and when only Bryn Oswald, Rennie Cooper and Karl Breuchner remained inside the hall, the dogs entered. Their deaths were brutal and swift.

***

"Goodbye, Paulus," Yama said, later. "You'll need this to help with re-building."

He handed his purse to Paulus.

"What will you do for money?" Paulus asked, surprised.

"There are two lieflings on the table at the inn."

"So there are," Paulus laughed. "I'd forgotten them. What will you do now?"

"Go home and tell Maisie the story of Dog Valley."

"Tell her I'd—"

"Tell her yourself," Yama interrupted. "She'll be waiting for you, once she knows you're alive. Maybe she'll come here to find you and her father."

Paulus nodded, smiling.

"Goodbye, Yama. Thank you."

"Paul. My name's Paul, she named me after you. Yama was the name I took when she told me the story of my family – he was the judge of all, tormentor of the wicked, and I reckoned my mother would approve. I don't need his name any longer."

"Maybe there's another valley like this one. More people that need judging. You're good at it – the magistrate was as much use as a tit on a bull, but you got it done. The world needs people like you."

Yama looked around. At the happiness on people's faces. At Elise and the baby.

"Perhaps."

He smiled, then turned and walked away. Paulus limped after him, taking his arm.

"Wait," Paulus said, quietly. "Who was the father?"

Yama stepped close to him and spoke softly.

"Ben cried because his own father murdered him. Never speak of that, or I will return and judge you as you deserve. Elise and Ben need you all."

Yama left the village and was never seen in Dog Valley again.

MINISTER FOR GHOSTS

hank you Jeff and long may it continue that you cannot afford a television. Being poor sometimes can be rewarding! That story was beautifully delivered, so please accept my grateful thanks.

So, onto my next lesson, Damaris Browne was not an easy vessel for me to channel. Because of her work as a solicitor, she keeps her cards very close to her chest and her spiritual centres battened down. But she was too much of a talent to miss, so I persevered.

Her ancestors included Spanish aristocrats, Somerset horse-dealers, various soldiers, sergeants and generals, and one wife-murderer. I have met most of them in my work as Minister for Ghosts.

For the spirit, the purpose of life is to evolve. So as you would expect, Damaris has been through many lives and now, as a consequence, she is a wise and knowledgeable vessel of my ministry. I will now put the words into the ether and let her tell this next tale.

FUTURE TENSE

by Damaris Browne

"... help ..."
"... kill ..."
"... stop ..."

Booth jerked awake. He was in the armchair, the TV still blaring at him, lager spilling from the can he was holding. For a fraction of a second he thought the calls had come from the film he'd been watching, some time-travelling piece of crap, everyone jumping back to the past to try and change history, but then his eyes focussed – whales swam across the screen, and beneath the over-loud music a calm voice whispered about their majesty.

He dropped the can, struggled to his feet, and stumbled across the unfamiliar room to the window. Cars roared down the street; two women tottered along the gutter in heels they couldn't control before the first one stooped and threw up over the second one's shoes, then they both started screaming at each other. They weren't the voices he'd heard. The two slags were white, but the voices had been foreign, hard to understand. Asian, perhaps, and one of them a boy's, he thought. He craned his neck looking up and down the street. No Asians. No three people. No boys.

Properly awake now, he made for the door. Someone else in the flats, probably. That was all he needed. New job, new flat, new city, and still some wanker beating up on his wife and kids at all hours. He peered through the spyhole and held his breath. No one out in the hall and stairwell. No one thumping on walls, telling the wanker to keep the noise down. He waited another minute. Heard nothing but the screaming slags and a heavy baseline of druggie music pounding somewhere.

He went back to the chair, ripped off another piece of pizza, sat down and watched whales.

***

"... kill us ..."
"... get help ..."
"... please, stop ..."

Booth jolted upright. He was in bed. No TV, no time-travelling whales, no music. Headlights shattered the darkness for an instant, flashing across the cruddy wallpaper, then fled; tyres screeched into the night.

No point looking out the window or peering through the door's spyhole. A week of it had told him that. The voices would stay quiet till he fell asleep, exhausted from trying to stay awake. Not just voices now, either. Images, too. A small woman, coloured, black hair pulled back from a pock-marked forehead, a faint black moustache above a scarred lip; a girl, not yet in her teens, bushy eyebrows, gappy teeth; a boy, a year or two older perhaps, thin nose, thin face, thin hair glossed back.

Booth reached for a cigarette and lit it, hands shaking. Every night same. The voices he couldn't properly hear, couldn't properly understand., so only scraps of words came to him. Scraps of words trying to tell him something.

***

81

"Here, reckon they're ghosts?"

His workmate, Jaz, leaning against the pub wall, pint in one hand, fag in the other.

"Don't believe in ghosts," Booth said.

"Dun't matter what you believe if they're there." Another pull at his beer, another drag on the cigarette. "Here, what if it's someone's been murdered there? The ghosts haunting the place. You said you got it cheap. P'rhaps that's why."

Booth sneered, but...

***

He asked around the flats first. The crazy old cow on the ground floor knew everything and everyone. "Never heard of no murder," she said. "Had a family of Pakis here ten month back. Kept theirselves to theirselves. Stank the place out but no brawling. Left when the council rehoused 'em. Saw 'em go. No one got killed."

Then he asked at the next door house, and the one beyond that, at the pub and the Spar shop and the Polish deli. No one knew anything of any murder.

He asked at the offices of the local paper , where a flat-chested, hard-faced bitch would hardly give him the time of day, and at the library, where the cripple behind the desk got everything set up for him so he could look through the records.

Nothing. No deaths. No murders. No reason for ghosts.

***

"... must get help ..."
"... will kill us ..."
"... please, please, stop ..."

He heard them in the day now. Saw them, too. Still

couldn't make out all they were saying. "Speak up," he yelled at them. "Talk proper English."

The factory chargehand gave him a lecture, told him to go home, get some rest. The doctor gave him tranqs, told him he was overworking, get some rest. The woman at the Chinese medicine shop gave him some muck that turned his stomach, told him his spirit was angry, get some rest. The woman across the hall gave him an earful, told him he was a loony, get fucking lost.

Then he saw them. Really saw them. Getting out a clapped-out old Ford at the house across the way. A small coloured woman, pock-marked forehead, hair scraped back; a girl, about twelve, eyebrows like something had crawled there and died; a fourteen year old boy, scrawny, unwashed hair. Not ghosts. Real.

**

He stood at the window, watching. A week they'd been in the house. No one came to see them. They hardly went out, only to the Spar and the deli. He followed them, then, listening to what they said, checking what they bought.

There was a man, he knew it. A man beating up on them. That's what the ghosts were telling him. He had to stop the man from killing them. But he never saw the man. Never saw him go in, never saw him come out. At night he went and stood in their front yard, listening. Stood there all night, by the privet, as the cars raced down the road, lights and ghetto drums thumping, and the slags slobbered by, drunk and moaning and throwing up and screaming. But he never heard the man. He still heard the voices, though. Still heard the broken voices telling him to stop the man.

**

"... will kill us all ..."

"You must get help ..."

"... please, please, stop this ..."

Three weeks. Three weeks of watching and listening. Seeing nothing there, hearing nothing there. She had to be hiding the man. Inside the house. The woman had to be hiding him, because he was hitting her, trying to kill her. He had to get into the house to stop the man, to stop the voices.

He waited till she went out to the Spar shop. The kids were at school. He went over to the house. Stood in the front yard, by the privet, watching, listening. Nothing.

He jemmied the lock, but quietly. Quietly, to catch the man. No one in the front room. Just an old sofa, the cloth worn, the stuffing leaking. A table, three chairs. But he knew all that; he'd stared through the window often enough. No one in the backroom. Another sofa, a better one. An old TV. Fraying cushions. No one in the kitchen. Broken tiles, mouldy grouting, curry smells. Washing up still wet. Plates, cups, spoons, knives.

Back to the hall. Upstairs. Slowly, quietly. Two bedrooms. Shelves. Books. Beds. Bathroom. Brown fittings, piss-stained lino. No man there. No man hiding under the beds, inside the bath, on the shelves, behind the books.

Back downstairs. Back to the kitchen, the door to the garden.

A noise. A door – the front door – opening. He crept back to the hall, under the stairs. The woman. Two carrier bags in her hand, frowning as she looked at the door.

"Samit? You are home?" she called. Her voice the same. The voice he heard every night, every day, every hour.

He was right. She expected someone. The man. He stayed quiet. Only as she passed did he move.

"Where is he?"

She dropped the bags, jumped back from him, a cry half-buried in her throat.

"Where's the man?"

"I have no money," she said. A whisper, a whimper.

"Where is he? I've got to stop him."

She went to run by him, but he caught her. She cried out again. He felt wet on his hand. He looked. His hand was red.

She fell at his feet. He looked down. A carving knife jutted from her stomach.

He lurched back. Then came forward again and pulled the knife out.

The man. The man must have done it. Must have pushed his hand, pushed the knife into her belly. Booth shrank back into the space under the stairs, listening, watching, waiting for him.

"Hey, Mum, we got let off early like I said. Mum?"

The boy came forward with the girl. She cried out and dropped to her mother's side. The boy saw him, went for him. Just like the man would do. The boy fell. The girl screamed. He had to stop her screaming, else it would warn the man. The man. The man. The man who would kill them.

***

"You must get help for this insanity ..."

"You will kill us all ..."

"Please, please stop this madness before you kill us ..."

The voices. He hears the voices clearly now, the ghost-voices of three dead people. Hears what they had been trying to tell him all along.

He sees them clearly, too, as the ghosts pad around his cell still pleading with him, though it's too late now. He's learned to ignore them, and he sits and watches TV, and falls asleep during the film, always the same film, some time-travelling piece of crap, everyone jumping back to the past to try and change history.

Minister for Ghosts

Damaris will be back later to give us another lesson in life. My next opportunity for channelling is Violet J Cooper; a dedicated mother who lives in Northern Ireland with her family.

Passion is a word that inspires the imagination. It runs wild. It runs deep, but with the wrong person it can lead to all kinds of bad things. In a marriage, passion may well be fine, but in an affair it might lead to guilt... and that is only if the indiscretion is with the living.

THE TRAGEDY IN ROOM 13

by Violet J Cooper

The curtains on the four poster bed cast shadows across the room that Annalisa found vaguely sinister as she awoke. She reached for the light, then stopped herself. There was nothing there, she knew that. Just shadows, crossed with her over-active imagination. A glance at the glow-in-the-dark hands of the clock told her it would start getting light soon. Holding her breath for a second told her that her husband Raymond hadn't come to bed yet. She knew he'd snore when he finally fell into bed, drunk, if he ever managed to tear himself away from his new golfing mates downstairs in the bar.

"So much for the romantic weekend away," she said aloud with a deep sigh. She knew that by the time Raymond came to bed he'd be much too drunk to enjoy the four poster bed, the soft yet springy mattress, the satin sheets. When morning came he'd pull the covers over his eyes to avoid the light, and her gaze; besides, she'd never counted hangover breath as one of her turn-ons. Annalisa wondered if it was the fact they were in room thirteen causing bad luck, preventing them from reigniting the lust in their marriage. But there was no room thirteen at home, and things were the same there.

The bedroom was warm, so Annalisa tossed the covers aside and let the air flow over her naked body. She closed her eyes and took a few deep breaths to relax, so when she felt a firm hand grasp her breast, her first thought was that she'd fallen asleep and Ray had come to bed at last, then seen her and been unable to resist reaching out for her.

When she opened her eyes and saw no one, she realised she was wrong. Sure that it was just a breeze cooling her, she reached for the sheet. Before she could pull it up over herself however, her breast was rubbed softly, then grasped more firmly again, and what felt like a finger began to trace the outline of her other nipple.

"Who...what?" Annalisa stammered, and tried to sit up. She felt a finger at her lips, then it returned to her nipple, which hardened under the strange touch. Although Annalisa was terrified, she was also starting to feel turned on. The finger left her lips and softly traced its way down her neck, making its way to her other breast.

"I must be dreaming," she whispered. "I must be dreaming. I'm dreaming. Dreaming." She closed her eyes and reached for the invisible hand. It was cool but not cold, undeniably masculine. Annalisa lay back and allowed it to caress her breast; now willing to believe it was a dream, she didn't fight it. She moved her own hands along the arm and found broad shoulders and a smooth chest. The torso was muscular. It was nothing like the flabby middle-aged spread of her husband. It was like nothing she had known for the past eight years, at least.

"Who are you?" she asked in a hoarse whisper. The finger touched her lips again, and she felt soft kisses on her earlobe. It was clear she was not going to get an answer, and she just couldn't quite continue to convince herself that it was a dream.

"Stop," she said. "Please, stop." Immediately the lips left her ears. One hand remained on her breast, but did not keep caressing it. Instead it just lay there. Annalisa gently moved it off, and pulled the covers over her head. A tear rolled down her cheek.

Ten minutes later she heard fumbling at the door. She kept her head under the covers as her husband staggered into the room. He collapsed onto the bed without even undressing, and she pretended to be asleep. Within minutes he was snoring softly, and Annalisa allowed a few more tears to flow down her cheeks.

Annalisa woke up early. Raymond was still asleep, fully dressed, face down on the bed. His snores told her that he was still alive. She watched him angrily for a few moments before going for a shower. When she emerged, there was no indication that he had moved.

"Ray!" she said. "Ray, are you coming down for your breakfast?"

"Nmph," he replied, talking into the pillow.

"What? Is that a yes or a no?" she asked.

He turned his head slightly. "Not now. Need more sleep. It was a late one. You go, I'll be down later," he said, then grunted and turned to face the pillow again. Annalisa sighed as she finished getting dressed and went down to breakfast alone after leaving the "Do Not Disturb" sign on the door so he wouldn't be woken by the cleaners.

She saw little of him until lunchtime. In the meantime she amused herself in the pool, and walking around the gardens. She also visited the library, hoping to learn more about the old castle that housed the hotel. As soon as Raymond saw she had a book when he finally joined her in the restaurant, he grinned. "You'll be busy reading for the day, then?" he asked. "I might as well go get another round of golf in," he continued before Annalisa had a chance to answer. She resisted the urge to throw the book at him.

"Sure," she said, and held the lunch menu in front of her face so he wouldn't see her hover on the line between despair and fury. She wasn't keen to allow him to see her cry, but she didn't feel ready to confront him with her rage yet, either.

After lunch, which they ate mostly in silence, Ray

took off for the golf course, and Annalisa decided to take the book back up to the room to read in bed. When she got there however, she regretted her decision not to have the cleaners disturb her husband in his slumber, as the whole suite had a lingering smell of stale alcohol. She opened the door to the balcony and sat out there instead.

The history of the castle was in fact quite dull. Many nobles had lived there over the centuries, but it had never really seen any major battles or played host to anyone of true historical importance. Annalisa was about to give up on the book in boredom when a chapter title caught her eye: <u>The Tragedy in Room Thirteen</u>. Her curiosity was aroused. The sun had gone in behind a cloud however, so she went back inside, relieved that the room had benefitted from a good airing and now smelled fresh once more. She curled up on the bed and started to read.

As Annalisa read about the man named Arthur and his beautiful bride Elspeth, who had perished in a fire in the eighteenth century, she didn't realise that she was crying. It was only when she felt a delicate finger wipe a tear away she realised it had rolled down her cheek at all. There was no one there – or at least, she couldn't see anyone. Annalisa reached for the hand, and noted that it felt smaller and softer than the one that had touched her the night before. She glanced at the book again and stroked the hand.

"Elspeth?" she asked.

There was no reply, but the hand grasped hers and interlocked fingers with her. "It's such a tragic story, but so beautiful," Annalisa continued. The other female hand stroked her face, and then her neck. "My husband wouldn't go back for me if the place was on fire. He probably wouldn't even notice," she said, allowing another tear to slip down her cheek. Another hand wiped it away. Annalisa sensed it was the same one from the night before. "He'd be too busy playing golf," she sobbed. The male hand touched her lips again, with one

90

finger. The female ones unbuttoned her shirt and reached inside her bra. Annalisa almost told them to stop, again, but hesitated. With her eyes open it felt strange, feeling two people caressing her and yet being unable to see them. However, when she closed her eyes she realised it felt good. Exciting and wrong and dangerous and weird – and good.

Annalisa looked toward the door, but knew that Raymond wouldn't be back from his game until dinnertime. She closed her eyes again and helped the hands remove her shirt, and then her bra. As a soft mouth kissed each nipple in unison, she let out a soft moan and arched her back. Her ethereal lovers seemed to find her reaction appealing; they kissed her breasts more firmly and after a little while, she felt the man's hand reach for the button on her trousers.

"I can't," she whispered, and reached for the hand to stop it. She stroked the hand as she pulled it back to her breast. When the female hand, which she presumed belonged to the ghost of Elspeth, trailed down her abdomen toward the button, she felt a tear forming in her eye.

"You really want me?" Annalisa whispered. "Both of you? You really find me attractive?"

It seemed Arthur and Elspeth could not speak to her, but they each took one of her hands and held it to their respective faces. She could feel them nodding. Keeping her eyes closed, she nodded as well. They both stroked her face gently, before the hands returned to her breasts. They took the time to caress and arouse her again, before making a move toward the button on her trousers once more.

This time, Annalisa did not reach out to stop them. She exhaled sharply as they removed her trousers and began to stroke along the outline of her underwear. She remained quite passive. With Ray she was often the one who initiated things, and usually had to persuade him, one way or another. Allowing these two pairs of hands to fondle her made her feel special in a way her husband hadn't for some time. For several years, if she was honest. She allowed them to continue to take the lead.

She paused briefly when she wondered if she had taken the sign off the door and momentarily wondered about a staff member entering the room and being confronted by what would surely look like a strange scene. Her eyes shot open and she tried to envisage how someone else would interpret the scene. *It's just like masturbating,* she thought. *Not like cheating on Ray. Not really. If anyone walked in, they would just think I was touching myself.*

She smiled slyly and closed her eyes again. She liked that no one else would think she was anything but alone. For herself however, she wanted to imagine the faces and bodies that she was touching and that were touching her and it was easier to do that with her eyes closed.

"I never had a threesome," she murmured as she assisted the hands in removing her underwear. "I was a good girl. Only ever had a couple of boyfriends before Ray. Never been with anyone else since the night I met him." She knew by now that there would be no reply, but Arthur and Elspeth seemed to interpret her speaking about her marriage as needing reassurance, and they slowed down. For a while they gently kissed and caressed her all over her upper body before the smaller, feminine hands began to stroke her thighs while one of the male ones traced a line from her breast down her stomach. She shuddered a little as it crossed through her pubic hair and a small gasp escaped her lips as it lingered on her clitoris.

"Don't stop," she whispered when the hand grew hesitant. "Don't stop." She guided their hands first, then reached out to touch them in return. Elspeth's breasts were small and firm and pert, and with her eyes closed Annalisa pulled her ghostly female companion close and began to stroke them gently, moving closer to the nipple in the way that she liked. While Arthur used his firm yet

92

gentle fingers to massage her clitoris and bring her to the brink of orgasm only to stop and pause and start again, she and Elspeth stroked each other and Annalisa grew in confidence. When she felt her legs tensing in anticipation once more, she moved quickly to open them and pull Arthur toward her.

Elspeth continued to kiss her as Annalisa felt Arthur's erect penis slide inside her. She gasped once more as he thrust powerfully again and again and couldn't prevent a scream of pleasure as she climaxed.

After she lay on the bed for a few minutes getting her breath back, Annalisa took each of their hands in turn and kissed them. "Thank you," she said. "That was beautiful. Thank you." They returned her soft kisses, and the trio held hands for a little longer until Annalisa slowly got up and went toward the shower.

As she looked at her husband across the table that night at dinner, she wasn't sure what she felt toward him anymore.

"What did you do this afternoon?" he asked.

I fucked a ghost, she thought. *Two of them in fact. And it was better than it ever was with you.* "Not much," she replied with a shrug. "Read a book for a while. There was a couple that died in our room, you know. Room thirteen. Maybe it's haunted."

"Oh, don't be bloody ridiculous," Raymond dismissed. "There's no such thing as ghosts."

"Well," Annalisa began.

"Come on, Annalisa, you'll bring my headache back talking about that nonsense," Raymond said as he rubbed his temples.

Annalisa blinked away tears. "How did your game go?" she asked.

Raymond shrugged. "It was fine," he said, sighing. "I'm sorry," he said, and reached across the table to take her hand.

Annalisa almost flinched as he touched her. "What for?" she asked, trying to keep her voice steady.

"You know," he said softly. "This was supposed to be

93

a romantic break. Just the two of us. And I've spent two afternoons playing golf."

"And last night in the bar with the other golfers," Annalisa snapped before she could stop herself.

Raymond just nodded. "Yeah. I'm sorry, babe," he said. "I guess I was just afraid."

"Afraid?" she echoed. "What were you afraid of, exactly? Being alone with me? That's just what a woman wants to hear!" Annalisa withdrew her hand and looked away.

"Of course not. Well, not exactly," Raymond said. "I guess I was afraid that...well. Even if I tried to be the perfect husband, that I would fail."

Annalisa looked at him again. "So...what? You thought you've be a bad husband instead?" she asked.

Ray shrugged. "Yeah. I guess. I mean, at least that way I was in control, sort of. Better to not try at all than to try and fail," he said.

"You're an idiot," she said, unable to stop tears flowing down her cheeks now. She wiped them away, hating that she was crying in the middle of the restaurant.

"I am an idiot," Ray agreed. "I'm sorry. Will you let me make it up to you?"

Annalisa nodded.

"We'll have champagne then, and chocolates?" Ray suggested. "In our room?"

Annalisa hesitated briefly. "Why not out by the pool?" she asked. "It's a lovely evening, it might be more romantic."

Ray smiled. "Sure," he said. "I'll get it organised."

"I'll be back in a sec," Annalisa said to him, smiling as she got up from the table. "I just want to fix my makeup."

Raymond reached for her hand again. "You look beautiful to me. You always look beautiful to me," he told her.

"Stop," she chided. "You'll make me start blubbering all over again!"

He kissed her hand before letting it go. As she hurried toward the bathroom, Annalisa could feel tears welling up in her eyes again. She stared at herself in the mirror for a while after taking a few deep breaths and fixing her eye makeup. "It was just my imagination," she muttered under her breath. "Nothing happened. I just dreamed it. That's all. I mean, it's absurd. Just a silly fantasy. There's no such thing as ghosts."

Somewhat convinced, Annalisa rejoined her husband, and as they sat by the pool sipping champagne, she almost felt they were flirting again as they talked and gently touched one another. The champagne made her feel giddy and the flirting helped her recapture her confidence, and as they finished the bottle she led her husband up to their bedroom.

She focussed entirely on him as they entered the room, kissing him so passionately they didn't even turn the light on as they fumbled and stumbled toward the bed, but as they reached it she decided that she wanted to take full advantage of the sexy lingerie she had packed.

"Wait here," she said softly to Ray, kissing him before grabbing her bag and pulling it in to the bathroom.

As soon as she closed the door she felt a hand close around her throat. The light flickered as it came on, and she saw that the mirror was steamed up.

JOIN US was written in an old fashioned, cursive style on it. The hand around her throat was Arthur's. Just a few hours ago she'd allowed it to caress her intimately, and give her all sorts of pleasure, but now it felt sinister. That feeling increased as the grip tightened, while he underlined the message in the mirror three times.

"I'm sorry," Annalisa said, half in a whisper, half in a gasp as Arthur's hand continued to grip her throat. "I can't. What happened earlier was beautiful. Wonderful. Honestly!" she said. "But now Ray and I..." Annalisa turned toward the door as it opened. Arthur touched a finger to her lips to shush her as she turned out the light.

When Annalisa's eyes adjusted to the dark, she could see that Elspeth had blindfolded Raymond with one of his ties, and used another one to secure his arms to the bed. Judging by the movements of his erect penis, and the noises he was making, Annalisa figured Elspeth was either fucking him or sucking his cock. He was clearly enjoying it every bit as much as she had earlier, but her mind was no longer on those transgressions.

She tried to call out, but Arthur was too quick for her. One hand remained at her throat while the other clasped her mouth, preventing her from speaking. The hands also forced her to keep watching – though Annalisa knew she could have closed her eyes, she couldn't quite manage to look away as Elspeth brought Ray to a climax. A tear rolled down her cheek as he called out her name. She wasn't sure if she was pleased that he referred to the ghostly Elspeth as Annalisa, or upset that he didn't know the difference.

When Ray started to snore softly, the light came on in the bathroom once more and Annalisa guessed that Elspeth had entered.

Join Us appeared on the mirror, in more delicate handwriting, indicating to Annalisa that she was right, Elspeth had returned. This time she only underlined the words once, tracing a finger along the bottom of the mirror slowly.

Annalisa shook her head. Arthur relaxed his grip. "What you guys did for me earlier," she began softly as tears streamed down her face, "it was special. I'll never forget it. But...I'm married. And it looks like Ray and I, we're going to be able to work things out. So please, just let me go."

Annalisa turned her attention back to the mirror as she saw another message appear.

We want you to stay. We're lonely.

"I'm sorry but no," Annalisa whispered. "But you have each other."

We want you. She watched as Elspeth underlined the 'you' three times.

"I can't," Annalisa said. "I am sorry. I truly am. But I belong with my husband, not with you."

96

Elspeth didn't reply straight away, and Annalisa wondered if she and Arthur were communicating in a way she couldn't understand.

<u>We would have preferred it if you had agreed</u>, The message read when Elspeth finally wrote it. Annalisa opened her mouth to apologise again, but the writing continued.

<u>We would have preferred it. However, we are willing to do it this way as well.</u>

"Do what?" Annalisa asked, as she felt Arthur's hand close around her throat again.

The light clicked off and Annalisa made a grab for the door, but Arthur was too strong for her. She could feel her throat being crushed as she desperately tried to scream her husband's name, but there was no time, she had no chance. Arthur was relentless, and the fact that Elspeth gently stroked her hand while he killed her wasn't really any comfort to Annalisa as she struggled in vain against her death.

The first thing she noticed when she regained consciousness was that her throat was still very sore. Apart from that, however, Annalisa felt quite light. Everything was still dark though, until she heard the click of the light again and found herself looking into Arthur's cold, blue eyes.

"You bastard," she hissed, trying not to look down at her body where it lay on the floor.

Arthur shrugged, and gave her a smile. "Sorry, I guess," he said.

"We just really wanted you to be with us," Elspeth said, and Annalisa turned to her, realising suddenly that all three of them were naked, though her body on the floor remained clothed.

"You don't talk like you're from the past," Annalisa said accusingly to the couple.

Elspeth shrugged. "Talking is like sex," she said. "It gets remarkably boring if you do it the same way for two hundred years."

Annalisa wasn't quite sure how to reply to that. She

soon realised that she had no reflection, however, so between not wanting to look at the floor nor in the direction of the mirror, she couldn't avoid Elspeth and Arthur's gazes for long.

"You can keep him too, if you want," Elspeth said, a jerk of her head indicating that she meant Raymond, asleep in the other room and still oblivious to the fact his wife was now dead.

"Keep him?" Annalisa repeated.

"You should consider it," Arthur said. "I can't hide the fact that you died from strangulation. The best I could maybe do would be a slightly dubious suicide, but otherwise, I imagine he'll probably be charged with your murder." His tone was so matter of fact that Annalisa thought that she would have felt nauseous, if she could.

"Then what?" she asked. "We live here, forever, with you? Trapped in this room?"

"It isn't so bad," Elspeth said. "We've been here a long time. We find there are plenty of ways to amuse ourselves, and each other. Sometimes we scare the guests, sometimes we screw them. You're the first one we've kept."

"Kept?" Annalisa echoed. "I'm not a pet!"

Arthur smiled. "No, not a pet. More of a plaything."

"Plaything? How dare you!" Annalisa shrieked, but neither Arthur nor Elspeth seemed bothered. She looked toward Raymond again.

"I can't do that to him. Why did you do it to me?" Annalisa asked.

"We like you," Elspeth said with another nonchalant shrug. "We had fun with you. And we wanted a bit of a change."

"So you killed me?" Annalisa asked.

Arthur took her hand. "Sorry," he said. "But asking people who have been dead for a couple of centuries to feel outraged over you being dead is just, well, silly."

Annalisa withdrew her hand. "RAYMOND!" she shrieked at the top of her voice.

Elspeth giggled. "He can't hear you. We can touch things, and people. But no one can see us or hear us. You know that already," she added.

"We'll leave you alone for a while. To consider what you want to do, about him," Arthur said.

"He wasn't too bad really," Elspeth giggled. "Bit dull though, I think having him once was enough for me!"

Annalisa shuddered, and wordlessly left the bathroom, closing the door behind her. She sat on the chair beside the bed and watched as her husband took slow breaths, in and out. *I wish I could cry*, she thought. This seemed like the kind of occasion that merited tears, but crying was something else that had been taken from her, apparently.

After some time, she thought of a plan. She reached for her handbag, and began to write a note. After 'Dear Ray,' however, she got stuck. She couldn't tell him she'd been murdered by a ghost. He would never believe it. What sane person would? If anything, it might look like he'd forged it to try to cover up her murder.

"Arthur!" she called. The bathroom door opened a little.

"Make it look like I hanged myself," she instructed. "I'll write a suicide note."

"Are you sure?" Arthur asked.

Annalisa nodded. "I can't do it to him. At least this way, he has a chance to move on, and be happy."

"We're happy, sometimes," Elspeth called. Annalisa ignored her as she began to write a suicide note. She detailed her guilt at having slept with someone else, which was after all, not so far from the truth, but did not go into any details about whom it was she had shared her passionate encounter with.

She told Ray she loved him, and was sorry, but she hoped that telling him she had been unfaithful would make it easier for him to recover from her death. To move on.

"Not bad," she had to grudgingly admit as she looked at how Arthur had strung her body up by the light flex in the bathroom. She left the note on the bottom of the bed.

"I'll live with you and talk to you," Annalisa told Elspeth and Arthur before shutting herself in the walk-in wardrobe so she wouldn't have to watch Ray wake up and find her body. "I don't have much of a choice about that. I'll probably even fuck you again when I get bored, as I imagine it'll be quite easy to get bored. But I'll never, ever forgive you. Never stop hating you," she said.

Elspeth shrugged and giggled again. "Never isn't a word that means much to a ghost," she said. "But you'll learn that, in time."

"Don't patronise me, bitch," Annalisa snapped.

Elspeth laughed a little. "I said the same thing to Arthur, after I died," she said. "The book you read missed a few of the finer details. Like how he started the fire, so we would be together forever."

Annalisa slammed the closet door shut, but she couldn't help but feel curious, and that just made her hate her new companions a little bit more.

"He started it?" she asked.

Elspeth nodded. "Yes, he started it. I was getting nervous, I wanted to back out, cancel the wedding. So he tried to burn the whole place to the ground. As death overcame me I thought I would go to Heaven. I was religious, in those days."

"Why didn't you go to Heaven? Why didn't I? And why isn't he in Hell?" Annalisa asked.

"I don't even know if there is a Heaven. We think perhaps it has something to do with the positioning of the room," Elspeth explained. "It's room thirteen now, and it's the thirteenth door along the corridor from either staircase. Right in the centre of the castle. Plus, each staircase has thirteen steps, so it's thirteen in three dimensions."

"So?" Annalisa said. "All that stuff about the number thirteen, there isn't really anything to it, is there?"

100

"Oh no, my dear Annalisa," Elspeth grinned slyly. "Just like there's no such thing as ghosts!"

MINISTER FOR GHOSTS

hristian Nash is a deep thinker and an even more profound soul. I like that. In his dreams, he Astral travels to places of the unexplained, and he records these journeys in his journal to escape the reality of life. I often flick through his papers late at night when he is in bed and I am somewhat shocked at what they reveal.

In this next lesson, the tendrils of evil pervade from this account of the terrible. The darkness and sorrow within slowly eats away at your soul.

As a loyal servant of Queen Victoria and Minister for Ghosts, it is my duty to share these lessons with you. However, I will not be held accountable for the horrors within and any nightmares you may have because of reading them.

GREY MEMORIES

by Christian Nash

ucas walked through walls and wondered why the others couldn't. *Are you my family? Where's my mummy?* They didn't answer. They never answered. A father and little girl shut the door behind them as they left the house. He tried to follow, walk through the door like he did the walls, but he was trapped. Trapped in a house he couldn't remember entering, and couldn't imagine being without.

Strings of control bound him to the building, pulling him back. *Mummy?* He could hear her breathing, but couldn't see her. Snippets of memories floated in and out of objects and he spent his days, weeks, months, trying to collect them. *Who am I?* He tried to follow them but was dragged in by invisible hooks. The house shook. Tears began to flow down his face. His footsteps splashed water and he realised the room was flooding. Water rushed up to his neck. He thrashed his head. *Help me mummy!* He blinked and he was transported to the iron bath upstairs, his head submerged.

Icy water stabbed at his eardrums. An invisible hand gripped his throat and held him down, nails digging in. *I won't be naughty. I promise!* The water disappeared and Lucas curled up into a ball, some memories better left in the dark.

He didn't know why he was there. Why every day he was dragged back to the iron bath to be drowned. *Do all*

103

little boys go through this? Where's mummy? He couldn't remember seeing her, or being with her, but he knew he had a mummy; every boy has to have a mummy.

His hand slid down to the flower in his pocket, its soft petals his only comfort. The door downstairs slammed shut and he heard the sobs of the little girl.

"You're always forgetting things, Emily!" he heard the father say.

Lucas reached out to a doll on the bathroom floor and a dagger-slice of a memory dug in behind his eyes. Emily. His sister. He glided down to meet them as if they could share in his moment, reunited. Layers of building flashed by until he stopped in front of them, his presence unnoticed.

The dad – his dad – threw the girl towards the stairs and she passed through Lucas's ghostly form. Everything went dark except the man's eyes that glowed red and pinned Emily down. *No!* Lucas placed himself between them, but daddy walked through him as he always did. The house began to tremble and Lucas grit his teeth.

Daddy's eye were glazed, focused on Emily. *Don't hurt her! Don't you dare!* Lucas forced energy into the tips of his fingers. His throat closed up, the air taken away in a fire of hate. He lashed out, but rather than hitting nothing, his hand slapped against his dad's leg. The red-eyed monster took a step back and steam spiralled from the pores of his body. Lucas's head shook as he began to choke on the darkness. Grey memories rose like smoke from the dining table to his left, and from cushions on the chair to his right. A distorted picture of a woman, a man and two children was ripped in two and the memories were gone.

"Who's there?" his Daddy said, the red evaporating from his eyes.

"It's me. It's me," Lucas replied. "Where's mummy?"

Daddy looked around before kneeling down to help little Emily. Light filtered back into the room as Lucas watched father and daughter embrace. All he wanted to do was join in and feel their warmth. A little boy needs a mummy and a daddy. A tear trickled down his face and he wiped it away before another could form, memories of the iron bath enough to force his eyes dry.

"I'm sorry," Daddy said.

"I know you don't mean it. Where's mummy?" said Emily, as if echoing Lucas's unanswered and desperate need for the truth.

"She did a bad thing. She had to go. You know this." Dad stroked her hair, a tear forming in his eye too.

Lucas reached out and tried to wipe away their sorrow, but his hand slid through. There was no anger to be drawn upon, no hate to fuel touch. *I love you.*

Emily shivered. "Did Lucas do a bad thing, is that why he's gone?"

"No! Lucas is nothing like your mum."

The glint of red flickered in Dad's eyes and Emily withdrew. Lucas knew he was a nice man, most of the time, but when the darkness came he was capable of anything. It was the same darkness keeping Lucas locked in the house. *I'll protect you, little sister. Don't worry.* Lucas moved next to her and hovered a hand over her shoulder. She scratched where he had wanted to touch, a smile daring to cross her lips.

Lucas's spirit wandered through the house as his sister and dad slept, searching for the grey memories and hiding from the darkness. Each search would lead him to his sister's room and if he didn't stop to think, he could be there for hours. Not that time meant anything anymore. Not that anything meant anything anymore, except Emily. She hugged the same doll she always had but it fell to the floor as she yawned. Lucas went to pick it up, but his hand glided through it. He ground his teeth. Heat built up in his heart and flowed out to his limbs, the burning need to exist bubbling behind his eyes. He tried again and the doll moved. With both hands he lifted it up and placed it back into her arms. *I'll be ready, Emily. If anyone tries to hurt you again, I'll be ready.*

Red light bathed the room, its glow radiating from his eyes. Emily took in a deep breath and Lucas's form was pulled in with the intake of air. His body was half absorbed before he realised and had to drag himself out, hiding behind the bed. Emily yawned again and he shot out of the room. He couldn't let the darkness take her too.

Daddy was snoring and the darkness within urged Lucas to him, red light still beaming from his eyes. *Where's my mummy?* Lucas felt the walls of the house as if they were alive, the sound of his mother's heart beating, the corridors contracting around him. Soft whispers gave orders to enter Dad's body, take control. *Mummy? Is that you? What do I have to do?* No answers came, just urges.

Black smoke obscured the doorways and windows. It was Lucas and the night. His red eyes focused in on Dad and he glided to his room. He couldn't control himself. Dad's bearded face was thin and old, deep lines unable to host a smile. Tired eyes looked to the doorway, right through Lucas.

"Who's there?" Dad called out.

"It's me," said Lucas, but the voice was not his own, the darkness throttling him.

"Who said that?" Dad said as he fell from the side of his bed.

"It's Lucas, don't you remember me? You killed me. Daddy. You killed me."

Dad started to cry. "Kill you? Lucas, I would never..."

The red light from Lucas's eyes burned hot and the glow made Dad's skin blister. The old man recoiled. Darkness crawled into the room from behind Lucas, black snakes heading towards Dad.

"Dad?" Lucas said, the image of a broken man wavering, control returning. "You need to leave. Get Emily and go. Daddy, go!"

"Emily?" Daddy said as if waking up.

106

"It's me, daddy, Emily's asleep. I'm so sorry. I won't be naughty again, I promise."

Dad's body went stiff and, as he tried to rise from the bed, his face was replaced with that of a woman. Her smile was wide and her lips blood red, her eyes glowing. *Mummy!* Lucas threw himself at her, expecting his mum to catch him, but she screamed. Daylight soaked the room from the window and penetrated the black smoke. Dad's possessed body recoiled. The snakes retreated into the hall and Lucas began to cry.

He could hear water and the clink of metal. He could feel the cold touch of death. Water leaked in through the floorboards and he was transported to the iron bath. The ethereal form of his mother leaned into the tub. She smelt like apples and her breath was warm like pie, but her eyes, her eyes burned red. Lucas's tears filled the bath and his mother's soft hands wrapped around his throat and forced his head under. *I can't breathe mummy, I can't breathe!*

It felt as if his soul was being torn from his heart, his mother's black nails ripping away at his innocence. As his head was thrust against the bottom of the metal tub, and his windpipe crushed, he could hear someone screaming. *Emily!* He kicked up and swung his arms. The water evaporated and the iron bath split in two. His mother was gone, but his sister's screams remained.

"I'm coming! Emily, I'm coming!"

Lucas flew to Emily's room. Dad had her pinned to the bed, his tongue licking out, saliva dripping to the pillow. Rusty springs squeaked in between screams, and Dad's heavy breathing produced clouds of smoke that even the daylight couldn't penetrate. Emily reached out to Lucas with her eyes and for the first time he knew she could see him.

"Get off her!" Lucas said as he tried to grab Dad's hair. His hands grasped nothing.

Dad picked up Emily by the throat in one hand and

grabbed Lucas with the other. It felt like the same soft hand of his mother gripping him and he looked up to see her face in place of Dad's, her spirit possessing his body, her spirit able to assault his. Those blood red lips. The smell of apples. The same warm breath like a kiss on his face. *Bring daddy back!*

Lucas swung a trembling hand at Dad's face. Heat built up in his heart and in into his limbs. Dad hissed, but Lucas's strikes bounced off. A smile crept onto his father's face. The house started shaking and contracting with each of Dad's breaths. He threw Lucas to the floor, pulling a dagger from his belt.

Lucas flung himself at Dad, but his small frame couldn't budge him, his spirit wavering between husk and darkness.

"Daddy, stop it! You're hurting her," said Lucas.

"Your dad is weak," said Dad, his voice contorted, their mother's spirit in control.

Emily's face was a mixture of blues and purples. Lucas floated by her side, unable to save his little sister. She mouthed the words 'help me', and Lucas bit down on Dad's arm. Fuelled by his sister's last breath, the bite sunk in and Emily dropped to the bed. The dagger fell to the pillow. Her chest vibrated with the manic beat of her heart. As she breathed in, Lucas jumped inside her, the intake of air sucking in his spirit.

Their minds merged, her memories filling in gaps, grey flashes bleeding with colour and warmth. They had been happy, once, but mummy's madness had torn their family apart. As one, they looked up at their father's possessed form, their mother's mask staring down at them. *We have to get away! C'mon Emily!*

Lucas took control and forced Emily's body to move, grabbing the dagger. She was weeping, but Lucas had no tears left. Their father chased after them, his heavy boots thudding against the floorboards as they scrambled down the hall. Lucas's spirit guided Emily and they sped down the stairs, her nightdress torn and bloody.

Escape was a few steps away. The corridor started to stretch, putting the door out of reach. Black walls appeared in the gaps left by the retreating exit. They tried to move forward, but the black snakes curled around Emily's legs and bit into her knees. She screamed out, slashing with the dagger in vain, Lucas's cries for help merging with hers.

"Run!" Daddy shouted as he fell down the stairs. This time it was his real voice and Lucas could see their mother's spirit hovering above, no longer in control.

Lucas left Emily's body and flew towards his mother, knocking her away. "Get Emily out of here, please!"

The stairs began to crumble. *Why did you have to do this? You're the one who killed me. You're the one hurting us.* His mother writhed in Lucas's grip and he struggled to reach into his pocket. *I love you mummy. Just stop! Please!* Her scream pierced his ears and he daren't look back in case Emily and Daddy were still there. *Don't let her take you.*

Pieces of wood broke off from the crumbling stairs and he heard a gargled cry behind him. This time he looked. Dad was holding his throat. Blood dripped from the wound caused by the makeshift stake. Emily dragged him out, wood protruding from her gut, the temporary glimmer of daylight shut out as the door slammed back into the frame.

His mother still thrashed in Lucas's desperate embrace, but he was able to pull the flower from his pocket. Grey smoke rose up from it. Memories danced and flickered within. A petal floated to the floor.

"I picked this for you, mummy," he said.

She stopped, the black snakes hissing in her place. "I-"

"You don't have to worry, mummy, I won't be naughty again. I forgive you." Lucas placed the flower into her hand and her spirit dissolved, leaving dust in place of a mother.

Lucas cried. The tears pooled on the broken floor, but he wasn't transported to the iron bath. And, instead of being strangled, a rough hand wiped away the tears from behind. He turned to see Daddy and Emily smiling. He took Daddy's hand, Emily on the other, and they walked through the door.

Light embraced them as they floated into the street. The dead bodies of Emily and Daddy were lying in a pool of blood, people flocking to them. Lucas blanked out the screams of horror and squeezed Daddy's hand.

"I love you," said Lucas and Daddy squeezed back.

The house tried to hook into them, the darkness lingering, but they didn't look back. On a hill to their right, a woman sat twirling a flower in her hand. It was orange like the morning sun. *We're coming home, mummy.*

MINISTER FOR GHOSTS

Evolution of the spirit is to inhabit many human bodies; living lives, learning lessons that help the spirit to grow. Susan Boulton has lived numerous times as a man and currently her spirit enjoys life as a woman, a very talented woman, I might add.

I knew her well in Victorian times when we both worked for the ghost ministry so it was inevitable that our paths would cross again.

So what is the subject of this next lesson? One of the biggest dreams of humanity is to overcome death, to be able to live forever, avoiding the transition into the spirit world and past lives. However, there are possible downsides to immortality. Is it something we should pursue, are we able to be more than mortal or are their consequences we just cannot conceive of?

DEATH WON'T BE CHEATED.

by Susan Boulton

The words came softly, rustling wings against the plastic over his face. "Death won't be cheated."

"Yes it will," Carter laughed, watching his breath mist the thin bag. "Yes... it... will..." Each syllable formed a different structure on the shiny surface. A haze of connecting atoms, which mirrored the chemical structure he had spent most of his working life on. He had a right to celebrate; wasn't he the hero and the darling of the world?

God, could anything be better?

Carter squirmed under Agrona; the dampness of her thighs where she straddled him adding another layer to his enjoyment. Her hands held the plastic bag tight on his bulging neck. Her dark hair dropped forward hiding her features; black wings brushing his chest and filtering the shimmering glow of the candles surrounding the bed.

"Death won't be cheated," The words penetrated the roaring of blood in his ears. His breath came in shorter and shorter gasps, as his body fought the lack of oxygen. Lips blue. Nostrils flared. Carter shook his head, not even making the effort to answer. His doubts did not matter, their voices would soon be stilled by the cries of a grateful humanity.

He gloried in the success of his team, just as he did over his persuading Agrona to join in this little game. At first she was concerned and frightened, but he soothed her and coaxed the passion in her awake, stimulating it until it was, he believed, equal to his own.

Agrona had joined the research group when they were at their lowest ebb. The months of failed experiments, dead ends and false leads had worn lines on Carter's forehead and brought doubts into the minds of all involved. Was their grail unobtainable? Yet, within in a week of this young, dark-haired laboratory assistant slipping quietly onto her stool things began to change. The results started to form a clear line pointing in one direction. Check and recheck. Test and prove. Test again. Blind tests, clinical and field. All were done. Over and over. At each stage improvements made. The drug refined. The genetic markers recorded. Side-effects logged and monitored.

The complete mapping of the human genome had been the beginning of Carter's quest. It had provided him with the trail. It was the first breadcrumb and Carter had willingly stumbled after it. The Holy Grail. The desire of millions. His goal was to stop the biological clock from running down into brittle bones, senility and weakened heart muscles. To end the loss of all that experience and knowledge locked in failing biological machines.

Forever young, firm and beautiful like Agrona. Soft, shy Agrona, whose fingers now tightened on his neck. How Carter had watched her, as she had catalogued the slow progress of their work. He had played games with her in his mind in the dark, lonely hours. He had wanted to take her innocence away, just like he did the creeping death that awaited humanity. Innocence and death, both in their ways were barriers, one to knowledge the other to being able to continue and enjoy that knowledge. Both could be conquered.

The lack of oxygen was blurring his thoughts, his excitement thundering out of control. Carter could feel death. His doctor's knowledge charted its attack on his failing system. He slapped at Agrona's arms. Her hands loosened their grip on the plastic bag. The inrush of air made him dizzy, then euphoric. He ripped the covering off, his fingers shredding the thin, manmade fabric. The same fingers then dropped and pushed Agrona's hips back, ready to consummate their union, to taste her innocence and give her knowledge. It would be a double victory mimicking his, over death.

The buzz of his phone cut through his laboured breathing. Agrona's head went back. Her body inched off his. *No, fuck-it, no.*

"No, let it ring," his voice came rough-edged, tainted by the lack of air and anger. He gripped her thighs tight, sweat-damp fingers marking her flesh. Climax. Brutal. Unstoppable. Incomplete; his victory tainted. The phone wailed on and on; the caller refusing to give up.

Agrona shook her head and slid off him, stepping gracefully from the side of the bed. Carter felt the cool air of the room waft over the slick layer of sweat on his body. Ice needles, which brought a shiver he could not deny, only rile against.

She straightened up; her young body the symbol of what Carter wanted for the human race. He desired all to keep the bloom that before had been so fleeting. Agrona's slender hand hit the speaker button, as she moved away into the darkness beyond the yellow haze of the candles set close to the bed. She became a darker shadow within the velvet blackness. Only her breathing told Carter she was still with him.

The phone clicked, hissed and through his cursing Carter heard the voice of his lieutenant, Mason. "You there?"

"Obviously," Carter snarled, as he rolled onto his side. Sweat dripped from the edge of his thinning hairline. It peppered the crumbled sheets like tears of frustration, marking the ebbing of the excitement in his blood. So close. The moment was lost - it could never be recaptured.

"We have a problem..." Mason's voice was hesitant.

114

"Problem?" Carter sat up, swinging his legs over the side of the bed.

"Five law suits hit my desk early this evening, just as I was leaving," Mason answered. "They are from women that took part in the beta testing three to four years ago. The twenty-five to thirty age bracket. From what their lawyer said it's the tip of the iceberg."

"What do you mean? Those women are healthy, we looked at their recent tests just before the launch of the drug last month. Their biological clocks have stopped, same as our male test subjects," Carter snapped, his hand going to his neck and tugging at the less than firm skin. His miracle had come too late for him to regain his youth, but he could, with its help, horde what life he had left.

"Yes, but they are infertile. They claim Seasle has made them sterile." Mason's words dropped into the gloom of the room. The candles guttered as if fanned by a release of a hundred hard-held breaths.

"That's impossible. Coincidence? Sheer bad luck," Carter scoffed. "We kept a firm eye on hormonal levels in both men and women. There was no indication that Seasle caused any imbalance in progesterone and estrogens that could result in any problems. The infertility must stem from another source. There are a dozen and one, you know that." As he spoke Carter rose to his feet. His fists clenched, knuckles white. It was impossible.

"Yes I know, but the..." Mason's voice stopped and the brittle sound of paper being turned echoed from the phone's speaker. "Medical data supporting the claims state that all the women are post- menopausal."

"That's not feasible, Seasle couldn't do that, it is designed to do the opposite. Are the women showing any other symptom of aging?" Carter looked round for his clothes. Agrona came out of the shadows, his abandoned shirt in her outstretched hand.

"None whatsoever."

"I'm coming over. You're at the complex?" Carter

115

snatched the shirt from Agrona and struggled to slip his right arm in. "I need to see this so-called evidence for myself."

"It's very convincing."

"You believe it?" A button snapped off Carter's shirt as he tried to fasten it.

"I didn't say that. By the way, news of the suits are already on the net. We need to get hold of Mathews, prepare a statement. The main media outlets will have it before morning."

"Yes....we need.... this is absurd...." Carter could not accept it. It was a hoax. A get rich quick scam. They had been so very careful. There were no major side-effects with Seasle.

"I'll round up the rest of the senior team," Mason added.

"Yes, I'll be with you shortly," Carter cut the connection. He stood there looking at his hand on the smooth plastic of the handset.

"Agrona, you best get dressed. Can you make your way home from the complex?" Carter did not look at the young woman.

"I don't have time for a quick shower?" she asked.

"No."

***

"Fuck! "Carter swore, as the lights glowed red at the intersection. The expletive did nothing to ease his rage. It frothed and boiled through his mind. Carter did not accept his grail was a false one, cracked and leaking. The production and sale of Seasle was already a multimillion-pound industry. By the end of the year, it would be a billon pound one. Someone wanted a slice of the pie, by fair means or foul. His fingers tapped on the steering wheel as he waited for the lights to change.

Agrona looked over at him, as he crunched the gears and swore again. The car stalled. A horn blared behind. "Fuck! Fuck!" Carter restarted the engine and pulled

116

away sharply from the lights, skimming through them as they already began their cycle again to amber, then red.

"There was an indication," Agrona said.

"What?" Carter shifted down a gear, as he indicated right. What was the girl on about?

"The side-effects." Agrona's finger now traced the hazy outline of the approaching complex on the glass window at her side.

"Were minimal. And no different than a hundred other drugs out there and in most cases a lot less. The benefits far outweighing the chance of a slight discomfort," Carter retorted.

"Night sweats. Irritability. Sudden tears. Disorientation and mental confusion. Itchy, crawly skin. Tinnitus. Aching, sore joints, muscles and tendons," Agrona quietly listed the symptoms.

"Yes I know, all part and parcel of the menopause, but there was no hormonal change and the side-effects were barely noticeable." Carter stated, barely controlling the anger in his voice.

"But they were there," Agrona answered. "You ignored them and dismissed them as unimportant. Perhaps fate, or what every God you believe in decided you can have your unsullied extended youth, but at the price of future offspring. Death won't be cheated, Carter."

"What did you fucking-well say?" Carter glared at the young woman by his side, eyes wide in total disbelief at what she had said. Those words? Where had she? It was nonsense. All of it. His left hand came off the steering wheel, making to grab her and to shake some sense into her. This thing had rattled her, that was all. He would show Agrona he was right. Seasle was a boon to mankind.

The car hit the speed bump at the entrance of the complex car park hard, and swerved to the right, its front tyre clipping the curb. The rear end began to spin out. The headlights danced across the tarmac. Carter swung the steering wheel, jabbing the brake with his right foot.

The front end came round and rammed one of the concrete bollards marking the edge of the black expanse.

Carter bellowed as he was thrown forward. His seatbelt tightened, cutting into the pit of his stomach and deep into his shoulder. The whole car vibrated and stopped. The engine roared then died, as Agrona reached across him and turned it off. As she sat back in her seat she looked right at him.

Confused. Dazed. Carter sat there locked in a web of surprise at what had happened. Then he began to laugh at the absurdity of it. He wasn't hurt. They hadn't been going at any great speed. A trickle of sweat began to creep down his back as the adrenalin flowed anew in his system. He welcomed it, as he had earlier that night, enjoying the sexual tightening of his groin in its wake. *Fuck. Not now he needed to think.* He tried to shake the feeling away, but it lingered, leaving him wanting to taste more of it.

The whole future, their future, was in danger from some cheap, gold-diggers. Carter fumbled with the seatbelt clasp, as he asked, belatedly. "Are you alright, Agrona? I need to get going."

"Yes you do," Agrona's reply was lost in the plop and hiss of the airbag in the steering wheel, as it suddenly and belatedly reacted to the impact.

The white bag filled the space between Carter and the steering wheel, pressing hard against his face. He could smell the rubber and the nondescript thin layer of powder that covered its surface. He cursed and tried to push the bobbing white mound to one side. His right hand scrabbled at the car door, trying to open it. Locked. "What the fuck?"

"Language," Agrona said softly, as her hand reached over and caressed the back of his head. "Death won't be cheated. I won't be cheated. Where there is life there has, and will always be, me."

"Agrona what the...?" Carter began to say. He was

118

confused. He tried to repeat his question, but his words became lost, as his head was pushed hard down into the airbag. What was the crazy woman doing? This was no time for games. He had to get out of the car and see Mason. He needed to get this problem sorted. The stupid girl was stopping him.

His hand lashed out trying to grab Agrona, but her seat was empty. Where was she? Behind him? "Stop it! This is no time for!" he bellowed, as he managed to raise his head off the white mound for a second. The relief was short-lived. Agrona's hands on the back of his head forced him forward again. He tried to reach back and grab her, but couldn't. Feet and legs braced, he heaved up, but couldn't move. He could feel other hands now. Small ones and large ones. Strong and weak. Thin fingers, crooked and wrinkled with age. Small smooth digits soft as a newborn's. Thousands of hands held him down, intent on pressing his head through the plastic skin and into the airbag.

Carter tried to scream. His fear warred with the rising sexual excitement in his blood stream. He felt the familiar growing state of euphoria brought on by oxygen starvation. The sensation he had once gloried in now terrified him. This time the pleasure was missing. It was no longer a game in which he was in control. His head was now totally submerged in the airbag, his features stretched and eyes wide.

The fabric filled his mouth coating the inside with a slick membrane, as his head was pushed deeper. His neck and shoulders followed, twisting to follow the path forced open by his head. He no longer fought the hands, as they carefully kneaded his body into the white sphere. His strength was gone, sapped by the all-consuming horror. Carter's screams became locked in his lungs, unborn to the outside world.

He couldn't die. He was death's master, not its victim. The oxygen-deprived remains of his conscious mind raced, then stumbled to their end in a total blackness of despair, as he realised his fate. He was not dying; he was being preserved just as he wanted, as he had hoped all humanity would be.

Carter's back curved; his knees came up, tucked tight to his chest. Both his arms wrapped round his legs. His thumbs were up; placed close to his head where it lay, chin on his knees in a foetal position. The white fabric of the airbag tightened around him, becoming the withered, swollen womb that rose high under Death's tired, shrunken breasts.

MINISTER FOR GHOSTS

Here is another story from a well-used but hugely talented vessel of my ministry. Bob Lock has a wonderful way of giving us a story that leaves us wanting more. And of course, there is always a lesson to be learned within his words.

OCD.

Obsessive Compulsive Disorder. It is something that most people have from one degree to another. In everyday life we do not even notice the condition. But in some cases, the symptoms can become a serious problem when mixed with superstition and a vulnerability to malevolent spirits.

Who would want to believe the claims from such an individual? Voices in their heads, strange visions, most of us would believe they suffered from mental illness. I can report that there is no such thing as madness, just varying degrees of attack from the dark-side.

Protect yourselves before it is too late.

LOCK THE DOOR THREE TIMES

by Bob Lock

Transcript of Dr. Henry Talbot's Final Notes on Shirley Parsons. Private Internal Memo Only. (not for public viewing)

lthough preliminary examinations and final diagnosis point to the patient (Ms Parsons) as suffering from post traumatic stress and obsessive-compulsive disorder, I am now torn by the possibility that Ms Parsons *indeed* suffered from the visitations she complained of. By admitting this I realize that I walk a tightrope of derision by my colleagues and peers, but I have no alternative. However, by reading on you will come to see that I have no other choice.

I met Shirley Parsons three days ago when she was referred to me after the court's decision (under section 35 of the Mental Health Act 1983) that she be detained until a report could be made on her mental health after being found in Mrs. Jordan's bathroom. Mrs. Jordan – her friend - was discovered in the bath. Mrs. Jordan had (I can only say) been reduced to... minced meat.

The first thing she did when brought into my office was insist I locked the door. When I asked why she became adamant. When I repeated the question as to why it was necessary to lock the door she began to scream and struggle. The two male nurses accompanying her had to forcibly restrain her and only when I left my desk and locked the door did she calm down.

'Now open and lock it again another two times,' she told me, her breath coming in deep gasps. Her eyes were wild and flecks of foam had begun to appear at the corners of her mouth and so I did as she instructed. I opened and then locked the door another two times. Ms Parsons calmed down immediately and I nodded to the two nurses.

'You can let her go,' I had said to them and indicated to a chair. 'Please sit down, Ms Parsons.'

She looked back at the door as if to confirm it was truly locked and then took three turns around the chair before dropping heavily into it. I could see she was exhausted. Dark circles like miniature thunderclouds orbited her blue eyes, eyes that were constantly searching the room as if looking for something. Finally they locked onto my own.

'It was *my* fault. I didn't really believe her. I let it in. She'd kept it at bay for months she said, but I didn't believe her. *I* killed her.' She went quiet, as if her mind was momentarily dragged back to that awful bathroom which had become an abattoir.

Throughout the examination Ms Parsons had difficulty explaining what had happened but insisted that her friend's death was *her* fault because she had neglected to lock the door three times and hadn't had the presence of mind to turn on the tap and leave the water running. Looking back, even though it was obvious that a petite woman like Ms Parsons (weight 8 stone) couldn't possibly overpower and place a woman of Mrs. Jordan's size (I understand she weighed approximately 17 stone) in the bath and then somehow grind her body to a bloody heap, it was still considered. With the benefit of hindsight, it beggars belief to have even contemplated the possibility. Nevertheless, as no other reasonable alternative was put forward by the investigating authorities at the time, she was placed in my care and my examination of her mental state of health began.

'It will come for me next,' I remember her saying and then, 'and once I'm gone I believe it will come for *you* afterwards.' She turned to the two nurses. 'Or *you* or *you*...'

Jenkins, a burly Welshman said something like... *as mad as a hatter*, but the other nurse, Reynolds, I think his name was, simply crossed himself.

'That won't do you no good...' she'd said.

'How exactly do you think you killed Mrs. Jordan, Shirley?' I continued and I asked her if she minded me calling her by her first name.

'No, I don't mind, call me whatever you want. It doesn't matter anyway. It's only a matter of time. I'm a dead woman,' she answered.

I recall trying to establish conclusively the circumstances of the terrible event. 'Do you want to explain what happened?'

She watched me for what seemed a long, long time and then she sighed and told me everything.

At the time... was it only three days ago? I remember thinking she was showing the typical symptoms of post-traumatic stress. Well, who wouldn't after walking into your friend's house and witnessing her being chopped up into little pieces in her bath-tub? Add to that the fact that she was an OCD sufferer. Therefore who could blame her for her outburst and for the misconception that she had killed her friend? Yet almost immediately it was apparent that, disturbed as she evidently was, Shirley Parsons *hadn't* killed Mrs. Jordan, but what she told me couldn't have been the truth either and so I wondered what she *wasn't* telling me. After all, how could I be expected to believe that Mrs. Jordan had been holding some sort of malevolent creature at bay by locking her doors and windows three times, circling a chair three times before sitting in it, and, if all else failed, or she hadn't adhered to those regimes then she could fall back on turning a tap on three times and letting the water run? If I was to believe Shirley Parsons then I had to believe she visited her friend that fateful night and had perhaps miscounted the times she had locked the front door and had thereby allowed the creature access into the house. Mrs. Jordan had been upstairs at the time, in the bathroom.

'I felt something huge and cold, yet unseen, pass me in the hallway and moments later I heard Agnes scream from upstairs. It was then I began to doubt – or perhaps I even knew - that I hadn't locked the door properly. I raced up to the bathroom,' Ms Parsons told me. 'The bathroom door was open and Agnes was fumbling with the tap on the washbasin. Then I can't really explain what I saw, but something transparently dark and shadowy lifted Agnes off her feet, threw her into the bath-tub and shredded her into little pieces. I ran downstairs and into the hall and felt that the *something* was following me. I grabbed the chair in the hall and ran around it three times and then sat on it with my eyes closed. A thing, a substance, vast and cold shambled around me and I felt its anger and hatred. Fetid and frigid breath raised goose-bumps on my neck... and then it was gone. I stayed seated with my eyes closed until the police came.'

Sometimes with post-traumatic stress it can be benevolent to gradually bring the sufferer into contact with the thing that caused the stress in the first instance but in Shirley Parsons' case I decided that would be impossible as the creature she described was unquestionably in her mind only. Nevertheless there was one way I *could* help her, of that I felt assured. I would make her confront her OCD problem and, perhaps in doing so, assist her with the monster she imagined was stalking her.

She baulked at this suggestion and finally got into such a state that I had to sedate her and have Jenkins return her to her room. Up until that last consultation I had adhered to her request for her to open and close the door to her room three times and then have the nurse to lock her in. I understand she would then walk around her bed three times before opening the tap three times on her small wash-basin before retiring. This last time, as she was unconscious, none of her obsessive compulsive actions were fulfilled and Jenkins, being a sceptic, did not carry them out on her behalf. It was on his last round of the evening, when he checked on her, that Jenkins discovered the terrible scene of carnage. I am not a squeamish person but even the most hardened mortal would blanch at the contents of that room. How a person could be reduced to such small slivers of blood, sinew and bone, inside a locked, secure room is a question that will haunt me for the rest of my days.

Now, as I conclude these final notes on the case of Ms Shirley Parsons, I can only wonder at the validity of her explanation of the event that occurred the night her best friend died. I have to admit a growing sense of unease as I go over my notes and dictate this private internal memo since Jenkins has not turned up for his shift today, and Reynolds, the other nurse who has been involved in the case, has begun to show signs of OCD by doing things in threes. I further have to confess an urge to lock the door three times myself upon reaching home, but to do so would dishonour my vows, my intelligence and my self-esteem. To consider these acts would ward off a creature intent on tearing me to shreds is farcical, but the fact remains that a woman in my care died believing them to be true. Should I err on the side of prudence and follow her protocol and therefore become one with those that I have attempted to assuage? Or do I retain my professionalism at the risk of at the least, my sanity, at the most, my life?

It seems I'm damned if I do and dead if I don't.

Dr. Henry Talbot

MINISTER FOR GHOSTS

As you can see from her previous story, Jo Zebedee is a great asset to my department. As a woman, her spirit is more in touch with reality than a man from the physical world whose judgement is usually clouded by testosterone. There is nothing quite as entertaining as a good ghost story unless, perhaps it is getting the better of a bully. So if you were able to combine the two it would be even better.

Enjoy my next lesson.

AIN'T NO GHOSTS 'ROUND HERE

by Jo Zebedee

The house stood on the outskirts of our village, right near the old Dead Pools, where the trees were all stunted 'cause of the power station's dirty water. It had no number, no roof and no ghost.

That much I knew; I'd spent my childhood in and out of that house, climbing along the roof-beams, in darkness when I was young, and then in patches of light as the roof started to collapse when I was older. Now, those rafters are either dry from the sun, or wet from the rain, and it's hard to tell just by looking. It gives a thrill, that, not knowing when you start to run along them if they'll be slidey or dry.

I've spent enough time there to tell you, hand absolutely on my heart, there weren't any ghosts. I've been there during the day, in all kinds of weather and I've even spent a night, locked in when a storm knocked the door tight-closed, waiting for my Pa to notice I was missing. I'm lucky it was only one night, I guess. So I know the house has rats, big ones like cats, and mice, and bird shit everywhere. But no ghost.

It has a great ghost story, though, one I made up. When I heard how Karl Dick-face from down the road made our Leanne, who's only twelve and has her own troubles with Pa, show her titties for some pictures, I just had to. I've seen those pictures, and it's not what a person should make someone's sister do. 'Specially not mine. After I seen them, and punched Jeff Ritchie for having them on his phone to show me, I came to the house for some thinking time. And as I perched up on the rafter beams, looking down over the village and the Dead Pools with their dark, still water, I got me an idea. As things went, it wasn't the best idea, but it was the only one I had.

What I did was, I made up a tale about the house, and I told everyone I knew if they came after school to the back playground, I'd tell them the story. And if they didn't they'd be eating their teeth from the tarmac. That did the trick, and I had a good crowd waiting for me, including Dick-face. I gathered them to me and told them what I'd found out about the old house.

"When you go in the first time..." I looked round the circle of lads – and a couple of the scrawny-type of girls who really wanted to be lads – and took my time. All their eyes were on me. "...the house, it feels you. A wind gets up, coming the whole way through the building, and it groans and rattles, and that's it feeling you."

"Lotta crap, Jase." Tom stood up, the straight-man I'd planned, and he pointed over at Dick-face. "What d'you reckon? You're smart. Ain't this a load of crap?"

Well, Karl got all puffed-out at being called smart, on account of the fact he's thick as shit, and he nodded. "Horse-shit, that's what it is."

I got to my feet. "Come on, then. I'll show you."

Well, it was hard for Karl to say no in front of everyone else, so he followed me from the playground, with the bunch behind us, and we reached the house not long after.

He looked at it, all puffed-out, and then at me. I jerked my head. "Go on, be my guest. If that old wind doesn't come asking who you are, then I'm wrong and you can say it. But if it does, then you'll know the house has greeted you."

He looked a little less sure. That's a trick I learned

from Pa. If you're confident, no one questions too much. Especially if you're confident with a belt in your hand.

I must have been confident enough, 'cause Karl walked his way up to the door, slow and sure, not looking back once. I admired him right then, and felt kind of sorry for what was coming his way. Then I remembered them ol' photos, and Leanne standing, all teary like, and all the boys looking at her, and I didn't do nothing to stop him.

He pushed the door open. It made a groaning noise that carried over the wind. He slipped inside and when that door closed, it sounded like the thud of his coffin. The crowd stared, silent. And then I heard it, and they did, too. The whoosh of the wind from inside the house, like a voice. I guess I could have told them it was due to the way the roof had come down the week before, that the house had a new echo from the draft, but I didn't.

Anyway, a few minutes later Karl came out. He looked a bit paler, and a whole lot shakier, but he wasn't scared enough yet.

"Did it feel you?" I asked. "Did you get a wind, all around you, like it knew you? 'Cause the first time I did, it cradled me for a moment."

He licked his lips and gave a nod. "I believe I did."

"Good." I turned around and started to walk away. "That's the first, then. Now it knows you."

"Hey!" I turned and he was running up to me, huffing a bit, 'cause Dick-face, he ain't light on his feet. "What happens the second time?"

I gave a lazy smile. I'd gone and caught him good.

"I'll tell you tomorrow," I said. "After school. Same place. If you're brave 'nough, that is."

I knew by his face he'd be brave enough, and I let them all go and then trod my way back to the house. I had a bit of work to do that night. I opened the door and the wind came around me, right up my legs and back, and it didn't half feel like a person. A woman, I reckoned, by the tickle of its fingers.

I didn't get home 'til it was my bedtime, which was a bonus of sorts. I got a good night's sleep, too, what with Pa out stalking the neighbourhood, which was another bonus, and when I woke up the next day I was ready.

I got to the playground late on account of having done no homework and having a de-ten-tion, but the kids were all waiting around for me. Lots of them. More than the day before. I stood in the centre of the circle and waited for silence. Karl Dick-face had his arms crossed, but he didn't look so brave.

"So, the second time," he said. I wondered if he'd slept last night, for he looked awful pale. He reached out and touched me on the shoulder, as if he wanted to grab me, and leaned right in. "What happens?"

"Well," I said. "The house knows you now. It'll know you jerked off last night, thinking about Steph Burley and what you might want to do to her."

He started at that, but by Christ, did he think I was stupid? His thoughts shone from his eyes every time she passed, and it wasn't a nice shining, if you know what I mean. I might be doing ol' Steph – who's a good girl, and doesn't have it too easy at home, neither – a favour. That thought, that I was helping others, gave me the strength to keep going.

"The second time," I said. "It calls you." I smiled, and I knew it wasn't a nice one by the way he backed away, all pale-like. "Are you ready to be called, Karl?"

You know, I don't think he was, but he didn't have no choice but to follow me and walk back up that path to the door. Either that or tell everyone what a chicken-hearted Dick-face he really was.

The sun was shining when we got there, showing up the white walls, and the dark ceiling with the missing parts. Around the house, conifers drew close, like they were listening, all scrawny from the Dead Pools' water, with branches like fingers. I gave Dick-face a wave and a nod, and in he went, back through the door that howled

131

its greeting. He didn't let it slam none this time; maybe he'd thought about the coffin, too.

Well, he came out just a few minutes later, and he was pale as a - a ghost, I suppose, if you can bear a cliché. He came haring down the steps, straight to me, and he grabbed me by the collar. Now, I'm pretty useful at taking a beating - my Pa's seen to that over the years - but he had me tight, and I couldn't breathe too easy. I told him to put me down. He did, eventually, and he stood, huffing and panting.

"So the house knows you, and it's called you," I said, choking a bit, damn him. "You're in trouble, Karl, 'cause it won't forget you." I leaned real close. "Tomorrow, I'll tell you what happens if you go in again." I spat. "Not that you will. You'll be too chicken."

Well, he drew himself straight, in front of everyone.

"I'm no chicken," he said, like he'd read the script, and I felt sorry for him, 'cause he finished himself right there, but you can't help some people.

I waited for everyone to go, and then I climbed into the house and got rid of the tape recorder I'd stashed, 'cause it was evidence, like. And I disconnected the little bit of wire I'd ran from the door to the on-switch. But I couldn't resist listening once more, and there was my voice, calling Karl's name, making it all long and spooky like. Well, I laughed and laughed, and then I stopped laughing and started to fix things up the way I needed them. And all the time I felt bad, but I remembered our Leanne telling me he didn't just take pictures, but he'd put his hands where he shouldn't. Like Pa did, she said, whispering it. When a guy does that, well you have to deal with him, don't you think?

Next day after school, I wasn't feeling so good, on account of Pa coming home a bit the worse for wear and beating me for the school calling about homework. So, I was sort of walking stiff and trying to hide it but when I saw the size of the crowd, all that sore just passed me by. I went

132

up and Karl was in the middle. He looked all scared, like he wanted to back down, and I think it might have been a neighbourly thing to let him, but we weren't private.

"So," he said. His voice was shaking. I looked around and saw Steph and Leanne standing next to each other, and the two of them smiled.

"Yeah?" I said.

"What happens the third time?"

"It knows you, it calls you. Then -- " I drew my finger along my throat, real slow. The crowd were silent. "It *takes* you."

I thought he might crap himself, right there, he went so pale and green, but he didn't. He didn't rush to follow me to the house this time, though, nor did he hurry up the steps. He took each one like it was his last, slower and slower and when he pushed the door, his hand was shaking. He went in. We waited and waited, and he didn't come out. No one offered to go in after him. I suppose that's what happens when you're a Dick-face with no real friends. Eventually only myself, Leanne and Steph were left.

"What happened?" asked Leanne.

I shrugged. "It took him. He ain't coming back for you no more, honey." I gave her a hug round her scrawny shoulders. "Ain't no one coming back for you."

They left, too, eventually. I went home and I goaded Pa 'til he chased me. I'm quick, though, quicker than him, and I led him a chase through to the edge of the village, and up the drive of the house. I darted round the back of the house, and hunched by one of the Dead Pools, before he could see me. He thundered into the house. It was only his first time but he didn't come out, neither. I stayed hunkered down, my sleeve over my nose to hide the stink of the pond until the darkness fell, and then I waited some more.

When the moon was high, I straightened to my feet. The wind had got up and there was rain in the air; a storm was coming. I opened the door of the house, and made sure to step over the missing floorboards. I checked down the hole, and neither body moved. They wouldn't, not impaled on the blades I'd hammered in. I smiled at that clever idea and tipped a hat to Mr King. I hope he don't mind me taking his idea.

I got rid of the bodies under the moonlight, and buried them next to the Dead Pool. I don't suspect anyone would notice the stink. I didn't say no prayers. And then I sort of moved into the house, and that's where I've stayed since, waiting in the dark. I got no option; that darn storm gone and closed the door after me, just as I was looking into my pit and wondering what other guys might deserve something of the same.

It's been two days now, and that old door's still closed over, and the rope going to the beams gave way under my hands, so I can't climb out. Our Leanne, she ain't coming for me. She too dumb-scared to tell anyone anything, that's why I needed the photos to know.

Now, it's just me, Pa and Karl Dick-face. I try to take some comfort that I was right, and the old house hadn't been haunted. Not then. But now...

Let's just say, I keep myself tight against the wall and try not to listen to the dark. And all the while I'm sitting, I'm waiting for the touch of the hand to take me into the dark earth where I belong. So far, it's only been a finger, but it's touched me and teased me for two days. That and the wind, writhing round me like some woman I can't get rid of.

I close my eyes. The touch runs down my cheek, follows my neck to my chest. I don't move, I can't move, and then it's in me, filling me and tonight's the third night and it's gonna take me. And, my sweet lord, it's sore.

MINISTER FOR GHOSTS

Stephen Palmer is a fascinating character and inside his mind is even more captivating. As I do with all my spiritual vessels, I enter their consciousness to get to know them better and to access their worthiness of becoming members of my ministry.

The experience with Stephen was truly a wonderful one, and it certainly took longer than expected. He took me to worlds of monochrome, a city where waves of exotic and lethal vegetation wipe out humanity and to a Gentleman's club where a wager is made on discovering the answer to the age-old dilemma of, "What is love?" Sadly, before they could find the answer London was covered with hair.

The visit to his mind left me breathless and wanting more so without further ado, I will let Stephen allow you access to his crazy world.

Be prepared for a journey.

THE CHOSEN ONE

He raked his surroundings with a steely gaze. "Are you certain she will come?"

"Indeed, my Lord. She has walked Green Lane every one of their Sundays for a whole season, and now the Solstice is here, she approaches."

He couldn't take his eyes off her. She was tall, slim, yet not without curves at the hips and where else it mattered; dark eyes, wide mouth if thin lips, and dark shoulder-length hair with a hint of russet that suggested a Celtic heritage. She walked with a slight limp, and often seemed lost in thought, giving her a most attractive vulnerability. It was no surprise that He lusted after her.

It turned out that she had family in the area, that, without pleasure, she would visit. Then she would go for walks, alone along country paths and lanes; and that was when He first saw her. Perhaps she noticed him in his white mantle, perhaps she glanced into those fierce orange eyes. Or maybe not. But it did not matter. She was the one.

He fretted, tense, poor-tempered, sometimes argumentative, not knowing what her plans were for that special day. But she did turn up on the Winter Solstice weekend, and she did go for a walk on her own.

In the furthest, most isolated part of Green Lane, where He knew she would tread because she always took that route, He set out a table. It was small, made of pine, with a pure white linen cloth upon it, and on that cloth were laid a silver bowl of water – warm water – a silver plate with bread on it, and the silver camera. This table He knew she could not miss.

That day before the Solstice the weather was overcast, though not cold. No snow or ice. He saw her approaching even when she was further than a mile away. He was high in an oak tree – the Oak King overthrows the Holly King on the Winter Solstice. She slowed as she saw the table, staring, smoothing her hair down with her fingers, in a charming gesture: a delight to him, who enjoyed this kind of hint of a woman's inner turmoil. She glanced around, intrigued; saw no one, as He'd intended.

She approached the table and leaned over it, bending at the waist. Though He was high up He was behind her, and so would have received a marvellous view of her haunches. It must have been difficult for him to restrain himself.

I watched as she put her fingers in the water. Confusion appeared on her face when she realised it was warm. Then she took the bread and sniffed it, and for a moment I thought she was going to take a bite – but she did not. Instead she put it back on the plate, stood upright, and looked around again, mystified.

Open fields: cows and sheep and cow dung and sheep pellets. Damp green grass and mud. Nothing more.

She turned back to the table and took the camera. It was an old large-format film camera, an oblong box with two lenses at the front – a beautiful thing, and one of the most valuable things He owned. She hesitated. Tension wrapped the scene, though she felt not one iota of it.

She took the camera then left, continuing her walk along the lane.

***

She brought the camera to her uncle, who was an old man with white hair and yellow teeth. He lived in the same little town as the mother.

"Hello Tara," he said, when she knocked at his door and he opened it.

"Hello. Look what I found down Green Lane."

"Gosh! That's a stunner." He examined the camera for a while in silence.

"I think it's got film in it, could you develop it?"

He nodded. "Might well get a hint as to who the owner is. Hand it in to the police and they'll just open it and ruin the film."

"Do you mind developing it?"

He shook his head. "Nobody uses film these days, it's all damn digital. Be a pleasure, my dear. Shall I do it now for you?"

"If you can."

And he did.

There were two images on that colour film, and they examined the two photographs together. One was of him, taken from the most flattering angle: black hair, white skin, orange eyes. The other image was blurred, indicating that the photographer might have ducked as the snowy owl attacked – half a head, the body a blur of feathers, the talons outstretched as if to grab or slash something just above the camera body: the whole an extraordinary moment in time.

"What on earth are they?" she said.

Her uncle shrugged. "I don't know him, that's for sure. Not a local, I'm guessing."

"Gosh, he's really good-looking. I wonder who he is? Do you think he's the owner of the owl? Maybe he's a falconer."

"Maybe."

She looked again at the prints, studying them, drawn in by the images. "I almost feel like I've got to choose – him or the owl. Isn't that odd?"

"Odd indeed, my dear." Her uncle took the camera and examined it. "You better had take this to the police. Did you know it's made entirely of silver? I checked with a magnet, there's no steel in it."

"I *will* hand it in soon, don't worry."

He smiled. "I know you will."

Really good looking! That would be wonderful news for him. That would give him the strength to bear the agony of his lust for another day.

***

On the day of the Solstice she was in town again, dealing with the wreckage of her family. Driving her old red motor she visited her mother, and then her uncle. She didn't visit the police. Towards the middle of the afternoon she went for a walk, deliberately taking the long way round, past a couple of farms, along the recently ploughed field, over the main road out of town then along the little lane that leads over the railway line and into deeper farmland. After half an hour she was walking along Green Lane; slowly, warily even, distant bleating and the cawing of crows her only company.

He waited atop the tree again, hoping she would eat the bread, or at least take a sip of the water. A sip of that water would take her half way out of her world.

She was probably too sensible to eat the bread. She was a country woman, and anyway intelligent. Strange bread on strange tables would perplex her, worry her. There would be in her mind the possibility of poison, or at least, if not poison, of stomach-churning germs. Not nice.

But the water... He had warmed it against his fevered body and scented it with beads of sweat from his brow. A single hair floated in it. If she happened to take a sip...

We had no way of knowing whether or not his plan would work. I tried to calm him, to counsel him, but He hardly heard me. He imagined tearing her clothes off, rolling on the winter grass with her, and she full willing. Of course full willing - nothing else would do. He'd thought of little else, I expect, since I told him that she thought him good-looking.

But on that Solstice walk she behaved oddly. She must have known something was afoot. A table, laid like that... the camera, the photographs.

He had moved the table so that it stood in the centre of the lane, but she avoided it, did not even stop, as she continued her walk. He was hardly able to contain his fury, so on silent wings He glided away in the opposite direction.

***

We talked that night. "Do you think she will come tomorrow?" He asked me, agitated.

"It is their Sunday," I replied. "I think it likely. She is visiting her family a lot."

"I *must* have her! I must feel her heat."

"I know, I know... but there is one day still left. Tomorrow." I hesitated, wondering if I should take a risk in order to calm him. I smiled. "No doubt she will walk the lane tomorrow-"

"No doubt?"

I hesitated again. "Little doubt, sire. Nothing is certain for them. Yet she will come, I believe she will come. But you must lay something before her that she will find irresistible."

"But all I have is bread! You think she will eat mice? Voles? All I can offer is bread..."

"Yes, sire. They do eat bread."

"There is always the camera... yes, yes, if she brings the camera with her tomorrow—"

"Sire! That way is a last resort. Violence is always the last resort."

He nodded. "If she brings the camera tomorrow she may see with different lenses. You shall tell her—"

"Me?"

"Yes, you, Thrush. You can speak her language. I cannot. She must come over to our side, and you are the one to make that happen. I am relying on you. There will be a wedding."

I bowed. "Yes, sire."

***

The day after the Solstice dawned cold and clear. Ice-edged puddles glittered, and there was hoar frost on tree branches. I was nervous. Very nervous.

She drove into the little town in her old red motor. She visited her mother and there were words, harsh words that perhaps the old woman would regret later. But I cared not about the ruins of her family.

It being a cold, clear, sunny afternoon she seemed keen to take a walk. I watched her from my perch on a gatepost. To my great relief, but also great concern, she took the camera with her as she departed the house. Light from the cirrus-shrouded sun reflected off the twin lenses.

She took the longest possible route, as though she had surplus energy to burn. Fully an hour passed before she stepped on the frosted grass of Green Lane. Yet she did not slow, and she held the camera in her hand, raised slightly, and I knew with a thrill of horror that it was at the forefront of her thoughts. I realised then that she planned to put it back on the table. Her deliberation, the way she held it, her lack of wariness... it was obvious.

He would have my life if the ritual failed! He more than wanted this woman, He *needed* her. Something in her looks, her smile, her walk spoke to him on a primal level. I had to act.

But what could I do? She was unlike me: we were unlike her. She *had* to come over to our side. We were of the land, she was of her kind - sprung from the womb of her mother. We knew little of the messy conclusion of that process. We were nature eternal.

And so she approached the table.

It lay waiting for her, and she slowed as she neared it, the camera held out, away from her body as though she was repelled by it. Clearly she was going to put it back.

Now she was but a yard or two away.

I fluttered up behind her and landed on her right shoulder. "Do not put the camera back!" I said.

She jumped, looking to her right; seeing me from the corner of her eye, she raised her left arm to swat me away. I flew off, banked, then hovered as best I could before her.

"Do not go!" I said. "You must keep the camera. It is for you!"

She took a couple of steps back, appalled at my speech I suppose; in shock.

"Eat the bread!" I continued. "It is for you. It is of the land."

"What are you? Is this a trick?"

I heard the screaming cry of an owl. There was so little time...

"Eat the bread! A great reward awaits you!"

"What is this camera?" she asked.

"Raise the viewfinder to your eyes and look through. You will see what the lenses see."

This she did. Probably she had done it before, but I knew that would have been at her uncle's house, or at her own. But this was Green Lane, this was the land, and only here would she see the truth of the land.

She gasped. She twisted her body around, seeing the panoply of our country: the gem-encrusted trees, the feathery boughs, the steaming leaves. The paths and the palaces and the silver coaches.

And then, having spun right around, she looked down the lane again and saw him flying at her, talons outstretched. She screamed, but too late - He was upon her. She dropped the camera and shrieked as He clawed out her eyes.

With mighty wing-beats He spun away, droplets of blood arcing to the ground.

"Get the camera lenses!" He shouted to me. "There are but moments left! My talons are too large, my beak too sharp for her delicate face. You must do it!"

"Sire, I'm only a thru—"

"Do it!"

I landed before the camera and with one wing righted it. Already the twin lenses were melting. With my beak I grabbed one, then flew over to her; she lay spasming on the ground, in shock. I landed on her face and popped the lens into her blood-soaked socket. She felt my presence, felt my sharp claws on her skin, but she was too traumatised to respond. I flew back to the camera, but the second lens was a pale puddle on a frost-encrusted leaf. Too late.

One lens was in however – the lens of her right eye socket. If she closed her left eye she would be one of us. If she closed her right eye she would be one of her own kind. If she opened both eyes, as naturally she would, she would be forever bewildered.

He flew down and slapped a muddy oak leaf over her left eye.

"Mine, I think," He said.

And He grinned at me.

Minister for Ghosts

As you all already know from my first introduction, Damaris Browne is a former solicitor, so it is perhaps unsurprising that this next lesson should be concerned with Justice, something long held by her to be not only desirable, but in this account, admirably meted out by the victims of an awful crime.

UNLUCKY 13

by Damaris Browne

He sighed. He had greatly enjoyed his time in his den, but the pleasure was over.

The expected feeling of mild depression, even of slight revulsion, crept over him as he viewed the remains – the shreds of flayed skin, the dissected muscles, the pooled blood. Post-coital tristesse, he had diagnosed for himself, save there had been no coition – the very thought repulsed him. His pleasure was more refined, more fastidious, more ... clinical.

The mood wouldn't last, he knew; by morning it would be gone. Before dawn he would feel able to return, to clean away and dispose of the mess the girl had made of his chamber. And then – with the thrill of anticipation which always came to him – he would begin considering his next pleasure, his next girl, and the long delicious days of choosing her, stalking her, befriending her, persuading her, then bringing her to his locked vault, his lair, his den of pleasure. She would be his fourteenth.

A ripple of pride and arousal ran through him. Thirteen girls already. Unlucky for some.

He put his scalpel down on the tray of bloodied instruments, ready for the morrow's careful - loving – cleansing and sterilisation. He switched off the cameras and recording equipment, already contemplating the long exquisite hours of editing it into the perfect film, then turned to the brazier to remove the white-hot pliers and extinguish the coals – the remembered hiss and piquant aroma of human fluids drizzling onto the burning metal exciting him a little again – but he stopped as something caught his eye.

Her blood still dripped from the gurney, but as it trickled over the stone tiles it appeared to form a pattern. With a little imagination he could see letters in it: a P, an R, an E ... He continued watching as the liquid dribbled and flowed. Another P, and an A perhaps. A strange phenomenon; one he had never noticed before. Another R, another E. Almost he could ... yes, he could read a word in it.

PREPARE

He smiled, a thin line of near-amusement, the ridiculous flight of fancy pushing aside his melancholy for an instant. Next he would think he could hear the girl talking.

He started. A puff of air had escaped her lips. Escaped where her lips had been.

He shook himself. Low spirits, that was his problem. Low spirits and imagination. What he required was supper and a well-earned rest. He took the pliers and double pincers from the brazier, laid them aside to cool, and dowsed the coals with the fire blanket. One final check and –

The flayed skin. He'd allowed it to fall haphazardly onto the tiles, the arousingly blood-splashed tiles. Tomorrow he would sweep the skin up and feed it delicately into the incinerator, but for now it lay in little heaps, sweet piles of succulent flesh. Save in one place. One mass was sliding, slithering, the strips forming one long line topped with a shorter line, quite like a T, other strips still moving, coiling around into a loop. The idea was preposterous, but they might almost make another word.

TO

A sound came, like a gasp from a lip-less, tongue-less mouth.

He stumbled back, colliding with his dissection trolley – which was closer, far closer, than it should have been – knocking it to the floor. His scalpels, his knives, his lancets, his skewers, ceramic and steel, serrated, razor-edged, acid-steeped, everything fell, some shattering, all skittering along the white stone of the tiles, where they began to jink and jerk and twitch. He watched, fascinated, horrified, as the blades shuddered into spikes ... into spiked letters.

MEET

A gasping shiver. From a dead mouth, the birth of a laugh.

His cords had also fallen from the trolley. Knotted cords for tying, for tearing, for blinding, garrotting. They writhed and coiled and curled below the knives, forming – his mouth dried as he watched, his eyes burning wide in terror – forming ... forming ...

OUR

He turned to run. The brazier ... It had been behind him; now it stood ahead of him. Between him and the stairs. Smoke boiled and eddied from the coals, the impossibly still-burning coals, the fire blanket tossed aside, the flames leaping, pirouetting, as thick choking clouds swirled patterns in the air, snaking into letters.

PLEASURE

More shivering laughing gasps from the body, from the blood, the strips of flesh.

He hurled the brazier aside, pain searing him, and he ran, tripping, tumbling, for the stairs. With fire-blackened, fire-burnt hands he threw back the top bolt and reached for the second. The first slammed shut again; the second resisted all his strength, his panic.

One key shot from the door's lock, another flew from his pocket. Both cart-wheeled down the stairs, then hung above the newly upright brazier for several mocking seconds before plunging into the glowing, glaring, coals.

The brazier dragged itself along the ground, towards the stairs, towards him.

He pulled and hammered at the door. He screamed. He begged. He pleaded.

The knives, his knives, strutted on points towards him, mounting the stairs with dainty precision. The cords, his cords, snaked over the walls, then wrapped themselves around his arms, his legs, his throat. His pincers, his pliers, white-hot, sizzled the air around him; flaring coals shimmied and span before his eyes. Then his scalpels began slowly, delicately, slicing through his clothes.

He screamed again.

The long, long, bloody night began – and ended – in screams.

Laughter rose. From the gurney, the incinerator, the gore-spattered stone tiles and walls. True girlish laughter. Mingled, blending, laughing at last, thirteen young voices.

MINISTER FOR GHOSTS

When my next vessel, Toby Frost was a young boy, growing up. He was a passionate young aspiring writer. I used to peer over his shoulder and read his early scribblings and I always knew we would meet again. We did and the next insight into my world is proof of that.

Though he loves humour, and has shown he is more than capable of producing excellent published-works, this adventurous tale shows the dark side of love, and its unintended consequences, when society decides two people should not be together, and one cannot act to disobey.

DEAD WITNESS

by Toby Frost

Some men are trouble. I should have thrown him out the moment I saw him. I was holding the day's first cup of wine-and-water, thinking about eating the lump of driftwood on my table that was passing itself off as yesterday's bread, and when I looked up there he was, standing in the doorway, looking at the sign that says 'Degarno the Thief-Taker', his hand raised ready to knock.

"Come in," I said.

He walked in as if it hurt the soles of his feet. He was thin, that kind of thinness where something has sucked all the fat and joy out of a person. His face was pale, his mouth small and red as if he'd been drinking wine.

"Guilia Degarno?" he said.

I nodded. I was the only person in the room, the only woman, and the only one with a face-full of scars. There wasn't much other choice. "Come in."

He entered and closed the door. I gestured at the other chair, then held out my hand.

"Renzo Calda," he said. He took my hand and did that thing rich people do when they kiss the air about a yard from it. Then he sat.

"How can I help you?"

"Do you really catch thieves?" he demanded.

I said, "Yes, sometimes. I do a lot of things, though.

I've helped people write letters who can't read, been a bodyguard for ladies, sometimes just told people what I think they ought to do. Pretty much anything... anything legal, of course."

"Of course."

A moment's silence. "So," I said, "what can I do for you?"

"I'm here on behalf of my master. It's rather a delicate matter."

"Fine. I'm a delicate person."

People come to me for a reason, and the reason is almost always a woman. Maybe they need something brought back - love letters, trinkets - that it would shame them to admit to a male thief-taker. Or maybe they think I'll have some magic understanding of women that they can't have. It's not true: I don't understand anyone much at all. But I *am* good at getting things done.

He said, "I need you to take a package to a girl."

I waited.

"Her household are unwilling to speak to me. Or my master," he said.

"Ah."

"And we don't know where she is."

"Who is she?" I gestured at the wine, and he shook his head.

"Louisa Forni. She lived at the house of Luca Sciata Calverno, on the west of town."

I knew the name Sciata. Our beloved prince, Mavlio, had hanged several of them when he seized power about five years ago. It's a flexible thing, treason. The rest he'd exiled, apart from a few minor relations who had bent the knee, before Mavlio bent their necks. Calverno must have been among that wise and humble group.

"I'm taking it that they don't approve of your master, then."

"No. Not at all."

"And might I ask who he is?"

"At the moment, I'd rather not say."

151

"Right. Who's this Louisa, then? A niece of the family?"

For the first time, he looked awkward. "A maid."

I let it pass. He probably had a good idea of all the things I could have said. If his master had been dallying with another house's serving girls, I could see why he might not want to be throwing his name around.

"I tried to give the package to her myself. It's a gift, you see. But they told me that she'd gone away, and they wouldn't let me leave it there. It's important."

"Alright," I said. "You give me the parcel, and I'll try to get it to her tonight. I'll see if I can talk to somebody, maybe get it in through the other servants."

He seemed to smile and deflate at once. "My master would be very grateful," he said. "It's important to him."

The parcel was small with a slight weight to it, like a wad of folded paper with a coin inside. It was sealed. There was a very slight smell to it, an alchemical smell.

I asked for some money and he showed me twenty shiny ones in a bag. Even better, he gave them to me with the same to follow if nothing went wrong.

***

The house was a solid white lump, three storeys high, with big pieces of glass in the upper windows and a little clockwork weathervane to show that its owners were moving with the times. It sat in a garden, surrounded by a six-foot wall to keep the riff-raff out. It wasn't a very good wall, because I climbed over it in three seconds flat.

I crouched at the bottom of the garden in a dark blue shirt, man's britches and a workman's cowl, watching the windows. The ground floor was shuttered, but light still leaked out from candles and fires. I doubted Louisa would be in there, but it wouldn't hurt to see who else was.

The night air was warm, the grass spongy under my boots. It was very easy to scurry across the grass, keeping in the shadow of the wall, bent over to hide my outline. I reached the house and put my eye to the gap between the shutters. The floor was stone. A long table lay heaped in cloth; at the far end a big pair of candles threw light over the woman sitting there. She was stitching something - mending a hole in a sheet, perhaps. The scene did not drip with menace. She looked up and spoke to someone out of view. I thought I saw the hem of a dark dress flick out as the second person turned around, but it could have been shadow.

A cheer went up to the right. I froze for a second – it was muffled, but it still took me a few nervous seconds to realise that it had come from the playhouse. They were showing *A Fool on the Solstice*, a comedy. I'd seen it the week before, and it hadn't been bad, although revengers are more my sort of thing.

I looked again. The sewing woman was gone.

To the right, in deep shadow, a bolt rattled and drew back. I ran.

I shot across the grass and as the door opened I ducked behind a statue of a fat cherub with wings smaller than my hand. The statue was good cover: he was wide and with wings like that, he wasn't going anywhere.

Light flowed out of the house. "Hello?" a woman called. Middle-aged, from the sounds of it, and big. "Is someone there?"

I quickly counted out coins in my hand. A dozen ought to do it. "Hello?" I said, uncertain and timid.

"Who's there? Come out."

I stepped out, coin-purse in my fist.

She was large, not fat: like a farmer's wife scaled up by a third. Her broad face was one big scowl. She wasn't tapping a rolling pin against her palm, but that was only because there wasn't one nearby. "Who're you?" Hostility, but not a lot of fear.

"Messenger," I said quickly, trying to sound scared of her. It wasn't difficult. "I tried knocking at the front door, but I don't think anyone heard so I came round the back."

"What're you doing here?"

"I'm here to deliver a parcel. My master sent me. He said there'd be trouble if I didn't give it to you."

She glared at me, arms folded. I needed to work fast before she pitched me over the wall like an apple core.

"It's for Louisa Forni," I said. I took out the parcel, and held it out. "There's some coins for your trouble."

"She's not here."

"Could you give this to her, please?"

"No," she replied.

"No?"

"She died."

"God," I said, and it wasn't forced. I don't like death, and I don't like losing money, either. "What happened?"

"She got taken ill, in the stomach. She died two days ago," she informed her.

"Taken ill?"

"She ate something bad," the woman said. "It poisoned her." There was a stress in her voice, an emphasis that I didn't understand. She'd sounded sorry when she mentioned death; now she was getting tough again. The gate was closing on me.

"Did Louisa have any relatives, anyone I could give this to?"

"No. She didn't."

"My master will want to pay his respects."

"Oh, I'm sure he will. He can explain himself to the priests in the death-house. Now get out."

There was nothing else to do. Nobody would mistake me for Our Lady of Condolence, but I'm not going to get difficult with someone whose friend just died. Especially someone who could break my neck like kindling. I left as discreetly as I'd come, except this time, being a sophisticated sort, I used the gate.

***

I broke it to Renzo as quickly as I could: I didn't want something like that hanging over me.

154

"Ah," he said when I'd finished, and he sighed as if deflating. "I suspected it. To be honest, I was pretty certain she was dead when they told me that she'd gone."

I wondered if he really had thought so. Sometimes when I get bad news, it feels as if it could never have worked out any other way. But that's just the Melancholia talking.

We sat in the Cooper's, an inn that used to be owned by the barrel-maker next door. A lot of people came and went; it was one of those places where nobody's journey ever ends. I was nursing wine-and-water; he sipped a cup of wine as if it was medicine.

"I have a further proposition for you," he said.

"Go on."

"They told you that Louisa Forni had been taken ill, am I right? That means if she really was dead, she'd be laid out. If they didn't know what it was that made her ill, that is." He took a sip like a hen pecking at the ground. "Did that woman say what the illness was?"

"No," I replied. I drank to hide the expression that my face was trying to pull. I had a nasty feeling that I knew where this was going.

"So she'd still be there, then. In the church –"

"In the death-house. And you want me to find out."

Renzo looked at me for a second. "You'll be paid well for it, Madam. If you want, you're welcome to hire some people – I don't mean any offence, but it's not work for a woman, really."

I knew then that I would do it, and that I'd do it myself. After all, it's the only way to make sure that a job's done properly. "Don't worry," I said. "It'll get done."

***

Saints Coelia the Mournful, Lacrimas the Remembrancer and Pietro the Binder of the Holy Wounds didn't have a lot to do with my life, or indeed the life of anyone who hadn't turned blue yet, and I was happy to keep it that way. Yet it looked as if I'd be visiting them a lot earlier than I'd expected.

The Church of the Blessed Mournful was near the edge of the city, not far from the wall. You could hear the workmen building the prince's new ramparts, and the grunting and swearing as they packed the dirt in thick enough to stop a cannonball. The church itself stood in its own grounds, unusual for a chapel, with a high wall around the edge to keep trouble out – or in.

Two years ago, there was a scare about the Grey Ague. The word was that most of a village about ten miles south had died from the ague, got back up, and wandered off looking for new people to give it to. So now they kept a vigil on all unexplained deaths, and if you were still lying down three days later, they did the rites and stuck you in the ground. I had it on good authority that they pushed a knife through your spine first just to make sure you weren't getting back up: they say morts can dig their way out of the earth.

So, how to get at her?

Anyone could bring a body into the church: after that, the corpse would be in the keeping of the priests inside. It was them I'd have to get at, and I had serious doubts that they'd be open to a bribe. They'd be dedicated, probably monks, sworn to poverty as much as they were sworn to their job. Fat deacons with one eye on the wine are one thing: dedicated followers of the three most miserable saints around would be another.

Besides, I was pretty sure that interference with the prevention of disease was a hanging offence. The prince hadn't strung anyone up for two weeks now, and he was probably starting to get the shakes.

Which left burglary.

The front of the church had a wide range of niches and statues, featuring a range of the unhappy and virtuous. Some of them were women: we're allowed to become saints provided we do enough weeping. Any of the statues would have made a good hand-hold. But the damn place had two guards on the front who looked as if they broke femurs and sucked out the marrow for fun, and a batch of alchemical lights in the grounds that lit up the sides of the church so they were whiter than a summer cloud. And besides, the death-house didn't have any windows that weren't more than thirty feet off the ground.

So that was that, it seemed. But it was a lot of money to give up on.

There *was* a way to get inside. I could get straight in under the saints' noses, and they'd be too busy crying their eyes out to know that I was there.

Forgive me for being disrespectful. But I did my share of weeping when Publius Severra's men carved up my face, and nobody gave much of a damn back then. The saints I pray to now are the ones who get things done: Senobine, to whom all secrets are revealed, and Cordelia, Our Lady of Battle.

Breaking into a church is bad. Breaking into a church full of stiffs, any of which might be considering getting up, is much worse. Renzo's master knew it, because Renzo offered a hundred and fifty for the job. As I took seventy-five as a down payment, it occurred to me that whatever was waiting for me in the death-house, Renzo's master really wanted to lay it to rest.

***

They called him the Friar. The story went that he'd once been a monk as well as an alchemist, and sometimes, when he looked down at the alembics on his desk, you'd see a reverence in his eyes that would have suited a holy man. But they also said he'd got caught up in a feud in one of the other principalities, and he'd had to flee. I never found out if it was true. He never asked me about my scars, and it seemed only fair to return the favour.

"Ah, you!" he said as I walked into his shop. "How goes it?"

"Not bad. And you?"

"Very good, my dear. Much better for this." He tapped a charter of practice from the Velonian Guild of Apothecaries hanging above the shelves. I'd pointed him to the right people for obtaining it. The charter was forged, but then Velonia is a long way away. "A man needs to practice his trade honestly."

"You do realise that it's not real?"

"Of course. But only until I can get a proper one. Now, what do you need?"

A few months ago, I had a bad bout of Melancholia. It happens sometimes: you get miserable, nothing seems worth doing, you just sit about and feel like hell. You find ways around it, usually. But I couldn't pull myself out of this bout, so I got a tincture to sort it out. Whatever they said about the Friar, his stuff had got me out of bed. You couldn't fault it.

I told him what I needed.

"No," he said. "No, no, no. I am not getting involved in that."

"But I need to get into the death-house."

"Then break a window."

"Look, it's just me. If anything goes wrong, nobody else'll care."

"I will."

"That's sweet of you. But I'll manage."

He looked at me for a few moments, and then he said "Hell", as if it was *me* taking money from *him*. "Come back at dusk."

I spent the rest of the afternoon arranging the details with Old Triss, the broker. I paid for two strong, reliable lads to do the carrying, and a sheet and a board to use. I spent some of Renzo's money on a decent meal, and drank no wine so as not to interfere with the potion. Then I went back to see the Friar.

"Here," he said, passing me a little clay bottle. "It'll do what you want. Just be careful."

"I will be."

Back in my room I heard the bells tolling vespers. I put on my second-best boots. My dress was dark blue, good for hiding in shadows. There was one knife in my belt, a bit longer than most people carry, but hardly a broadsword. Nothing suspicious.

I took a few deep breaths and thought about the money. There was a little copper mirror under the bed: I put it on my lap. Then I unplugged the bottle and swallowed the contents.

It didn't taste too bad. I lay back on the bed, feeling myself start to slide towards sleep. I picked up the mirror – my hand felt as heavy as a rooftile. The face in the mirror was losing its colour the way old cloth loses dye. By the time I fell asleep, the scars on my face were purple, my skin like wax.

***

And I was awake.The first thing that hit me was the cold. The special sort of cold you only get in big buildings; a feeling not only of temperature, but of emptiness. I could smell the stone, the dust. I lay wherever I was, staring into the hollow dark, feeling the hardness of stone against my back. Slowly, rafters appeared above me; a roof like an upturned boat.

I listened and heard nothing at all. Carefully, I sat up.

The sheet lay open around me. I sat on a plinth in a hall. On the far side of the hall was a row of plinths, all with a person lying along the top, like the figures on crusaders' tombs.

I was still wearing my boots. I swung my legs down and stood up. Any movement in that place seemed loud. The hiss of the sheet sliding off my body seemed to fill the hall.

159

Moonlight seeped in through high, thin windows. At the far end of the hall, a set of wooden steps led underground. Everything was drained and grey. I looked at my hands, and they were almost purple, blue around the nails. I had about eight hours before the Friar's potion wore off: come morning, I'd slip out when they brought tomorrow's bodies in.

I walked into the middle of the hall. My limbs felt sluggish, as though I moved through water. Maybe the potion was doing that, dulling my mind like strong wine or pixie-leaf.

I reached the plinths along the far wall and looked at the people lying on them. They were dead, of course, loosely wrapped in sheets with the faces and upper bodies uncovered. They had the ungainly, useless look of bodies from which the life has gone. They made me think of landed fish.

The nearest was a man of about forty. His head was tilted back, lips slightly parted. He had thick, black curly hair. The sheet hid whatever it was that had killed him. I looked at his face, made gormless by death, and thought about closing his mouth. I didn't, though.

The next was a woman, fifty perhaps but hard-worn, and God knows what had happened to her. Drowning, I suppose, but don't ever say the dead all look at peace. There were flecks of black dirt on her puffy cheek, a couple of dots on the white of her eye.

The third was a lad, twenty or so, yellow-haired and foreign-looking: a Teut, perhaps. He'd been stabbed in the side of the neck. The wound was deep and wide, and he must have bled to death. He wore no shirt, and his pale chest had no other wounds. One lucky hit, if lucky was the word.

My girl wasn't anywhere to be seen.

It was only then that I realised how alone I was. I could have stood there forever, a fake dead person looking down at the real thing. With an effort, I lifted my hand and made the

160

Sign of the Sword across my chest and silently called on Saint Cordelia to watch over me. Then it was time to get moving. Somewhere in this place, Louisa was waiting to be found.

Assuming that she hadn't been hidden. Or that she'd been taken here at all. Or that she hadn't got off the slab and walked away. *Stop it.*

Blue light flickered at the edge of my vision.

It could have been a trick of the light, bad as it was: the motes of dust dancing above the slab. But there was a film of blue light around the first dead body, the man with thick black hair.

I stepped back. The Friar's potion was making me see things. I glanced at the doors, and realised that they would be locked. I'd got myself locked in here, full of a drug whose effects I could only guess at, alone with the dead.

I should never have drunk it. I never should have let the stuff inside me.

The thought came unbidden, but it was right.

There must have been something upstream, something rotting into the water. Oh, my guts...

Where had that come from? What upstream? I was talking about the potion, not drinking from some poisoned river. But the words weren't coming from me at all.

The blue light was around all three corpses now. It was so dim that it didn't seem there when I looked straight at it, only in the corner of my eye.

He held me under – he pushed my face in and held me under. I can't breathe –

You want to fight me, eh? Come on. I can take you. Oh shit, he's got a knife –

I could hear them: their last thoughts, in my mind.

I ran to the back of the church, to the set of stairs leading underground. I hurried down them, my boots almost silent, and I swear that as I fled the hall, I saw the blue outline of a man rising from the slab.

I stood at the bottom of the stairs, one boot on the steps, trying to put my head back together. I took a deep breath and forced myself to look over my shoulder. Nobody stood there, no ghosts, no faint blue shapes outraged at the impostor in their midst.

I looked away and breathed out.

I was at the start of a corridor. The walls were whitewashed but the workmanship was far cruder than above.

The drug had messed up more than my skin. It had done something to my head, without a doubt, but what if it was more than just a kind of drunkenness? What if the stuff, in making me look dead, had put me halfway to being that way? Was that what I had seen?

In eight hours' time the sun would rise, and I'd be back with the living. Maybe I was wrong. Perhaps the combination of this cold place, the bodies in it and the look of my hands had given me crazy thoughts. I could just be scaring myself, and making a damned good job of it.

The passage turned left. I waited at the turning and leaned around the corner. There were rows of doors on either side, and each had a little window set into it, like in a prison cell. The air smelt sweetish, vaguely sickly, and under it there something harsh and unnatural. It was the smell of alchemy.

A candle on a shelf gave a little light. I took it down and held it in my left hand. My right was at my waist, near the knife on my belt.

I don't know what I expected to find, but my guts knew it was going to be bad. My insides had tightened, twisted somehow. My heart beat quick and hard. I've been in places I shouldn't have been, trespassed and burgled and thieved, but the sense of being somewhere I never should have gone was almost strong enough to freeze me to the spot. I was in their world, at least part in it, and maybe the dead didn't like intruders.

There were four doors. It wouldn't take long. I stepped over to the little barred window set into the wood, keeping back and to one side, and held the candle up.

It was a cell or maybe a storeroom. A table stood in the middle of the room, and on it lay a dead body, covered by a blanket. Lumpy feet stuck out of the end of the blanket. A shelf stuck out from the wall, holding a row of things that looked like butcher's tools, because that's exactly what they were. I wedged the candle on the windowsill.

A hand dropped onto my shoulder.

I'm a professional, so I didn't jump more than ten feet and yell any louder than my lungs would let me. I drew the knife as I leaped away and I was standing with my knees bent and feet apart, left hand open and raised to block, right hand holding the knife down at my side.

She stood in the middle of the corridor. She wore a white robe held together with a leather belt. Her feet were bare and must have been cold. Her hair was black but going silver-grey. She had a headscarf just resting on the top of her head, not pinned. She looked like a nun, and like some statue of an empress.

"It's all right," she said.

I wasn't so sure. I lowered my left arm, stood up a little. "Who are you?"

"I work here," she said. "I tend to the dead." She looked at my side. "You can put the knife away. I won't hurt you."

I looked at her for a moment. She seemed pretty solid. I slid the knife back into my belt. "Sorry. You caught me by surprise. I, ah, well - when I saw you, I thought you might be a ghost."

She shook her head. "Not me. You look like one, though. Or maybe a mort."

"I'm not a mort."

"I know: morts can't speak. You're just pretending." She smiled, but wasn't letting me go past. "May I ask what you're doing here? And why you've gone that colour?"

"I need your help," I said.

"There's a price," she replied.

"What is it?"

"Talk to me. I don't get many visitors."

***

One of the little rooms was empty. There was a bench against the wall, and we sat on it. She lit a lantern and asked me about the city.

I told her what I knew, about the new walls and the fortified towers full of cannon. I explained that the engineers were building a great statue of the prince on a rearing horse, which they couldn't have done in the past, and apparently it was a great achievement. The playhouse was doing good business and the city had its third printing-press. The philosopher Lannato was said to be making a boat that could sail through the sky.

As I recounted it all, I realised that she had been down here a long time. Anchorites, that's the word: women who shut themselves away to do nothing but pray until they died. Pious, crazy or both, depending on how you look at it. I always wondered if they made the choice themselves.

"Who cut your face?" she asked. I suppose that living in a crypt probably doesn't make you much of a conversationalist.

"A criminal," I replied. "I saw something I wasn't meant to. He thought I'd go quietly. I didn't. At least I got away."

"Ah."

"One day I'll pay him back," I said. "Maybe in a year's time, when I've got all the money I need. But I will do it. Nobody else will if I don't."

And that's why I'm here, I thought. Looking through a bunch of corpses nobody will care about unless they're carrying disease, looking for a serving-girl on behalf of her rich lover. If I didn't find out what had happened to her, nobody else would. If I didn't take revenge on Publius Severra for what he did to my face, who would?

"So what did you come here for?"

"I was paid to find out what happened to someone. A girl, twenty or perhaps a bit older than that, brown hair, quite long. Probably in servants' clothes. I think she was brought in a couple of days ago."

164

"Ah," the woman said. "Is that why you made yourself look dead?"

"Yes. It was the only way to get in, and I had a feeling that I wouldn't get an answer if I asked."

"You probably wouldn't have. Yes, I know who you mean." She stood up and took the lantern from its hook. "This way."

She led me down to the end of the corridor. All the doors were bolted on the outside, but not locked. They must have left the bodies here for a day or two, in a sort of quarantine, and if a corpse turned out to have the Grey Ague, it wouldn't be able to do much except stand around and bump against the door.

My new friend pulled back the bolt. The door swung open quietly, and we walked in to see the body.

She lay on the table, head tilted to one side. The yellowness of the lantern gave her face a glow, and for a moment it seemed as if she had just closed her eyes to listen to something. Then she was a corpse again. She had long, thin hair, and a round, friendly sort of face. Her neck seemed very long, although it might have been the angle of her head. The muscles at the side of her jaw were clenched.

"She was brought in three days ago," the anchorite said.

"That's the body, all right," I said. I felt tired. Finding her didn't seem like much of an achievement.

"Bodies," the woman replied. "Two bodies." And she gestured at the dead girl's belly.

***

I got out of there with the daylight, in the commotion of bringing the first corpses in. I stood in the road and thanked God I was alive and looked it. Then I stumbled home. The bed opened up before me and I fell into it and slept until midday.

For a while I sat in bed, thinking about what I'd been told. There was no reason to think the woman in the crypt had lied. I thought about the dead girl, and all I felt was sad and tired in a way that sleep wouldn't heal.

The packet still lay on the table where I'd left it, sealed with a blob of wax. Louisa wouldn't need it. It still smelled vaguely alchemical.

Using a candle-flame, I heated the blade of a stiletto until it was almost too hot to touch. I used it to prise the wax away from the paper, so I could open it. I had a pretty good idea of what it would be, but I needed to make sure.

***

"It's what you thought," the Friar said, looking up from his bench. "You dissolve the powder in wine, get the woman to take it twice daily for a week. Gets rid of unwanted pregnancy. Once the side-effects wear off, nobody would ever know."

"Side-effects?" I stood at the door, feeling weary and slightly sick. I knew such powders existed – only the most sheltered fellow doesn't – but I'd never had cause to use them, thank the saints. It had been a long while since I'd had much to do with any man, since before I acquired my scars. I'd once been jealous of women who had their looks, but right now, I felt strangely relieved to be out of it all.

"Stomach pain, I gather." The Friar started collecting up the dust. "Illegal, of course, but not too hard to locate. The problem isn't finding it, but finding medicine that's good. The stuff they gave you to deliver was top-quality powder, but if you took badly mixed medicine... well, it wouldn't just be the pregnancy it got rid of."

I took the parcel back from him. I wanted to change the subject, so I said, "That potion you gave me."

"Ah, yes, my dear. Did it work?"

"Too well. Gave me nightmares. It did bad things to my mind."

166

"Really?"

I told him about what I'd seen: the blue haze I'd thought to be the spirits hanging over the dead bodies, waiting to escape. I told him about the anchorite, and our conversation. Then I turned to go.

"This woman you spoke to," he said as I reached the door. "Have you ever heard of a graveyard guardian?"

I shook my head.

"First person buried in a graveyard. Looks after the other spirits. Helps them on their way, so to speak." He looked straight at me, and then shrugged.

He turned back to his work and I walked out.

***

I met Renzo out in the open. He paid for us to enter the little garden in front of the counting-house, and we walked between the statues as if he was a merchant escorting his daughter.

"We both knew what had to be done," he said. He spoke to the air before him. "So my master sent me to sort out a powder she could use. He told me to get him the best. It took the apothecary almost a week to make the thing: he said if it was any quicker, the potion might make her ill. But by then, the girl had taken her own potion."

"So she bought something else. Something a servant girl could afford." Neither of us said: *And it killed her.*

A woman laughed somewhere off to the right, and a man joined in. Somewhere, distantly, a wagon rattled by. We strolled on, past the statues of heroes.

"My master meant to marry her," Renzo said. "Just – not yet."

"But she couldn't keep working in the house, not while she was pregnant."

"Not unmarried. They'd have thrown her out."

I thought about the woman who had confronted me in the garden, and thought she probably would have done.

"I'm sorry about it all," he said. "Really I am."

167

We walked quietly for a while, the rows of statues raising hands and weapons to salute us as we passed.

"Listen, Renzo." I stopped and faced him. "You're not a bad man," I said, "and I don't think your master is either. You tried to sort it out. If you had just walked away and denied it all, who'd have cared except you? It'd be your word against hers. But at least you tried to help out."

Renzo said nothing. He looked angry but defeated.

"But you got it wrong," I replied. "So the next time, if you want something done, you come to me. And I'll make sure that it doesn't go wrong, provided you come early enough. And maybe sometime you won't need me at all."

"I'll arrange for your pay," he said, and he stiffened suddenly, like a puppet whose strings have been pulled. Renzo gave me the smallest bow I'd ever seen, and left me standing in the gardens, surrounded by marble men.

***

They put her in the ground the next day, and I went to watch. Nobody deserves to be buried alone. It was the usual winding-sheet affair, and the priest did what he had to do, then moved on to the next. Two men stood nearby, though: Renzo and a young fellow, well-dressed, no more than eighteen. He had this dumb, awful look on his chubby face, like a soldier who's just had his first taste of war.

Good, I thought, but I knew neither of them could truly know what had happened; they could only see its aftermath, and regret without quite understanding.

I felt sad looking at the grave, but as they shovelled in the earth I felt something else. It was a sense of obligation, of responsibility, as though Louisa had entrusted me with an important task. Don't ask me why, but I knew it for a certainty. I would make the money I needed, get the training and the gear, and then I would find Publius Severra, whose men carved me up and left me to die, and I would settle the score with him.

After all, nobody else would do it.

168

MINISTER FOR GHOSTS

amanda R Primeau is a vessel that is psychically open to the spirit world and all its wonders. This is an enviable ability to have as it helps communication between the two dimensions. There is a downside to this gift, though. Sometimes, a malevolent spirit will take advantage of a person's openness and try to get past their spiritual-protection. I am regretful to report this happened to Sam and she has suffered because of it.

As Minister for Ghosts, part of my job is to protect the people with whom I work. Sam was attacked by such a malevolent entity so it was my duty to help. I called in Sam's mother, who was more than happy to take on this evil. She protected her daughter in life and now does it from beyond the veil. When necessary, she manifests herself as a Tawny owl and is accompanied by an aerie of eagles. As her protection, they gather up the necessary spiritual energy to dispel these vile attacks.

Thankfully, Sam is safe now and lives out her new life in Colorado USA with her husband and two children. Her mother watches over her and the family.

MY BROTHER'S KEEPER

by Samanda R Primeau

I don't like the way that guy talks to my brother. Being in prison for killing his wife is hard enough for Neal, without his cellmate yammering all the time; Neal barely hears me when I visit with him, and it's tearing me up. Sometimes, the way he talks to me is so disordered he sounds delusional. Well, I'm not a delusion -- a delusion couldn't protect my brother. I'm his guardian angel. I'll be with him forever.

His cellmate won't.

***

It's my job to remember our past lives, and make sure we end up together each time; Neal has always been the best brother. In our last life, when I was Jesse -- he had another name then, but I won't confuse you with all that -- we were the best of pals. As kids, we swam in the river and fished in the lake and hunted in the woods. When we grew up, I met and married Chris; Neal moved in with us, and life was just perfect.

Then Neal started talking to Chris' cousin, Claire. He asked her to marry him, and they made plans to move into a house of their own.

He didn't seem to understand why she had to die.

It was so confusing for Neal - I think he told Chris, because next thing you know, we were both poisoned. Chris yelled about us killing the cousin, and just walked away and left us dying on the floor - after kicking Neal in the head.

I shot Chris in the back.

I tried to bring us into another great life, here, but it got a bit screwed up. Still, I've made the best of it, and he's still my brother. He needs my protection. I've kept him from so many mistakes, and the sad thing is that he doesn't even know it. He will one day, and we'll look back and laugh.

When he was six, that little tramp down the street -- Maddy something - took him behind the school and kissed him. She was nothing but trouble. She saw what she'd gotten into, though: I gave her a look, and she screamed her head off and ran for home so fast she got hit by a car, crossing Oak Street. After she got out of the hospital, she never spoke to Neal again, and good riddance. She was a little off from the brain damage, and nobody believed her stories of devils in the eyes - or if they did, they kept it to themselves.

Neal didn't talk much to girls for a few years, but then when he was ten, the girl who had just moved in next door -- I think her name was Ellen or maybe Helen - took a shine to him. She wouldn't leave him alone. Neal started spending all his time talking out his window to the little floozie. No matter how much I talked to him, he wouldn't do anything I wanted to do. He'd never been that way before. I had to act, which is something I don't like to do - after all, I'm not here for myself, I'm here for my brother; I do what's necessary to protect Neal.

I took that little slut swimming in the river that ran by the back of the house. The kids had hollowed out a swimming hole that was plenty deep to hold her under. She washed up at the bridge a couple days later. The man next door tried to say he'd seen who took her down to the river, but I took Neal over to see him and cleared that up. I guess he didn't like the look in our eyes. He changed his story, and the police stopped looking at us - which was good, because Neal was innocent, after all.

Neal's teen years were a trial for us all. When the hormones kicked in, he started to change, and ignore me. Me! Can you imagine? I had to protect him a lot during that phase, when he took up with the bunch that called themselves Satanists at school. That leader boy was entirely too friendly, and he was nothing but bad news. He was telling Neal all about how he should get this girl for the group - I told Neal she was used goods, and he told the boy, and the boy got mad and shoved Neal, so I confronted him.

The look I burned into that kid scared the piss out of him - literally - and he screamed and jumped in front of a car. It was just like that little tramp in first grade. Witnesses told the police that nobody'd touched the boy, and everyone could see he was in shock. They ruled it a suicide.

The Satanists kind of drifted apart after their leader killed himself. I think it worried Neal that I'd jumped in to protect him, because he took to calling me his sidekick - meaning he was a superhero of some sort. As superheroes do, he kept that quiet, which was just as well. For a couple of years, things were really great. Neal listened to me, and talked to me, and it was just like it was meant to be - loving siblings, sharing everything.

Then, the unthinkable. His hormones leveled off, puberty settled down, and Neal just wouldn't listen to me at all anymore. I was all alone. It was worse than before, because we'd had those wonderful years.

We drifted apart, though I could still steer him away from trouble, usually - but then he acted like it was all his own idea, and when he thought about those years at all, it was like everything he'd done had been his own ideas. You can imagine how I felt, but I managed all right until the breakdown.

A few years ago, it got to be too much for me and I confronted him; I demanded to know why he ignored me, when all I wanted to do was protect him. Turns out, Neal was terrified of me. Me - his guardian angel, his protector, his sidekick. I love my brother so much, and he cowered on the floor and crawled into a corner to hide, holding his head and sobbing - as if I could ever hurt him.

I held him as well as I could, and tried to comfort him; I talked to him about all the good times, all the lives that we've been together. I told him how I've always kept him safe and never let any harm come to him. I'm not sure how much he really heard, but he stopped crying and settled down.

We were able to talk to each other like old times, for a while. He did things I wanted to do, and it was looking up. I loved spending time together again. But it came and went - one day he would be talking to me, and the next he'd try to ignore me, and sometimes he acted like I wasn't even there.

I didn't know anything about medications, never had any use for doctors, so I didn't realize Neal was taking something for "depression." He'd always taken vitamin pills and whatnot, every morning, so another pill was nothing to me. This stuff, he would take it for a while, then start feeling "better", so he wouldn't listen to me anymore, and then he'd think he was "cured" and stop taking it. Every time we started talking again, he'd get upset and start taking his pills again.

Once I figured out what was happening, I put a stop to that -- I made him get rid of those pills.

Then he went back to the doctor. By the time I realized what it was about, it was too late -- he was going under anesthesia, and as I discovered later, it was for electro-shock treatment. It went on for weeks and his suffering really hurt me, when I couldn't protect him. I was pushed out of his life for a while, but tried to keep an eye on him now and again.

It was during one of those periods he didn't want me around, that Neal met Sandra. She was the new receptionist at his doctor's office. I guess she came on pretty hard, because it was only three months later they were married. I just couldn't believe Neal had been taken in so fast. What was she doing to him?

Changing him, that's what she was doing. Neal had new clothes, a new car - and a new person to hang out with. He was being somebody I hardly even knew. And worse, he was acting like he liked it. I tried to talk him into going to our old hangouts, but he always seemed to have these headaches. He'd just moan and hold his head like it was gonna fall off.

Obviously, this woman was no good for him. He'd never had headaches like that before. I tried to tell him that, but he would just moan louder. And then she wanted him to go back to the doctor. What if the doctor gave him a bigger shock and he forgot all about me? That's what she wanted, the greedy bitch - she wanted Neal all to herself, so she could dress him and take him out and play with him, like he was her little doll. Neal shouldn't be made into a puppet for anyone to order around and make him do stuff. He's my brother.

Before Neal could go to the doctor again, I acted. After all I'd been through for him, I knew I must protect him.

I should have realized, when she was setting out that fancy dress and running the smelly bubble bath, they were having company for dinner, but I slipped in without Neal knowing. People normally cook something when they're having a dinner party - how was I supposed to know a caterer was bringing all the food? Who does that?

I caught her getting into the bathtub and pulled her feet out from under her. She hit her head on the tub as she fell, and I just held her under for a while to be sure. I didn't turn off the water - what should I care if the bitch's house flooded? Neal wasn't going to live there anymore. But I guess that was another thing I ought to have had the strength to think about, because the caterer came in as the water was running down the stairs, and when she ran up to see what it was about, there I was.

I wish I'd been stronger. Poor Neal is here in prison,

now, and it's because I wasn't strong enough to protect him from everything. And the pills he gets from the prison doctor only make me weaker. I can talk to him, a little, and sometimes I think he hears me, but only when it's quiet and he can listen to the sounds in his own head.

My name is Jesse. At least, it was in our last life -- I didn't get a name in this life, because I died before we were born. We were triplets, for that first few weeks, but I didn't come here to share my brother. The other one was a weak little girl - I thought it would be easy to cut her off, and it was, but the bitch was stronger than I thought, and she took me out with her. Poor Neal was left as the only baby to be born, but I'm still with him; there's a tiny piece of me, the sister-that-would-have-been, embedded in his brain, and there I ride.

It would be quiet enough for us to really talk to each other, if it weren't for his cellmate. I don't like the way he just keeps talking and talking to my brother. And after being afraid of him for a few weeks, Neal is starting to talk to him now. I think the guy's nothing but trouble.

I have to protect my brother.

I'm his guardian angel.

MINISTER FOR GHOSTS

The meaning of life is to evolve. Evolution is gained by loving more to the people around you and to your surroundings. If you have love in your life then hold onto the emotion and cherish how it makes you feel as in your next incarnation it may well not be as pleasant.

My next vessel is Canadian Nathan Hystad. He has contentment with his life and a love for his wife that is reciprocated. His mother has moved on to the spirit world but she still loves him with all her heart, as he does her.

Nathan was recommended to me to become a member of my ministry. I watched him for a while and the decision was truly a simple one. He has a good heart and an even better imagination. As a spiritual vessel of the Ghost Ministry I tasked him with the responsibility to explain how a spirit could be grounded and he does it so well.

His mother still watches over him from her little corner of heaven and is so proud, as I am.

A HAUNTING PAST

By Nathan Hystad

He watched her from the corner of the room. She was pretty; small and brunette. He imagined her to smell like lilacs though he couldn't remember what lilacs smelt like. He had been here for weeks now; seemingly anchored to this building. He knew her name was Sarah; the fat man who came to check the electricity had called her that. The fat man was no danger; he couldn't sense anything strange about Sarah's apartment.

He hovered near the ceiling, trying to be careful to keep his "head" from moving into the floor above. It was a strange balancing act he had gotten used to over the years. *Years... I have been this way for years.* He could have cried if he was able, but he couldn't. He would have yelled if he could, but he couldn't. He was not sure what he was, who he was or why he was ... he just was.

His memories failed and it angered him. As his thoughts went to a dark place, the lights began to flicker. The radio turned on and Sarah got frightened. Her cup fell to the floor shattering. It startled him out of his anger. The lights came back to normal and the radio turned off. The classical music started again and Sarah cleaned up her mess. *What am I doing to this creature? Why am I here?* He tried to leave, but as she sat back down on the couch he stopped. She looked so beautiful.

He couldn't leave. He was here for a reason.

He watched her from the corner of the room.

***

"I'm telling you toots, there's nothing wrong with the place. Electrical system is a go, no frays, no breaker issues and it never does any of this so called flickering when I'm around. Why is it that no other unit has any complaints?" Earl said.

"Fine, Earl, it's not my imagination but whatever, don't worry about it. I'm just tired right now and have work to do. I'll try to take a video if it happens again," Sarah replied as she shut the apartment door on him.

She decided to get back to working on the case her law firm was in the middle of. The accused, Klutterman claimed he was innocent of the multiple murder charges. His fingerprints had been found all over the scene; his clothing covered in blood. Sarah opened the file and flipped through the black and white photos. There were four bodies in total on the floor. He claimed to have nothing to do with the deaths of the three women but stated he killed the man in self defence. The case seemed fairly cut and dried but the District Attorney's office couldn't leave anything uncovered.

Colin Klutterman had a sordid past, starting from being a trouble-making kid in school. He moved on from bullying and pranks at seventeen when he stole his first car. He had a series of misdemeanours with a few days in jail and community service leading up to the murder charges. Nothing that screamed psychopath, so what had set him off and turned him into this monster?

Sarah flipped open her laptop and clicked the file labelled - "Klutterman Apr 21, 2009". His voice began to speak through her small speakers and as always it had a raspy tone.

"I've told you guys a hundred times, I didn't kill those girls!

I was there because I was invited and maybe for some recreational habits. It was self-defense! The guy snapped and started killing them. I stepped in and stopped him from killing me ... I was lucky to make it out of there alive."

He went along this line for a minute before he started sobbing uncontrollably. Sarah thought he put on a good performance. He was tested after the murders and they found extremely high levels of alcohol and heroin in his system, which have a tendency to cause blackouts.

Just as Sarah was about to close the file she heard Klutterman mumble something about an INXS song, being played over and over. Something struck her as familiar about that and years of looking for small details convinced her it meant something. At the moment she couldn't link anything so she closed the laptop and went to bed.

***

He watched her from the corner of the room. It was surreal at times, like he was in a dream. She worked at her desk; papers strewn everywhere and the computer light making her delicate features glow in the dark. He could hear the computer play a man's voice speaking in rushed tones. The volume was too low to hear from across the room. What was playing on the computer wasn't important. The girl was. Sarah was important. There must be a link to her and his past - but what?

He felt better in the past week since he had scared her. His mind was becoming clearer every day. He could remember brief moments from his life. A flash of a little league game - he hit a game-winning run. He could almost see what his parents looked like and he was sure he'd had a sister. Her name was Molly - no Holly, her name was Holly. He knew it now. He smiled inside at his new-found knowledge as if he would become human again, if all the pieces were there.

He still had no idea what his name was, but right now

179

that didn't seem important. He watched Sarah listen to her recordings and from the look on her face she had a 'Eureka' moment. She gathered all of the paper in a heap and ran out of the room with pages falling out of her briefcase.

The lights were off so it was hard to see, but he floated over to the desk where a solitary picture lay. It showed four bodies lying across a messy floor. Blood was everywhere. There were needles on the ground and beer bottles on the table beside them. He couldn't make out faces but he recognized the shoes on the man. He floated back into the corner of the room. The lights flickered the whole way now from the kitchen to the living room. The radio turned on...Never Tear us Apart quietly played through its speakers. He knew who the man was.

He waited for her from the corner of the room.

***

Sarah sat in her office downtown. She knew there was a file on the man Klutterman said was the real killer, but they had done extensive research on him and he came up as clean as a whistle. The crime scene was a ratty motel room that typically housed cockroaches and prostitutes with the occasional hitchhiker.

The male victim was Harold Chester. Five eleven, one-ninety, brown hair. He worked in a small investment firm and mainly dealt in insurance. His record was squeaky-clean, maybe a little too clean for a thirty eight year old. Not even a speeding ticket to speak of.

The three female victims were known prostitutes. Klutterman's story indicated he was lured to the room by one of the girls with promise of sex and drugs. Chester being there was always the big elephant in the room. But with Klutterman's priors he was always the suspect. Something felt wrong about this whole scenario. She was sure that the jury was going to find Klutterman guilty but she needed to dig more on this Chester character; she didn't want the defence finding something that would ruin her case.

Sarah leaned back in her chair and took a deep breath. The air felt lighter here than at home.

She turned her attention back to her laptop and started to do some research on the previous known places Chester had lived, to see what she could dig up. It was going to be a long night.

**

From the corner of the room, he watched her enter the apartment. Her dark hair was pulled back in a pony tail and her baggy eyes didn't do much to lessen her beauty. He knew why he was here now, and it had nothing to do with the fact that he was now in love with this woman. As much as he longed to take her in his arms, he knew that could never happen. He was here to make sure the man who murdered him was brought to justice.

Klutterman had killed him. This was a fact. He had no strong memories of the event but he could see the wide eyes crying as he was stabbed repeatedly. He almost remembered lifting from his still warm body. Floating. Floating away. Not sure how to control his movements like a balloon in the wind. He drifted around the city for some time, he was sure. The next thing he knew he was here...but a few years had passed between. *Where was I? Who was I? And what happened that night?*

Sarah distracted him as she strode into the room and threw her bag down on the desk. She tried turning the lamp on but it didn't work. After a few flicks she took the bulb out and could see that it was black inside.

He floated there, knowing he'd fried the light bulb when he'd been angry. It wasn't his fault. None of this was his fault.

He watched her from the corner of the room.

**

Sarah was feeling more and more uncomfortable in her apartment. The air felt thicker...the radio was buzzing and her light bulbs were burnt out. Something was wrong and she even had an outside electrician come in to check it out. He couldn't explain any of it. Everything seemed up to code from his side.

She was also sure that things had moved. Pictures she laid out. Notes about the case. She felt like she was being watched. *Could someone from Klutterman's defense team be spying on me?* She doubted that, but something was off.

Some of the news she had dug up while searching for something dirty on Chester had been troubling. He had lived in five States in the past twelve years, both in small towns and in big cities. One thing stood out. There were cases of missing persons in all of those places while he was there. Even in the small town of Milton, Nebraska where he lived for only five months. He worked for a small State Farms Insurance company while there and three missing persons were filed in that time. Two women and one man went missing and all within those five months. He was never questioned. Sarah had even called the local sheriff station there and they weren't even sure who Chester was.

To this day none of the missing persons had been found in Milton. She'd discovered similar scenarios in the other towns and cities. Who remembers the quiet insurance salesman? What was Chester's motivation to kill? That was the question... and how could she prove anything? Her boss would not be happy if she kept digging. Klutterman was about to get life in prison this week and that meant a win for her office. Right now her boss needed a win. Either way, Klutterman was a killer.

She picked up her phone, pressed her contact list and scrolled until she found her boss's name. Dane Zimmer. She held it in front of her for a moment.

***

He watched her from the corner of the room. She was struggling with something. He could tell from her conversations with work that the case was close to ending and Klutterman was going to pay for what he did.

Images flashed in his head. Dead bodies. The women lying in blood. Fatal stab wounds in them. *Wait, those aren't the bodies from the picture where I was killed. What is this?* More images came to him. Death flashed in his mind. Men, women, children. All dead. A shovel. Dirt. Digging. Dirty finger nails. Always dirty finger nails. Must scrub them clean. *Where is the steel wool? I need to clean my nails.*

He snapped out of what could only be a ghostly sweat. It felt like his 'body' was dripping away. He concentrated on bringing it together. He wasn't done here. It had all come back to him. The lust for death. It came at an early age and started with animals. He killed his first person when he was a teenager. She had been a schoolmate's mom. Mrs. Lewington. They looked for her for months, but they never checked her own flower garden. He pictured her now and couldn't help but notice the similarities to Sarah. Same small frame and brown hair. Those eyes...he remembered how wide they went as he choked her to death. He had loved Tommy's mom, but she didn't take him seriously. For those last few seconds of her life she took him seriously.

He looked over at Sarah as she spoke on her phone. His energy was thrumming loudly at this point and it took everything he had to concentrate on what she was saying.

"Dane. Dane, I don't think this is Klutterman's doing. Sure he killed Harold Chester, but I'm sure there was good reason. Dane... just hear me out... We can't let Klutterman... Hello?? Hello?"

He floated to her from the corner of the room.

***

She took a long breath and pushed the dial button on her cell phone. It rang.

Dane answered with his usual greeting, "Dane here."

"Dane. Dane, I don't think this is all Klutterman's doing," she said.

"What are you talking about? The case is as good as over, Sarah."

"Sure he killed Harold Chester, but I'm sure there was good reason."

"Listen... I'm sure we could drag up all sorts of 'what ifs' but the fact of the matter is..."

"Dane... just hear me out..."

"Klutterman is going to prison for a long time Sarah. Let it be. Let's move on to the next one and celebrate locking up another scumbag."

"But Klutterman didn't... Hello? Hello?"

The phone went blank just as the lights flickered hard. Her music that had been softly playing on the laptop turned into Michael Hutchence's haunting voice. NEVER TEAR US APART boomed from her small speakers.

***

He floated to her and expelled angry energy. He was a monster... a murderer... how could he have ever forgotten this? He couldn't let Sarah tell the world. That was what made him so proud of his legacy. He had killed close to forty people in his life and never once had he been suspected. He would go out quietly and no one would ever know he had anything to do with any of this. He would be the quiet insurance man who was in the wrong place at the wrong time when Klutterman went on a booze-fuelled rampage and killed four people.

He grinned inwardly as the music blared from her computer. That song was playing during his first kill. Mrs. Lewington was in her back yard digging the spring ground, about to plant daffodils. He could almost smell them still. She had a small boom box on the deck and it was playing the Australian rock band's new hit. Forever it held a place in his heart.

As he neared Sarah, he became frustrated. He was a ghost. And ghosts were harmless. He needed a plan. He dug deep for energy and slipped a picture of Harold Chester from her pile on her desk. He carried it with him across the room and knew it must appear that he was a floating picture head. He would make sure the last person to die by his hands would know her killer was him... know his name.

***

She saw the picture floating towards her and screamed. *What the hell is going on?* She pushed back from her chair and knocked it over. The music kept playing and her light bulbs were popping and exploding around her. She backed into the dark corner.

Sarah could hear nothing... the room was silent and for a moment she wondered if she had imagined the whole thing. Then she felt the breath. It was like her face was just outside a freezer door when you first open it wide. The cold air enveloped her head and a scream stuck in her throat. She felt cold hands wrap around her neck but couldn't see anything in front of her. She kicked and punched but there was nothing there to hit. Her breath came harder and harder, white spots floated in her vision.

She fell to the ground, one solitary light coming back on behind her... then darkness.

***

The moment was here. The moment he finished her and moved on. Just like he always did. Only he didn't know how he would move on from this. He was a ghost now;

185

an anchored spirit. Would he disappear, would he stay here or be free to roam?

He managed to get his opaque fingers around her slender neck. With everything he had, he squeezed. Her arms and legs came towards him like so many he had seen before, but this time he wasn't really there for her to hit. He closed his eyes as he felt himself losing strength. Her eyes were beautiful... there was no time for that. He had to give it everything he had, in order to finish her. As she clawed at the air, he realized that for the first time he couldn't do it.

Sarah was different to him with her quiet ways and pretty face. Her resemblance to his first kill stopped him in his tracks. Sarah's eyes wide... confused. His strength failed him and she fell to the floor. The music stopped and the one light bulb still working went on. He floated down to the floor with no energy to do anything but that. She lay sprawled on the floor, breathing lightly but clearly unconscious.

It was over.

* * *

Sarah looked around the hospital room and saw a fresh bouquet of roses beside her. She grabbed the little 'Get Well' note and saw that they were from Dane. There was writing on it. 'We got him kid. Klutterman got consecutive life sentences'

She dropped the card on the bed recalling the events of the accident. She remembered being alone, then a picture of Chester had floated across the room. *This makes no sense. Did I hit my head?* She recalled being choked by nothing she could see and the music and lights blowing up. Then she remembered a flash of Earl in her apartment calling 911. He must have heard the music blasting and her screaming. *Thank god Earl was there.*

It still made no sense. She knew Chester was a bad

man; that he'd murdered a lot of people...there was no way it was coincidence. But maybe it was best if Klutterman just went away and her life could get back to normal. But first things first, she would get a new apartment.

***

He watched her from the corner of the room. She'd read the card from the flowers and now she was lost in thought. He'd followed her here somehow. He'd blacked out along with her and thought that was it for him, as a spirit. Instead he awoke here. His time with Sarah wasn't over. This drew a metaphysical smile from the ghost.

Sarah turned the lights off and he stayed in the corner. And he watched her.

Minister for Ghosts

I first met Ken O'Brien when it was brought to my attention that he had a gift; quite an amazing gift that enables him to see spirit, I might add. When he was a small boy, a rather splendid thing happened. He went to visit his recently deceased and much-loved grandmother who lay in state in her coffin. I am told this is the tradition in Scotland. As her spirit left her body to walk into the light, Ken witnessed the whole thing.

I shadowed him for a while and it was clear he could do a magnificent job for my ministry so employing him as another of my spiritual vessels was an easy decision to make.

Ken brings us this next tale of seduction holds a moral lesson for us all in our everyday lives. Beware of temptation.

LEUCOSIA

By Ken O'Brien

My life was going nowhere. The list of my sorry achievements consisted of a wife I had betrayed, two sons, oblivious to the failings of their errant father and a huge amount of debt. The affair had fizzled out like some acrimonious Roman candle - cheap sparks lacking substance or staying power.

Helen, my wife, never did find out about my adultery but I was sure she suspected something. I used to watch her in the mornings, all plump and matronly as she made breakfast for the boys, and wonder why I felt so dead inside. She was the mother of my children and yet I felt something close to resentment towards her. The routine of normal life assaulted my senses and aspirations like the incessant drip of water torture - she looked after the house and children, I went to work, I came home, we never talked, we never had sex. Day after day, the same routine was repeated over and over again.

The affair had been almost inevitable and, now that it was over, I couldn't stomach the return of the daily grind in an existence with no hope. I did what most pathetic self-pitying creatures like myself do at times such as these - I turned to drink. Spending what little money I had, I stumbled towards the oblivion of an empty whisky bottle. I used to tell Helen that I was having a night out with the boys. Sometimes she voiced her concerns that I was spending too many evenings drinking. Flying into a rage was my normal response. Like most guilty people, I'd learned very quickly that the easiest method of hiding your own misdemeanours was to turn the tables on the challenger. I'd accuse her of smothering me, of sucking me dry until I was nothing but a husk of a man. Did she resent my having a little fun in my life? Usually, the argument would culminate in her going to bed in tears and me staying out all evening.

There were no nights out with the boys and most of the time I spent drinking alone and wandering the streets between bars. I didn't know what I was looking for; I just felt the need to move between empty spaces.

***

It was on one particular rain-lashed night when I staggered between puddles and avoided being splashed by passing motorists that I found something. I wiped the rain from the face of my wristwatch and checked the time. Almost midnight. That was when I noticed the flashing sign across the road. It said: Welcome To Club Anthemusa. I'd never noticed this place before. A burly bald-headed, dark-suited man stood in the doorway framed by flickering blue neon signs. From within the building came the strains of a muted trumpet and the clash of a cymbal. I asked him if the nightclub just newly opened.

The Bouncer ignored my question. 'You want in?'

I felt the loose change in the damp pocket of my overcoat. 'How much is it?'

He let out a deep laugh and shook his head. 'For you, man, nothing.'

He moved his burly frame, unblocking the doorway, and ushered me inside with the sweep of an outspread hand.

***

The interior of the club was dimly-lit and sparsely-populated. A cluster of tables and chairs held a scattering of patrons in the area between bar and stage. Trails of tobacco smoke curled and writhed above the tables like insubstantial serpents. Every member of the audience watched the band on stage. I found enough money in my pocket to order a whisky and stood for a moment surveying the scene. The club customers were all men nursing drinks alone at their table listening to the music. The band on the stage played some strange kind of melody I'd never heard before. The tall female singer in a silver evening dress dominated the platform. She seemed incredibly thin and pale but I found her beauty unmistakable and chose a chair at an empty table close to the stage.

The curls of her hair cascaded over her shoulders as she stood singing into a microphone. Her fingers appeared to caress the mike rather than hold it and her lips brushed against the muffle. Her voice was almost a whisper yet clearly heard within the club. She didn't sing any lyrics but harmonised with the music, complementing the instruments perfectly.

She was staring at one member of the audience in particular. It seemed as if she sung only for him and that the rest of us were nothing more than voyeuristic intruders. Somewhere deep within my soul, I yearned for her to sing for me. Time became meaningless as I sat listening to the strange, haunting sound of her voice and, all too soon, it was over. The song came to a close. The lady bowed to a scattering of applause and I checked my watch: one a.m. The band began to pack away their instruments and the man she had been singing to rose from his chair and exited with the dark-haired beauty in the silver dress. Somewhat the worse for wear, I made my way home and sneaked into bed beside my snoring wife.

***

Helen was her usual cheery self in the morning. She busied herself with breakfast as I sat nursing a headache and a strong black coffee. The boys came running into the kitchen. They were arguing over some ridiculous toy. Helen dropped two pieces of blackened toast into the sink, clattered the grille pan down on to the worktop and scolded the children for their behaviour. The smoke detector began to beep loudly.

'Shut up!' I yelled. 'All of you! Just shut the hell up!'

Helen stopped waving her tea towel at the smoke alarm and looked at me aghast.

'Tony,' she cried, 'What's the matter?'

'Everything!' I yelled, slamming my cup on to the table. 'I'm going to work.'

'But, what about your breakfast?'

'I'll pick up something on the way.' I said as I grabbed the daily newspaper and made for the door. Then, I paused and looked back at my family. 'Don't wait up for me. We've got an important meeting at work so I'll probably be late.'

'How late?'

I ignored her question and slammed the door.

***

The working day did not go well and I was warned about my recent tardiness but I was beyond caring what my supervisor thought. I spent most of the day staring out of a window waiting for night to fall. I intended to return to Club Anthemusa. I knew I had to see the singer again. I wandered the streets trying to retrace my steps to the nightclub but couldn't find it. As the night wore on, I grew more frantic in my search. Then, as I heard the town clock chime midnight, I saw the club directly across the street from where I stood. I had wandered around this area a dozen times, how could I have missed it?

The doorman ushered me inside and, cradling a large glass of whisky, I made my way to the same table as before. The band was already playing and she took the stage. Her voice seemed to fill my whole body with sadness and I felt a tear trickle down my cheek, which I wiped away with the heel of my hand. She turned her attention on another member of the audience and seemed to sing exclusively to him. My heart felt ready to burst with despair. I wanted to cry Me! Sing for me! But, instead, swallowed all of my whisky in a single gulp. I made my way to the bar for a refill.

'Another, friend?' asked the barman. He was a bulky man with short dark hair and a matching beard. His combination of bright red shirt under a dark waistcoat matched the décor of scarlet walls and ebony beams within the club.

I nodded and held out my empty glass.

'Makes your heart want to break, that voice of hers.' he said, as he refilled the tumbler.

I took a sip of my drink. 'Who is she?'

'Calls herself Leucosia. Says she's the last of her kind.'

'You mean she doesn't have any family?'

The barman shrugged. 'Yeah. Something like that.'

'Where'd she come from?'

'Somewhere around the Med is all I know.' He held out his arms and gave a wide grin. 'I'm from Greece. Beautiful country. You should go sometime.'

'Perhaps.'

'You want another?' The barman nodded towards my empty glass. 'This will have to be your last drink. It's almost one.'

I glanced at my watch: twelve fifty five. 'You don't open very long.'

The barman shrugged. 'Don't care. It's up to the boss. He pays me a good wage so I don't complain.'

At one o'clock, the band stopped playing and I watched Leucosia disappear with the man she had been singing to. I felt a surge of jealous rage flow through me as I made my way out on to the street. As I staggered towards my dreary home, I wished to feel the thrill of a night with the singer. It was a prize I would be willing to go through the gates of Hell for.

***

Each night for the next two weeks, I found myself in Club Anthemusa at midnight.

My excuses regarding these evening excursions to Helen grew feebler as each day passed but she still meekly accepted the situation. As a consequence, my resentment towards her grew and I became less and less concerned with the wellbeing of my family. Seeing Leucosia was all that mattered to me.

The barman always gave me a friendly nod and had a glass of whisky waiting for me by the time I reached him. I would take up my normal position near the stage and watch the band for the next hour. Each time she sang, she would target an individual and sing almost exclusively for them. A few times I caught her eye and she would give me a smile, but her attention never lingered on me. I began to despair of ever being the object of her song.

***

One night, as the misery of being overlooked once more settled upon me, a stranger appeared by my table. He was a short man, perhaps seventy years old. His hair and beard were grey and he wore a tweed suit.

'Mind if I join you?' he asked.

I shook my head and gestured towards the empty chair. I only agreed to be polite and didn't really want any company. All I wanted to do was listen to Leucosia.

The old man looked around the club. 'Not too busy tonight,' he said.

194

I shrugged, unwilling to be drawn into conversation. 'Hope it gets better. I've got bills to pay.'

I looked at the stranger and frowned. 'You're the owner?' I asked him.

He held out his hand. 'My name is Achelous. Pleased to meet you.'

I shook hands with him and then slouched back in my chair. Half my attention was still on the captivating music. 'Perhaps,' I suggested, 'you should stay open longer. That would help with the bills.'

'No point,' Achelous replied and nodded towards the stage, 'she only sings for one hour every night and that's all that people like you come for. Once she's gone, that's it. No point in staying open.'

I absently played with the place mat on the table. 'I suppose you're right.'

'You know I'm right. Say, would you like a drink? On the house of course.'

'Sure.'

Achelous raised his hand and within a matter of seconds, the barman appeared with two large glasses of whisky. For a while, we both sat back savouring our drinks, enthralled by the beautiful music.

'She'd like to meet you,'Achelous said.

I flinched, startled. 'You mean Leucosia? Meet me?'

The old man nodded slowly. 'She has a room upstairs. Her room. She'll take you there at two. Dimitri, the barman, will let you wait in the club until she comes for you.'

I could already feel my heart quicken in anticipation. I wondered if she would sing to me. Achelous stood up slowly and pushed the chair away.

'Ah, these old bones. Too many summers and too many winters they have seen. Have you any idea how old I am?' He laughed and held out a hand, 'don't answer that. One of us will only get embarrassed. I will leave you now but I have ordered Dimitri to keep you supplied with this fine whisky. It's the least I can do for somebody who, I hope, will bring a little happiness into Leucosia's life. She is very dear to me. Remember that.'

'I will.' I held up a glass to the retreating form of Achelous. A toast to the man who made it possible for me to finally meet my love, I thought.

***

I sat watching the hour come to an end. At one o'clock, the band began to pack away their instruments and Leucosia disappeared with the man she had been singing to. Dimitri must have noticed my distress.

'Don't worry,' he said as he placed a fresh glass of whisky on the table. 'What you see there.....it's nothing. She'll be back and you'll be the happiest man in the world.'

I slowly savoured the taste of the whisky and recalled Dimitri's words as I waited for the return of Leucosia.

She arrived promptly at two and stood beside me at the bar. I noticed that, despite her natural beauty, she had always looked pale and drawn under the stage lighting. Now, her skin was flushed and she seemed to glow with health. The slenderness of her body appeared more curvaceous under the softer illumination of the bar lights.

***

Dimitri took the half-empty glass from my hand and raised his eyebrows.

I felt her cold fingers entwine with mine. 'Come,' she ordered.

I followed willingly as she led me up the stairs behind the stage and into her bedroom. She turned to face me and put a finger to my lips before I could speak.

'No talk,' she said as she began to work the thin straps of her gown over her pale shoulders. It dropped to the floor. She stood before me naked but I couldn't wrench my gaze

196

away from her eyes. It was as if I looked into The Abyss itself and was filled with the urge to jump.

Slowly and deliberately, she undressed me and led me to her bed, where we lay on her scented pillows and made love until near dawn, when we drifted into sleep. The sensations I experienced that night were incredible and it should have been the happiest moment of my life, but I found myself disturbed by dark dreams. I was falling into the black pits of her eyes and somewhere deep within the recesses of this nightmare, I had the feeling that there was a price still to be paid.

Somebody shaking me roused me from my slumber. It was Leucosia.

'You must go,' she said firmly.

Startled, I had to ask the most important question. 'Will I see you again?'

'Perhaps. Yes.'

'When?'

'Soon. Achelous will tell you.'

Somewhat confused, I did as she asked and left Leucosia's bed. I made my way through the building but I saw no sign of Achelous. I resolved to return to the club that night and seek an explanation from the old man about her behaviour.

***

It was almost midday when I entered my home and saw a suitcase by the foot of the stairs. Helen stood next to it with her arms folded.

'Where are the boys?' I asked.

'At school,' came her curt reply. She pointed to the suitcase. 'Those are your clothes. Take them and get out.' After a moment, she added: 'I just can't take anymore, Tony,' she moaned.

I resisted the urge to smile. Helen had done the dirty work for me. I had lacked the courage to end the relationship but my wife had finally found the strength to be decisive and finish this charade of a marriage.

Without a word, I picked up the heavy case and made to leave.

'One thing before you go,' said Helen.

'Yes?' I replied.

'Your work called. You've been sacked. Apparently, you've hardly been in recently.'

'I see.' It didn't matter. Nothing mattered except being with my new love. Even at this early stage, I knew that I was completely smitten by the nightclub singer. 'Tell the boys I'll be in touch.' I closed the door and stepped out into the windswept street. At last, I thought, free from the drudgery and routine, free to pursue my love for Leucosia.

***

It was easy enough to get a room at a boarding house near the docks. I paid the landlady a month's rent in advance and spent the rest of the afternoon settling into my new home. I didn't expect to be there for very long. Once things were settled between Helen and myself, I hoped that Leucosia and I would find a place of her own. My work complete, I sat watching the clock, anticipating being with my love once again.

***

My one evening of bliss became a week of turmoil and confusion. Each night I went to Club Anthemusa and received free drinks from Dimitri but Leucosia ignored my very presence. She sang to others and disappeared with others but never came back for me. Each time, I would wait at my table until two and Dimitri would come across in his sympathetic way. 'Go home,' he would say gently. 'There's nothing you can do. It's up to her.'

Once, he even told me to go home and never to return. I gave him an angry glare and stormed out of the bar.

***

One morning after another fruitless night at the club, I took a walk down by the quayside. It was a cold day with grey skies. Despite the bracing wind, the broad expanse of dark water showed barely a ripple. I leaned against a handrail and watched the reflections of clouds slip by on the murky surface of the harbour.

'Ahh! Good to see you again,' said a voice I recognised immediately.

I turned my head to find Achelous standing next to me. He thrust his hands deep into the pockets of his coat. 'It's cold today, no?'

I nodded. 'Yes.' I was in no mood for conversation so deliberately returned my attention to the still waters below once again.

Achelous had no intention of taking the hint. 'You look unhappy,' he said.

'Can you blame me?'

'Leucosia?'

'Of course.'

'Ahh! It is so easy to judge that which we do not understand.'

I felt the cold wind hit my cheeks like a slap. I shivered as much with anger as with the chill. Like a fish I took the bait dangled before me by the old club owner. 'Tell me, mister Achelous, what I do not understand?'

He merely shrugged and gave a smile. 'Leucosia,' he said pointedly.

I blinked in surprise at the simplicity of his answer. 'She's beautiful, no?'

I nodded mutely.

'You love her?'

'Yes.'

'Then you must wait.'

'For what?'

'She will come for you when she is ready.'

'But, those other men....'

'Mean nothing. Do not worry about them.'

I shook my head in confusion and returned my gaze to the river. I was sick of these cryptic words from this crazy old nightclub owner. Was Leucosia some kind of prostitute? Was Achelous her pimp? The thought of such a thing made me feel sick. I felt his hand on my shoulder.

'Do not worry, my friend. When she is ready, she will come for you again. All will be as it should.'

I turned to face him with my reply, but Achelous was gone. Ignoring the old man's advice, I resolved that very night to confront Leucosia and learn the truth.

***

I found the Club Anthemusa at midnight in a place where I was certain that, moments before, no club had existed. As usual, a cordial greeting from the doorman heralded my entry. Dimitri grinned broadly and handed me a glass of whisky. The band played and the beautiful Leucosia caressed the microphone with her long fingers and bright red lips. I immediately discerned her target for the night. It was a balding, plump middle-aged man. He sat alone at a table and stared unblinking towards the singer in the silver evening gown. As the night drew to a close, the band began to pack away their equipment and Leucosia headed for a side door, her arm linked through the arm of the middle-aged man. I made to follow when I heard Dimitri call to me.

'Don't.'

I ignored him, followed the singer out of the side exit and immediately stumbled over something in the gloom. As things came into focus, the full horror of the vista before me was laid bare. I stood in an alleyway filled with the shrivelled and mummified bodies of men. Black and bloodless creatures that once were human beings littered every area of the narrow space, some piled high like bags of garbage against a chain-link fence, others scattered haphazardly along the length of the alley. Dark rain like blood coursed down the rough brick walls. In the distance, a single streetlamp illuminated the end of the passageway and I saw Leucosia.

I called her name and stumbled through the corpses towards her. The shrivelled bodies were as light as paper and crumbled beneath my feet. Leucosia was standing facing me and was holding the plump middle-aged man. She was kissing him and, as I approached closer, I could see him visibly shrink and shrivel before me. The singer opened her eyes. She did not look like I remembered her. Her dark, long hair seemed to writhe as if pulled by underwater currents. Her skin had taken on a pallid blue tinge and her eyes were like shadowy pools of decay.

She dropped the desiccated body of the middle-aged man and laughed.

I continued to stagger towards her, hands out wide, my face contorted with horror. 'What are you?' I rasped.

'She is the last of her kind and she must feed,' came a familiar voice from behind me. I turned to see Achelous standing in the corpse-strewn alley. He shifted his gaze towards Leucosia and bowed. 'He is not quite ready, my Lady.'

'No matter,' the singer replied. 'I'm still hungry. He will do as he is.'

Realisation struck me. I was to join these dry husks that once had been men. 'But, you and I...'

Leucosia once again gave a light, playful laugh. 'What? Did you think you were special? Did you think I cared for you any more than these others? You were merely an amusement to me.' She grinned with savage teeth and bloodstained lips, sweeping her arms out wide, inviting me to join her. 'Oh, Tony. Poor Tony. Come to me and have peace.'

As she began to sing for me, I knew that my fate would be sealed unless I acted immediately. I clamped my hands to my ears. 'No!' I screamed in desperation and terror. I turned and ran, barging past the old man and into the club. I dodged between a laughing Dimitri and the grinning bouncer, narrowly avoiding his large hands and finally made it out into the street bathed in the cold, stark night. There, I fell to my knees and succumbed to an overwhelming weariness.

***

Eventually, I regained consciousness and sensed my surroundings had changed. I opened my eyes and looked around. I was sitting by the quayside and felt a cool wind against my face. It was almost dawn. The club was gone, the alley and its hideous secret had disappeared. Leucosia was nowhere to be seen, as if she had faded with the coming of day. After a while, I got up and made my way to the boarding house, unsure of myself or my grasp on reality. Had these last few weeks really happened? Was the whole situation simply a fevered hallucination concocted by a pathetic drunk? I was no longer certain, and yet the bond I felt for her seemed to linger on like the dying ember of a dream.

As the weeks wore on, the recent events seemed to take on more of an illusory quality and, try as I might, I never found Club Anthemusa again. After a while, I gave up the search and resolved to stop drinking. Some time later, I called Helen and asked if we could meet to discuss things. Sobriety had given me clarity of mind and I began to see how appallingly I'd treated my wife. I harboured secret hopes that perhaps I could undo some of the damage to my marriage.

***

I sat in a small café down by the docks and waited for Helen to appear. I was nervous and smoked almost a whole pack of cigarettes as I constantly checked the time. Every now and then, I'd glance out of the café window and then slump into my chair with disappointment. It seemed as if she had changed her mind about the meeting. I was just about to pick up my cigarettes and leave when a slim, attractive woman sat on the chair opposite mine. I stared across the table in surprise.

'Helen?'

She shrugged. 'Were you expecting somebody else?'

'Eh, no...but you've changed.'

'I've been going to the gym,' she said. 'Shall we have some coffee?'

Still trying to recover from the shock, I ordered two espressos as Helen began to discuss the mechanics of our separation.

'I thought you could take the boys every second weekend,' she said between sips of her coffee. 'That is, when you get back on your feet.'

I nodded mutely, wondering how to broach the subject of a reconciliation when she suddenly began to wave at somebody on the other side of the window.

'There's John,' she said. 'I'll have to go.'

I glanced through the glass and saw a man sitting in a BMW parked just outside the café.

'John?'

Helen nodded. 'I met him about a month ago.'

'Oh,' was all I could find to say.

'Anyway,' she continued. 'I'm so glad that you've stopped drinking. I'm hoping we can divorce in an amicable fashion. It would be so much easier on the kids. Must dash. Bye!'

I watched them embrace before they drove off. My final hope had just been eroded before my eyes and I felt a pit of desolation form in my gut. I couldn't blame Helen. She deserved much more than I could give her.

Still, there was nothing left for me. I went to the nearest off-licence, bought a half bottle of whisky and wandered aimlessly through the town. Every now and then, I'd remove the bottle from my pocket and study it before secreting it away once more.

***

Eventually, I found myself leaning on handrails by the quayside where I stared into the dirty water and contemplated my future. Perhaps it would've been better simply to succumb to Leucosia's siren call or just drink myself to death? For a second, I thought I saw the images of my two boys on the water. It was only a glimpse but it made me realise that there was still something worth living for. I'd let them down so badly and knew I had a lot of ground to make up but perhaps, finally, I could stop being a coward and start to become something resembling a father. I pulled the unopened bottle from my pocket and tossed it into the harbour. As I walked away, I thought I heard that familiar, tinkling laugh and I knew with a terrifying certainty that it was not over. Leucosia would come back for me one day.

MINISTER FOR GHOSTS

im James works with the dead as a funeral director so opening him up psychically to give you this lesson to deliver was easy. I have been with him since he was a boy and I used to enjoy the look on his face, immensely when I merged the past and the present to surprise him with my old George III mahogany eight-day longcase clock which I had chime, unexpectedly.

The old-clock had beautifully adorned the hallway in my apartment in Knightsbridge so I enjoyed seeing it again. I also had a lot of fun moving objects in the old farmhouse where Tim lived with his parents. Of course it was particularly easy to play with his mind as the thousand year old building had absorbed a lot of spiritual energy over the years. I was able to draw on this to facilitate the paranormal-activity.

Nowadays he lives in a more modern dwelling, a two hundred year old farmhouse, so I cannot have as much fun with him, which is a shame. Of course, he is suitably aware to allow me to channel him in telling this next tale.

RAVENOUS

by Tim James

Auric Fortesque-Zaravich sat at the bar in a small pub, appreciating its rustic olde worlde charm. Part of him yearned for the days when all of the world had been like this, not just a few hold outs hidden away in small places where local public houses were closing, dropping one by one.

Just like people, or so it appeared.

It seemed as though locals were going missing in an area of Somerset. Centred loosely around Taunton, there had been a spate of disappearances. No set pattern to them, old people, young people, male, female, pensioners living alone, a solitary kid playing in a park, a couple camping in the woods, kids walking along a lonely country road.

All vanished without trace. Even though the police and other agencies had been called in there seemed to be very few trails and all of them had ended up cold.

So it had all come to a request to Special Investigations, an outdated governmental department attached to the Secret Service. The head of which knew there were very few operatives left, his purges and money-saving had very little funds for them.

There was nothing that actually marked the case as something that needed the SI's special attention, but no one else was having any luck, and with little or no staff

206

available, the head had only one recourse: to ask his predecessor for help.

And once he had been asked, Auric felt there was something a little bit odd, a gut instinct that should not be ignored.

So it was that he had travelled down to the South West, making his way from village to village, trying to see if anything caught his attention, painfully aware that a stranger walking around an area where there had been unusual disappearances would be suspicious in itself.

It was interesting to see how much the country had changed since he had been last here. How many of these quiet rural spots had closed down, become private homes or were just derelict? He had visited more than a few on his journey, pubs being an ideal place to sit back and gauge the atmosphere, to listen to casual conversations. If anything was going to be picked up it would be in a place like that.

There was a sense of something slightly subdued; conversations were muted, many faces drawn, touched by the awful things going on around them. Heads turned to stare at a stranger with a level of distrust that went beyond local curiosity. The pub Auric sat in was called The Lost Soldier, what he would have considered a proper, traditional establishment. Dark wood bar that could be dated back centuries, padded seats lining the walls, with chipped, polished wooden tables spread out around the lounge, fronted by a large open fireplace, laid in, but not alight.

The village, Hatchet St. George was typical, old houses clustered around a church, with newer estates gathered around these. Where once there had been two pubs, now there was only one and virtually all of the old shops, once commonplace in village life, had vanished.

Auric ignored the glances and walked up to the bar, waiting for a few moments for the landlord to approach him. A well-dressed man, not a stereotypical country innkeeper, thin, dressed in a smart modern suit, although he was not wearing a tie.

He looked Auric up and down, then gave a half-smile, "Afternoon. Can I get you something?" Not a local accent.

"Which of your Real Ales would you recommend?"

He nodded slowly, "I've got a couple, mostly bottled but the one on tap is the best"

Not very welcoming, he decided, not exactly what he would have liked in a pub, but then he did hark back to an older time. Things changed. "Anything local?"

"Not at the moment."

Auric took a deep breath and chose the tapped ale, "Is it possible to order some food?" he asked and the landlord rather reluctantly shrugged, "Standard bar meals mostly, you know the thing."

He almost seemed disgruntled when Auric ordered a Scampi and Chips, but left the bar to order it.

Auric retreated to an empty corner and sat down, slumping into a chair having a view of most of the lounge area. He placed his pint on the table, leaned back and closed his eyes, apparently relaxing, but actually listening to the buzz of conversation that filtered around the room.

He had been on the road for nearly three weeks, just travelling the villages around Taunton, trying to pick up anything that might be the remotest of clues to the disappearances. Apart from reaction to it, there was very little to draw on.

Worse, in the time he had been working, there had been another two. A hitchhiker, a man in his fifties on a walking holiday; and a twelve year old boy, apparently snatched when walking home from school.

Auric had made himself known to the police, but tried to keep as low-key as possible, letting them remain the main visible force in the investigation. But he was beginning to think that his low-key approach was having no effect at all. Just as the more traditional police search was fruitless.

He muttered a few words under his breath, allowing the magic field to open around him, casually combining a few gestures and whispered words to enhance his hearing. But it was virtually a wasted effort. The conversation in the room was mostly about mundane things, the weather, irritating partners, gardening.

There were a few comments that just touched on the unsolved crimes, but nothing suspicious, and a few more about the stranger sitting in their midst. In other words just what he would have expected, a carbon copy of all the other places he had been recently.

When his meal arrived after nearly an hour of waiting it was badly over-cooked, dry and surprisingly cold. He did not know whether the cook was just bad; that it had been done on purpose to drive him off quickly, or a ready-cooked meal that had been over-microwaved just for the hell of it.

He sat and ate it though, sipping at his second pint, which he acknowledged was a good one, and listened to the muttering around the pub, wondering whether it was time to change his current modus operandi.

He was nearing the end of his meal when he heard a sworn exclamation from the other side of the bar, guessing that it came from the main bar itself, rather than the lounge he sat in. Within seconds the door between the rooms burst open and a young man bulled through. He was dressed in a donkey jacket, rough jeans and dust-stained boots, marking him as a builder of some description, Auric guessed.

The fact that he was quite big seemed to add to that estimation, but it was him heading right toward Auric that startled him more than anything. And the look on his face was not welcoming.

The landlord slipped into the room behind the new arrival, "...calm down, you don't know anything!"

The advancing man ignored him, stopping right in front of Auric, slamming both hands onto the table with a heavy thump, looming over him threateningly. "Who the hell are you?"

Auric weighed him up; there was more than just anger emanating from him, distrust and perhaps fear, so he pushed himself back into the chair, "Uhhhh, my name is Auric..." he muttered, trying to appear as intimidated as he could.

"What the fuck do you think you are doing here? We don't want any strangers at the moment!" he spat the words with vehemence.

"I'm sorry," Auric gasped, "I was just passing through and my car broke down. The AA should be here shortly..."

"Bollocks!" the man snarled, "How do I know that you aren't just wandering around the area, picking out your next fucking target? You sick fuck! " His anger was rising faster and faster, very little reason in his eyes.

"What did you do with my sister? She was only thirteen for fuck's sake! What did you do with her?"

Behind the aggressive builder the landlord and one of the man's friends gripped an arm each. "Hey Matt, back down man," his friend hissed. "You're not helping anyone acting like this! He's just some poor fool passing through, you can't keep going off like this at anyone you don't know!"

"Listen to him!" the landlord hissed, "I've given you a lot of leeway, but I can't let you keep threatening my customers like this."

Matt shook them both off, his eyes still burning. "Bollocks!" he yelled, ignoring all the eyes on him. "You tell me you are not involved in this! Where's my sister, you bastard?"

Auric stood. "Perhaps I should leave."

Part of him knew what was going to happen, but he hoped otherwise. Almost immediately he stood, Matt swept the table aside and went for him, a large fist hurtling toward Auric's head, not even remotely pulled.

Smoothly, quickly Auric responded, slipping to one side, gripping the wrist as the hand slipped by his face, a whisper of wind following it. An application of pressure, a slight twist and Matt was on his knees, arm twisted behind him, locked into place.

He leaned forward his mouth close to the other's ear, whispering intently so only his attacker could hear,

"Calm down. You do not want to take this any further, I'm with the police looking into this, but I want to keep my identity low-key. You risk blowing my cover. Now stay there and shut up until I'm gone."

With a slight push that overbalanced Matt, causing him to slip forward, Auric turned quickly shaking his head to the others in the room and made for the exit.

Behind him, Matt's friend helped him to his feet. "What did he say to you?"

"Nothing!" the downed man spat, "A fucking liar is what he is!"

***

Auric slipped out of the pub, and began to stride away. For a moment he wondered whether his walking out so abruptly would look suspicious, but considering the anger being thrown at him, it was not a stupid thing to do.

He moved around the side of the building, heading back towards the car park where he could make a quick, hopefully unseen, exit. Before he even reached the small open area there was a sound of heavy footsteps behind him, and something big barrelled into with enough force to throw him to his knees.

He began to turn, and a solid weight smacked into the side of his head.

With a detonation of exploding stars he pitched forward and fell away into darkness.

***

Auric came to, hanging spread-eagled, arms stretched out above his head. He was still seeing stars, a testament to how hard he had been hit. He was in a dark room; it was next to impossible to judge the space, but what little light filtered in only served to deepen the shadows that lurked all over.

He shook his head to try and clear it, gathering his

senses. There were faint muffled noises, sounding like feet moving from above; vision may have been limited but the smells of the place were like nothing he could place. And they were not good. Stale sweat, rotting meat, blood, urine and faeces. Not good.

"You awake?"

The voice was strained, familiar.

Auric realised he had groaned, "I am."

"It's me, Matt, man. You've been out for hours, not sure how long, maybe a day!"

Auric slowly turned his head; ignoring the ache that filled his head, in the grey gloom he could see uneven shapes scattered over what looked to be a flagstone floor, and pinned to the wall much as he was, dangled the builder. Lost mostly to shadow Auric could see a trickle of dried blood running down one side of his face. It seemed he had received a blow to the head as well.

"Are you okay?" Auric managed.

"What do you fucking think? But nothing's broken. Is it true what you told me? You really police?"

Auric sighed, concussed, definitely. "Not police exactly, but working with them. And acting like a complete amateur."

"Do they know where you are?"

Auric chuckled sourly. "As I said, acting like a complete amateur."

Was it his imagination or could he hear something from the shadows on the far side of the room?

"So we're fucked?"

When he chuckled again there was a genuine humour there. "Not exactly." He took a deep breath and muttered. The magical field opened up and around him, motes of colour and shape that could be reached out and touched, but not with his hand chained to the wall as it was.

Auric continued muttering, words that would sound like gibberish to his fellow captive, but it did not matter. As he spoke he felt the concussion correcting itself, the wound on his head healing.

212

Without missing a beat, he changed the spell, the words continuing. With a crack the clasp on the chain that held him in position snapped open, and he felt his other arm take the strain.

He muttered a few more words, and whatever held his ankles snapped free and almost immediately the other wrist gave way, and he dropped to the floor.

He breathed hard, ignoring the pins and needles that exploded through his limbs with an overwhelming intensity. A few moments was all he could allow himself.

"What the fuck?" Matt gasped, "What did you fucking do?"

"Magic," he responded, knowing just what it sounded like, and just how Matt would take it, despite it being the truth.

He staggered to his feet, and slipped over to where Matt was hanging. The floor felt somewhat gummy, tacky beneath his feet.

"I'm going to free you now," Auric hissed, "but watch yourself when you fall, I'm not recovered enough to catch you yet."

"Don't fucking worry about that," Matt responded, "anything is better than being up here."

With a few more words and gestures the other chains cracked open and just as he had before, Matt slipped, dropping down to the floor with a heavy thump, and something that sounded wet.

As the big man sat on the floor, Auric looked around, his near silver eyes glittering in the dark half-light. "I'd close your eyes, I'm going to get us some light..."

"Okay, okay," Matt hissed. "But listen man, you gotta listen to me. It's the fucking landlord, he's the one behind this, the landlord!"

About to speak an archaic word, Auric paused. "The landlord? I did not see that coming." He frowned as he moved his hands in mystic patterns, touching the lights that fluttered around him like butterflies. The ancient words slipped off his tongue just as thoughts danced through his head.

Although he had not intended it for a trap when he used his talent to listen in to casual conversation, it was also a simple way of noting any others like himself. But the landlord had not even reacted, so either he was a good actor or his abilities, if he had them, derived from a different place than Auric's own. And that was very unusual.

A small sphere of white light appeared in the air above his head, growing and stabilizing, banishing the shadows around him like a mini sun.

On the floor Matt hissed, squinting from between half-closed eyelids, a look of disbelief ingrained in his face.

Auric ignored the other man, taking in his surroundings. A large room, with solid stone walls, the kind of uneven stonework that was most certainly not a modern build. Various racks and shelves were dotted around the room, stocked with bottles, cans and crates. Barrels stood clustered together, upright, one on top of the other.

The cellar then, Auric surmised, but there were no signs of stairs, and a quick glance up showed no visible trapdoor, so no easy exit. The far end of the room was more modern, red brick and concrete blocks: a mélange of building materials as though whoever built it took what was at hand and just slapped it together with badly mixed cement.

But it held two doors, which looked as though they were bought off the shelf in a standard DIY store, but were more than a little solid.

He took a deep breath, and in that moment he heard a whispering, scratching sound again, a bit like the noise a puppy would make rubbing against the door to get out. And there was the rancid smell of blood, masking the scent of damp and old beer that just had to be there.

"It's time we were gone," Auric decided quickly, holding out a hand for Matt and hauling him to his feet.

Without a pause he headed to the first door, the one without a noise behind it, took hold of the handle, turned and pulled.

It was locked.

A few words and there was a deep click, and the door swing open easily.

He glanced at Matt. "Go, I'll be right behind you!"

Matt looked at him, almost as though he were going to argue and then he slipped past and began to walk up concrete stairs, toward freedom, or so Auric hoped.

It was then that he heard a voice, sing-song but hopelessly off-key, dribbling from behind the closed door, "Husband of mine, is that you out there? Have you brought more treats for our beautiful children?"

He froze, a grim chill creeping up his spine like skeletal finger tips.

"Carry on," he grunted to Matt. "Get out of here!"

The other glanced back down at him, "Are you sure?"

"Certain."

"I'll call the police and get back!" His feet thumped on up the stairs and Auric watched out of the corner of his eyes as Matt reached a door and pulled. It opened without protest. Auric turned away and pulled the other cellar door open.

It creaked, a garish red light seeped outwards, tendrils stirring and coiling through the air with a life of its own.

Something moved.

In the same moment there was a thump from the top of the stairs, a grunt like some stunned animal, and Auric felt things starting to slip, falling out of control too quickly.

A figure slowly stepped through the doorway, pulling his attention back to that, a figure from a nightmare. A thin woman, dressed in a clothes that did not seem to fit properly; her hair had obviously been styled, but it had just not worked; strands seemed to fall in all directions, across her face, almost floating in a chaotic halo around her head. Her eyes were half-sunken in their sockets, dark and dry, faded mascara, although no powder was present. Lips over-rouged in a face that was too pale.

Her body though, was that of a classic carnival grotesque, twisted at angles that were not quite right, as though she were a puppet held up by strings cut to the wrong length, hands up in front of her, her head crooked to one side.

But there was worse. Clinging to her waist with disjointed spider-like legs was a creature that might have been a child, a twisted face half-peering from her uncovered chest where it suckled at a breast that seemed milkless and dry.

More things slipped around her feet. Something with a face like a dog that walked on extended arms, dragging undersized legs behind it. A boy of relatively normal appearance followed it, all dark hair and big eyes; and other things moved, slipping, sliding, tumbling, staggering and walking like a menagerie of twisted deformity.

Auric could see twisting, spiralling shapes orbiting her body in undetermined revolutions, the multi-hued colours of the lights and symbols of a magic field, as vibrant and alive as Auric's own.

In surprise, even horror at something that was outside his five hundred years of experience he took two or three paces back, and, step by step, the monstrosity advanced.

In the same moment, there was the uneven sound of shifting weight, thumps, a sack of potatoes falling, and Matt, limp and broken, came to rest lifelessly at the bottom of the stairs.

Standing at the top was the landlord, a dark shadow clasping a length of iron in one hand, that dripped blood.

The woman gasped, reaching out with dislocated fingers, her eyes fixed on the lights that moved around Auric, a mirror of her own. "What butterflies," she breathed gently, "Just like mine, did they escape, such pretty, pretty moths and lights?"

He realised that she did not know anything about

her heritage, the magic she had access to. Somehow, probably at an early age, impossibly, she had accessed the magic field, and it had clung to her, open, never closed for the rest of her life. With no understanding, with permanent exposure, there was no way of knowing what it could have done to her. Only one thing was definite: it was not good.

As the light from his sphere penetrated the gloom Auric could see the floor, a carpet of blood and offal, bones and shit, countless victims discarded and consumed.

The landlord descended, "I don't know how you got free," he snarled, "But just like that idiot it will do you no good. You are only one thing - food!"

At the sound of his voice the woman's head snapped to one side and a smile twisted her features. "Husband mine comes. More delicacies for me babies. We are so grateful." Her discordant tuneful voice lilted poetically.

The dog-faced one shook its head, its jaws separating in an array of jagged serrations, far too many teeth crammed into too small a face, but the jaw just kept widening, revealing at least three tongues that lapped at the air.

The thing that clung to her side scuttled down over her hips, down her legs and onto the floor. Mewling like a drowning kitten it slipped across the uneven floor, sniffing at the fresh blood that escaped from the hole in Matt's head.

Even the normal-looking boy seemed to react with anticipation, its mouth opening, the jaw clicking and cracking as it dislocated, revealing far too many teeth.

Auric took another two steps backward, thoughts cascading through his mind at the horror and the madness of the situation.

If he spent too long he would die.

With a gesture he touched upon her field and with a word dispelled it.

Like a hundred fireflies extinguished at once, the second set of lights blazed brightly for a moment, and then were gone. Her disjointed advanced stopped. Her eyes widening, glinting in the glare of the sphere of brilliance, trying to focus on things that were no longer there. Only one set remained. Auric's.

"Where have they gone?" She spoke with genuine alarm. "What have you done to my butterflies, have you stolen them? Give them back," she pleaded. "Put my butterflies back!" She stamped her foot in temper.

The landlord reached the bottom of the stairs, frowning in the light above him, for the first time realising there was more going on than he had been aware of, a poker clasped in a white-knuckled fist.

"I'm sorry," Auric muttered looking at them both, the woman a pathetic tragedy, a man who killed for misbegotten love and their damned offspring.

He raised both arms, speaking words as ancient and powerful as the memory of time, and fire blossomed around him, coming to life on its own, and began to rotate around him.

Faster and faster it moved, forming trails in the air; trails that seemed to ignite of their own accord, growing brighter and hotter.

The broken woman dropped to her knees, uneven arms reaching out imploringly, but whether she was asking for release or the return of her butterflies did not matter; the landlord turned to run; the children began to hiss and scream, pulling back from the glowing conflagration.

Still the fire grew. Spinning, churning turning, expanding into a whirlwind of fire, bright orange then white. There. Right in the heart of the storm Auric opened himself to the magic, letting it run through him as though it were a living thing, some strange entity blending with his own.

He rose into the air and let it loose, a force of pure elemental fury.

It exploded outwards, consuming all it touched; the body of Matt was cremated where it lay, the woman kneeling in supplication transformed from broken to a thing of wonder, becoming a flare of heat, a pillar of salt; while her husband half-turned, darting toward the stairs, even as he smouldered, smoked, screamed and combusted, turned into ashes.

The floor itself was scoured, racks and bottles exploding into fire, beer barrels collapsing in on themselves, popping and vanishing into the growing inferno, something that consumed all it touched. Walls, doors, brick, bone, blood and steel.

Still the twisting fire continued to grow, intent to wipe the memory of this place of atrocity from the face of the Earth. The children evaporated like fluid, leaving nothing but the flame and the man at the heart of it.

Like something escaping from the pits of hell itself, the fire lanced straight up, a tongue of flame climbing toward the sky, passing through the roof of the pub as though the beams and slate were non-existent. The walls of the empty establishment bulged outwards and then were sucked inwards, disintegrating in the twisting pyre that reached into the night, a beacon of power and purification.

Auric floated in a blaze of nothing, the heat all around him but not touching him, almost at one with everything.

The pillar of fire shrank, drawing back into itself, so it was little more than a sphere of white, a miniature sun.

Auric. A shining light. Golden. It was at the heart of his being, it was who he was, the name that defined him. And just like that he let it go, floating away into nothing, and at long, long last he was free.

With the suddenness of a light being switched off, the flame was gone, and darkness claimed everything. In that few moments of blindness something moved and then as torch beams penetrated the gloom a single ragged figure was found in the heart of the extinguished conflagration.

A lucky victim saved from a terrible fate.

His name was Richard Golding.

Of Auric Fortesque-Zaravich there was no sign.

219

MINISTER FOR GHOSTS

Well what can I say about my next vessel. She truly is an angel walking the Earth. A S Besham lives in Iran. She is a very deep thinking, and very talented lady but living in a developing country is not easy. She always manages to do it with a smile, though.

Sadly, a while back it was time for her brother to join us in the spirit world. He made an appointment to see me and vociferously recommended Aty to be appointed to the Ghost Ministry. It was an easy decision and she channels her emotion into this lesson on how a loss of a loved one can have the most terrible and profound effect upon a person, nothing more so than the loss of a child. I am sure this story will make you think about your own loved ones.

BILLY'S LULLABY

By Aty S Behsam

DAY

My days are scheduled to remind me how to keep breathing. Drink coffee, take a shower, and call Thomas to let him know I'm okay. Each morning starts the same way; I open my eyes and the world crushes on me - every morning. Because Billy isn't here.

My Billy is seven. He has the most beautiful smile in the world. He wants to be a pilot, and he loves the colours of the sky. We lost him on a rainy night.

Thomas must be at work, so I am alone. I stand in front of the mirror in our room, tying my curly hair without the slightest attention. There is a piece of paper taped to the mirror frame, right next to a picture of Billy laughing in a pool. My son has his father's blue eyes, and the brown colour of my hair. The piece of paper says in my own handwriting, "Billy is alright."

How would I know? I crumple the paper and throw it in the trash bin, leaving the room with two bags under my eyes and faint colorlessness on my lips. I make myself coffee and sit in the kitchen, watching my son's empty place and drinking the poison; everything I eat tastes that way. Because Billy isn't here.

Reluctantly so, I take my medicine. When I take a

shower, I think of the times Billy was so little, a bird without wings, I'd washed his tiny soft body in the sink.

***

When I call Thomas, he repeats the same thing he does every single morning. "I love you. We can make it. We're not alone. We have each other."

All I can give in return is my silence, and one single sentence in the end. "Time goes by."

Time goes by and we're surviving. Time goes by and Billy is not here. I can't tell if I say this as something good, or the worst thing that's happening. Or maybe both. We are dead people walking. The parents of a missing child.

I promise him to go shopping. I do everyday. I quit my job and he doesn't want me to sit in the house feeling sorry for us. He doesn't want me to think about Billy. We both know it's not possible not to. In Mrs. Linda's shop, I try to hide behind the shelves to escape her. I'm afraid she'd ask about Billy. I can't talk about Billy. I barely talk about anything at all. I don't even complain about things, even to the woman who knocks my groceries to the ground and walks away without apologizing, as if I'm not even here. I pick up my things and use the self-checkout before heading for exit.

As soon as I walk out, my exhausted eyes catch someone walking toward a silver car on the other side of the street. "Heather?" I murmur. Then I call louder, "Heather."

Thomas's sister is easily recognizable with her long ginger hair flooding on the black leather jacket she always wears. She opens her car door. I call her name again, crossing the street rapidly, but she drives away.

***

For the first time after eight months, Billy isn't the only

one I think about on my way back home. Heather and her husband Jack have been acting not only rude, but really odd. She used to be in our home almost every day. Heather and Jack have been married for years, but they can't have children. I still think that's the reason why they loved Billy so much, because ever since he went missing they stopped calling and showing up. They wouldn't even answer our calls.

Thomas always says it's the sadness. People don't like being around sad people because sadness is contagious. He says that because Heather is his sister.

I'm about to turn the car into the garage when I see something in front of the house; I stomp my foot on the brake, eyes wide on the sign.

FOR SALE

Thomas wants to sell the house. I park the car and storm toward the wooden sign, sweat settling on my forehead. I force it out of the lawn and take it inside with me. I drag it to the basement door, then throw it inside and watch it hit the stairs and vanish in the darkness.

I sit in Billy's bedroom waiting until Thomas comes home. Once the sun goes down and darkness swallows the room, I take my pills and prepare dinner to calm myself.

***

Around seven, I hear the door open. Thomas and I hardly ever fight. Mostly because he's a very calm person and it's affected me over the years. But tonight I'm in for an argument. I head outside the kitchen and lean on the doorframe, watching him taking off his coat. "Hi."

He turns to me. I frown and stand up straight; his skin is pale, his forehead shining with sweat. "What is it?" I ask.

He shakes his head. "I'm not hungry."

"We need to talk."

He pauses on the first stair. "Honey, I'm not feeling well, okay?" He takes another stair up.

"Are you selling the house?" I ask, my voice unusually loud. Thomas spins around, blinking at me several times with a scowl. I clutch my waist. "I saw the sign outside. I don't remember talking about this."

"What are you talking about? What sign?"

"'For sale' sign."

"Anne," he mutters. "I'm tired and so are you. I'm not selling anything. There are no signs."

"It's down there," I say, and point to the basement door. Anger colours his face red--he clenches his fist, his knuckles bright. He drops his briefcase on the floor and marches to the basement. I stand outside while he steps down and ten seconds later he shouts, "There are no signs."

I scoff and run down, almost slipping on the last two stairs. Thomas is right. There is nothing down here but our old clothes, some luggage, and Thomas's old trophies from our college, all drowned under a heavy layer of dust. Thomas opens his arms and shakes his head.

Have I already started losing my mind?

I look around the room. "I threw it down."

"Are you taking your medication?"

"What, you think I'm delusional?"

"Maybe it's the pills, I'm not blaming or judging you, sweetheart—" he told her.

"Blaming *me*? You're the one who's selling the house without telling me."

"But I'm *not*," he shouts.

"What were you thinking? What if Billy comes home and we're not here?"

"Billy's not coming home." His voice is so low, I can barely make out what he says. I only stare at him. He pinches the bridge of his nose.

"You're giving up," I say loudly, and I can feel tears coming; my throat hurts and my chest is tightening.

Thomas shakes his head, his ocean eyes shining.

224

"No. I'm letting go."

"Billy is *not* dead. He's not dead." I burst into crying. The mixture of anger and despair is gripping my throat. I catch my tears with the tip of my fingers, but Thomas doesn't wipe his. He lets them slide down his face.

"Billy is alright," he says.

I shake my head, crying. "No. Billy is out there. Alone. Scared. How can you do this? It's only been eight months."

"It's not been eight months."

"256 days since the night he vanished."

"Anne, I'm asking you sincerely ..." He swallows and takes in a shaking deep breath. "We should let Billy go."

"I won't!" I felt a fire burning all my insides. "I don't care what the police say or what you say. And you are *not* selling the house, half of it is mine and I won't allow it."

"Annelee, I wouldn't even try. I'm just asking you to consider letting go."

"I can't believe you're asking me this. You're just like your sister."

Thomas lets out a deep sigh. "Here we go again."

"She wouldn't even answer our calls or contact us to ask if her brother is okay. I saw her today and called her and she completely ignored me."

"Honey, I love you." He covers his face. "I'm trying to do what's best for us."

I hold my heart. "What's best for me is to find my son. I can't live without Billy. I can't, Thomas. I can't." I leave him alone in the basement.

NIGHT

I sleep in Billy's room, singing him a lullaby. The first thing I do next morning is bursting into tears. Thomas has covered me with a sheet, and left a note in the kitchen next to the coffee maker: "I'm sorry." He's cleaned the kitchen and taken out the trash, and the cold, untouched food. I drink my coffee, take a shower,

225

and bring myself to swallow my pills. Then I call him before going to Linda's.

On the way back, a block away from the house, I slowly stop the car. I can see Heather outside the house, big sunglasses on, talking on her phone. I tell myself she's finally decided to pay us a visit, which is still strange because she knows Thomas goes to work.

I get out and slowly walk to her; I don't want her to see me before I get close enough; I'm afraid she'd jump into her car and get away again. I can hear her talking on her cell. I open my mouth to call her name, but she says on the phone, "Hold on, Billy's calling me." I freeze on the spot. With her back to me, Heather starts walking to her car. "Hi sweetheart," she says. "I'm at your house. I'm going somewhere now, I'll see you tonight, okay? Yes, yes, I did. I love you too."

I stop breathing. My heart is like a big hammer in my chest, I fear it might explode. No matter how hard I try, I can't speak. As if someone has stolen my voice. I want to reach out and grab her, but my hands have turned into stone. Heather gets into her car and drives away.

***

My hands are shaking and my fingers feel numb when I push the buttons on the cellphone, forcing my foot down on the accelerator. "Thomas, call me when you get this message. Thomas, I think Heather and Jack kidnapped Billy." I cover my mouth for a second. "I'm going to their house. I heard her talking to Billy, I swear."

I don't know how I make it there, but when I stop the car outside the house and take in several deep breaths, I assure myself, "I'm not delusional. I heard her. I saw her outside the house. I'm not delusional." I step out and rush to the house. I hammer the door several times with a heavy fist. "Heather, open the door." Nobody seems to be home. I punch the door again, but it's no use. I go back to the car. I don't understand what is happening. I do not know. I do not know.

The sky becomes dark and night slowly takes over. Thomas doesn't call me back and nobody shows up at the house. Something tells me I should call the police, but the last time I talked to a cop he told me they've stopped looking for my Billy. My interpretation: they no longer cared. I don't need to be called delusional. And I don't want Heather alerted.

A familiar fire has started inside my chest, and it gets heavier, hotter by the second. I get out and cross the street to the house again. Then I skirt around to the backyard, take off my jacket and hold it on the kitchen window, and with an eye around on the quiet neighborhood, I break the glass with my elbow.

When I reach inside and open the window's lock, I feel a sharp twinge on my arm; the glass has cut my skin deep, but I ignore the throbbing wound. I climb up the frame and drop inside. With a hand on my arm, I stand frozen in the kitchen, listening to see if anyone is home, if anyone has noticed an intruder in the house.

There is only silence.

Slowly I tip-toe into the living room, heading for the second floor. My eyes catch the corner of the room and I stop. I walk closer, and as I do, I become more and more terrified of what I'm looking at. The family pictures on the wall and on the fireplace aren't only Heather and Jack with their families and friends; most of the pictures include a teenage boy I don't take a good look at. There's a picture of Billy at age six, Thomas and I holding him tight together. But what scares me is the picture in the center. I pick it up.

"Oh, my God." I can't draw in air: my Billy, a birthday cake in front of him with the number eight, Heather and Jack on either side of him.

They've had him this whole time.

"Anne."

"Jesus!" I clutch to my heart and wheel around; Thomas

227

is staring at me. "You scared me!"

He bites his lip. "What are you doing here?"

I look at the kitchen door. "How did you get in here?"

"Please, let's go home."

"Heather and Jack have stolen our son." I give him the picture. "See?"

"Honey, please."

I don't understand. He's supposed to be shocked. He's supposed to shout, his face angry red. But he only stares at the picture, a rueful smile on his face.

"Can you not hear me? Thomas? Wake up!" I grab the collar of his shirt. "They've had him the whole time!"

A *click* sounds. We both spin to the door to the house. My heart is in my mouth. Heather walks in with a handful of bags. She replaces her sunglasses with a pair of spectacles. I frown for a moment; Heather doesn't need glasses as far as I know. As she reaches to close the door, someone says, "Hi."

Heather smiles widely and opens her arms. "Oh, Billy. I removed the sign, sweetie."

As I try to find a place to hide, a tall young man walks into the house and embraces Heather, followed by Jack, whose sideburns are now gray, making me even more confused. The tall young man, I now see, is the same boy as in the pictures. I open my mouth to say something before they can see us snooping in their house, but as the boy, whose blue eyes are familiar, takes off his coat and turns to the fireplace, my heart drops the floor. I'm slowly sinking into freezing water. I start losing my senses, cold.

Thomas takes my hand, and I turn to him. He is looking at the boy, a faint smile on his lips.

"When do your classes start, Son?" Jack asks the boy.

"Next week," he says.

"You sure you don't wanna sell the house?" Heather asks him.

"Yeah, I might go back. Maybe. One day."

"Billy ..." My whisper chokes.

"Your parents would have been proud of you," Heather says, pulling the boy into her arms again. I study those lips and those eyes and how he smiles to them, and like bright light on water, everything becomes clear in my mind.

The rain was heavy. Thomas and I were arguing about being late. He said Billy was okay with Heather. I told him I don't like going to parties I can't take my son to. That we had to hurry and pick Billy up from Heather and Jack's, so he could sleep in his own room. Thomas said we needed some time together. I didn't say anything. He took my hand, and gave it a soft kiss.

He was smiling, his eyes on the rainy road; on the two lights that rushed in from the opposite lane. He shook his head and narrowed his eyes.

"What are you doing?" he muttered, flashing the car's lights as to signal the driver ahead that the car was slowly derailing from the road to our side. The car went back to the right line.

"We should tell Heather and Jack about the plans," I said.

"Billy's birthday?" he asked.

"Yeah, I think it's—"

Thomas shouted and spun the wheel. I screamed. For a second the whole world turned upside down. Then with a massive hit we crashed onto the asphalt.

When I opened my eyes, I couldn't feel anything below my neck.

"Tho—Thomas," I panted. I could barely see anything in the dark, and in the red. He was covered in blood, bent over the wheel.

I shouted his name, cried it, but he wouldn't talk to me, his eyes still open, he only stared blankly to my direction.

I couldn't move. How long it took me to fade away, I couldn't understand, but I spent the last minutes of my life in darkness staring at the love of my life whose eyes seemed like empty glasses, and I cried, hoping someone would come because our Billy was waiting for us to take him home. But there was nothing but the rain and the cold air, and the iron-tasting blood in my mouth. There wasn't any distant siren or anyone calling back. Nothing.

Slowly I faded away.

Death. The unbidden visitor arriving in the middle of a sentence. In the middle of a night. One who doesn't care if you have a child waiting for you. "We called the police," I say quietly, tears quietly running down to my chin.

"False memories. False imagination, I think," Thomas whispers. "I think everything that has been happening was how we imagined. I found out yesterday. They were talking about us in the office, and as soon I heard, as if a veil suddenly pulled up and I could see everything, people stopped noticing me and I stopped being real. Anne, it's happened before. I can feel it's happened before."

"I left myself a note," I say shallowly, remembering the note I'd thrown into trash.

"I'll prepare the dinner," Heather says. And Jack follows her out of the room.

Billy walks toward us. He reaches out and picks up the photo of himself with us. I can't get enough of him; I could stand here all night and just watch him, even if he never sees us. He's a complete combination of Thomas and I. He is us and so much more. I know he doesn't feel anything, his eyes only focusing on the picture, but as I touch his face and feel his warmth, something holy takes over me. My heart feels alive again.

Billy leaves us in the room. Thomas squeezes my hand. "You wanna go home?"

***

Thomas asks in the car that isn't really here, "You okay?"

"I am," I say sincerely. "Are you?"

He nods, turning the car to the garage. We don't talk until he parks and we go into our house that is no longer ours, climbing the stairs that aren't touched by us. Everything is okay. I felt more alive than I've ever been. Before going to bed, I leave a note for myself on the mirror frame, right next to Billy's picture. "Billy is alright."

Thomas wraps me with his arms. I fall asleep with

my eyes are on my note. My smile has never been so genuine.

MINISTER FOR GHOSTS

As Minister for Ghosts I do get to travel a lot and it is not always to destinations on the Earth plane. Sadly, I cannot enlighten you on those locations any more than I have.

When I lived in London, I heard how beautiful Jersey was but sadly never got the opportunity to go there while I was alive. So, it was an absolute pleasure to move my essence across the veil, and get close to my next vessel when I heard about Joseph Atkins and where he lived.

Of course travelling in the spirit world does not involve trains, ships or aircraft. The destination is only a thought away and a nano-second before arrival.

Once in the Jersey ether, I very much enjoyed shadowing Joseph. I had a lot of fun scaring his ducks. Animals are closer to the spirit world than humans so they could see me clearly. I think they read my thoughts about how I remembered how nice they tasted, as they tended to keep their distance!

WARLORD'S BONES

By Joseph Atkins

I sat it on the mantelpiece above the empty fireplace; the human figure made from forty cubes of bone.

***

The funeral was horrendous. Everyone stared at me like they were trying to work out why I wasn't crying. I definitely wasn't happy, but I wasn't sad either. Enduring Joan's relatives was the worst. Those familiar facial features, reflecting the very same expression I had seen a thousand times: the look someone might give you if you borrowed their hanky to dry your armpits.

I received the dirty-bone-doll at the reading of Joan's will. I went to the reading out of curiosity and also to support our children, I never expected her to leave me anything. I did have an inkling that she had squirreled something away to wrestle a last jot of love from the children. I was correct. My teary James and Laura were handed a rusty metal box filled with gold Saxon coins worth a small fortune. The box came with the express instructions that they sell the contents and share it equally between them, using the money to buy their own properties. Or, "move away from your poisonous father," as I heard it. The gold also served as a sharp slap in the face to me, revenge for all my jokes about her archaeology and broken pots.

When the executor of the will pushed a mouldy cardboard box across the desk towards me, I half expected it to be filled with dog shit – Joan was always irritated by my distrust for canines. I carefully lifted the musty flaps to see the chalky bone-man sprawled beside a sealed brown envelope. The children speculated that it must be very special and worth even more than their gold, while I kept myself from saying that it was probably a voodoo doll that would make my cock drop off.

At home, I tucked the box away beneath the stairs to gather dust.

***

Laura moved out first and it didn't take long for James to follow. It was during his packing that the dirty-bone-doll was rediscovered. James placed it on the kitchen table, a gesture I'm sure he felt was thoughtful, but just served to bolster Joan's triumph. The statue watched me from every angle.

The ghostly visage of the bone-man had long, drooping eyes with a hint of faded ink. The mouth was flat and expressionless. Rough slits had been carved in for the nostrils. It was a repulsive little thing, which got me thinking that so many ugly objects always seemed to survive the test of time. The sculpture was surely very old. Disgusting.

That same evening as I splashed my eighth or ninth measure of single malt into a glass, I approached the figure. I was humming rather energetically along to some Tchaikovsky by then, so I mustered the courage to open the brown envelope beside the doll. I thought Joan's last poke would carry her signature passive aggression, which of course it did, but far less than I had expected. In her scrawling style the note read:

Temu
1227AD
Ceremonial statue
(Temu is also afraid of dogs – he can keep you company now.)

Nothing more. A pathetic jab at my entirely rational

phobia. In my drunken stupor I chose to defiantly display the horrible bone-man, and that is how he found his way onto the mantelpiece.

***

The dreams did not begin in a subtle manner. At night I was thrown into a distant land of vast plains and tall mountains. Horse hooves always drumming deep within my medulla. I hunted in sparse woods and dwelled in a simple round tent. The first dreams always ended in the same way: I have a brother whom I love, but I find him eating a rabbit he has just caught, he has not thought to share. Without hesitation, I walk up behind him and open his throat with my knife.

I woke up each time, sweating and shaking. The man I had been in the dreams was as far from me as you could get. He was tough and fearless, the sort of man men wish they were, yet he was also a murderer. He showed me so much blood and battle. Not cinematic Hollywood battles, but real struggle and fight – ending other humans and watching their eyes turn grey. I shared in the adrenalin and bloodlust.

During the days, I felt shame and confusion at the acts I performed in my sleep. The scenes were so vivid I was sure they had actually occurred at some point in time. I juggled with the notion that it had been myself in a past life, though I had always been sceptical of such nonsense. I debated whether I should go and see a specialist but all I could imagine was some mad, wide-eyed woman with crazy hair, telling me that my energy flow is broken and I need a crystal.

***

It was then that my neighbour, Stephen, decided he would buy his little girl a puppy – some kind of labra-shitz-oodle. Stephen was the anal-retentive letter-writer in the road. The kind of man who never failed to keep his lawn exactly two inches tall, and complained to the council if the bin men sounded like they were enjoying themselves. Stephen also insisted on lengthening my name to Timothy, even though that is not what it says on my birth certificate.

It was the dog who helped me make the connection with my dreams to Temu downstairs. I was deep in the dream-world one night, with the warrior-man's wife, Borte – I loved her so much it made my mind boggle at the questionable coupling I'd had with Joan – when its howling woke me and set my hairs on end, followed by a raging anger in my veins.

Ever since I was bitten by a dog as a child, I have feared them. I avoided them and never befriended anyone who owned one. When I passed dog walkers, I always felt my pulse quicken and a faint weakness hit my knees. I had never before felt what I did when I woke up that night; pure hatred for the creature next door. My teeth clenched to the point I thought that they might shatter, and hot fury baked my skin. Those feelings, I knew, were not entirely my own, yet they enveloped me completely.

The whining dog would not let me sleep. I paced around the house trying to calm my nerves. When I passed the mantelpiece, Temu caught my eye. I could have sworn the bone-man's expression had changed, but on closer inspection it was the same flat mouth and gaunt eyes. The figure was warm when I picked him up and Joan's words came back to me: *Temu is also afraid of dogs – he can keep you company now.*

***

My dreams became darker still. I had decided Temu the statue was made from Temu the warrior-man's bones. His life-story progressed rapidly in my sleep, since dreamtime moved under different laws. Temu was no ordinary man it seemed, he was a leader of armies. A ruthless and cruel man to be feared and respected. I saw generals surrender before us and then we would boil them alive. We would feast at tables upon uneven planks, and when we looked down at our dancing feet upon the boards, pained eyes looked up from between the cracks; we danced upon captured soldiers, crushing them to death.

Each waking brought me back to my mundane life, but I am sure small pieces of Temu came with me. Losing my job should have been the warning sign I should get rid of the dirty-bone-man, but my boss deserved that fist in the face. Having no work meant I could spend more time sleeping and dreaming. There was so much more to do when I slept. We captured slaves and made the women parade before us, choosing the prettiest for ourselves. When we torched settlements we left none alive, not even the sheep or cattle, and we slaughtered every dog from horseback.

***

James and Laura tried to stage an intervention. We all sat around my living room, littered with sleeping pill pots, whisky bottles and blankets. I didn't let them see me smiling at Temu on the mantelpiece. I allowed my children to analyse me and decide that I was having a delayed reaction to their mother's death. Ushering them away with the promise of change, I returned to my dreams.

We were so powerful by then. People bowed before us and when we rode across the open plains, we could not see the end of our horse lines. Then we woke to the barking dog next door again.

***

When they found Stephen's dog, wet and stinking, its paws pegged into his precious lawn, I was taken away. I met many policemen and doctors in those few days. I missed Temu more than anything. In the courtroom, the judge was told I believed that I was Genghis Khan. That I had woken up one day and decided I was Temujin, the name of the great Khan before he became the oceanic ruler. I knew different. I was Tim; Temu and I shared our dreams.

I am moved to a special institution, an old Victorian

building with many white corridors and bare rooms. I smile when I see my room has a mantelpiece. They let me bring a couple of things from home, as long as I can't hurt myself with them. So I sit him on the mantelpiece above the empty fireplace; the human figure made from forty cubes of bone. Joan's gift. Temu keeps me company, he's also afraid of dogs.

MINISTER FOR GHOSTS

eresa Edgerton currently resides in California, along with her husband, assorted offspring, twin grandsons, the obligatory pets, a few courageous houseplants, and several thousand books in a house without enough bookshelves.

Teresa reminds me of Queen Victoria. She is very strong-minded and does not tolerate fools gladly. I like that. It certainly makes it easier to get the job done.

So, sadly we have reached the final lesson. And who better to bring it to you than Teresa. As a wise woman and former reader of Tarot cards, my job inspiring her to recount this tale of a plague-hit kingdom was an easy one.

A WREATH OF PALE FLOWERS FOR VITRI

by Teresa Edgerton

The Princess Vitri was dying. Everyone knew it. Everyone, that is, excepting the King, who spent long hours in his daughter's bedchamber, hovering over her bed, listening to the sound of her breathing, his lips drawn into a thin line, beads of perspiration standing out on his brow ... as if he meant, by a sheer act of will, by the force of his formidable personality, to keep her alive. Everyone except for Emerald, the youngest handmaiden, who went right on feeding, brushing, and playing with the Princess's pet monkey, and tending the flowers in her private garden—particularly the odd little shrub, the one with the silvery blooms, which one of Vitri's many suitors had fancifully named "the Rose of Charun" (though it was not a rosebush or anything like one) after the Princess herself. These things Emerald did, as though she expected the Princess to rise from her couch at any moment and take her pet down to the garden for some much-needed exercise.

Though half the court was stricken, the other half bereaved or soon to become so, no one wore mourning. A baleful omen for the Princess, a malignant influence—so King Jesahach had proclaimed it, and banished the colour black from his presence. And on the day that Vitri's doctors wrapped her up like a mummy in scarlet flannel and

240

propped her up in a chair by a roaring fire, in order to sweat the disease out through her pores, one of them had chanced to mention that red was a wholesome hue, much used by physicians. So now everyone had to be dressed in crimson, vermillion, sanguine, garnet, carnation, coquelicot ... any shade at all that could claim a close relationship to the colour of healing.

Poor Vitri's torments were dreadful, and not least among them those that were inflicted by the Royal Physicians. For besides that they baked her in flannel, they opened a vein in each of her feet to let out the old, dead blood, dosed her with potions laced with arsenic and grains of gold, covered her with ointments of dung and powdered worms, and every day brought a new treatment, even worse than the day before. But the King suffered, too. He was always beside her when the doctors were treating her, and though he sometimes flinched or cried out at the things that were done, not once did Jesahach turn away, no matter how cruelly it hurt him to watch.

"You will be well, my darling. Just a few days more, my lamb," he crooned, and it was something to see and hear, that cold hard man, so tender, so concerned. He was a widower with no other children (they said that the Queen had died under the burden of his vast contempt, his crushing indifference) and the Princess Vitri was all and everything that he had ever loved.

***

Meanwhile, in Alöepaticum, the city that surrounded the palace on three sides, the plague raged on, and ordinary people were dying by the hundreds. Physicians and healers went from house to house, wearing charms soaked in camphor, tireless in their efforts to save as many as possible, but for all their dedication ... for all their bleeding, purging, blistering ... for all the great tuns of barley water and hydromel that were poured down parched throats ... still,

241

they had only succeeded so far in delaying the inevitable.

The magicians, sages, and astrologers tried their best, too—with no better results. They scratched runes and other magic symbols on the doors of every house the plague had not touched—yet the contagion eventually crept into those places as well. They painted an immense golden pentagram on the stones of the market square. They pored over star charts, consulted tablets made of wax and of stone. There was no counting the number of chickens, pigs, goats, and rabbits that were sacrificed to their divinations, as they searched for the cause of the fever. There had been a similar pest thirty years ago, one that had killed and killed and killed, and then ended by apparently slaying itself, because, even though no effective treatment had ever been found, it had only lasted for three months during the summer, and no cases had been reported or even suspected since. But there was some question whether this was the same disease or not—and besides, no one wanted to wait three months and see.

It was a bad time for wandering beggars and for foreigners generally; people were terrified and they were looking for scapegoats, somewhere to place the blame. A mob set on and killed an old man, for no other reason than because he was seen making mysterious gestures. It later developed that the man was mute, and he had only been making innocent signs with his hands in an effort to communicate.

***

Into this atmosphere of wild-eyed credulity and rabid speculation came a majestic stranger, who entered the gilded gates of the capital in a dark chariot drawn by a team of extraordinary crimson horses. A visiting prince, some thought him, but many were unfavourably impressed by a swarthy complexion, hair that whipped in the wind of his passage like a black flame, and a face that was cruel as well as proud.

Soon the cry began and was just as quickly taken up: *"The Lord of Discord has come! Charun is surely doomed if the Prince of Eternal Night rides through the streets of Alöepaticum."*

But he was not the Lord of Discord, as they soon discovered, when he drove right up to the porch of the College of Magicians, and two white-bearded sages threw wide the iron doors of the College and welcomed him inside. He was a foreign magician named Clyssus, greatest of necromancers, who had arrived to consult with the city mages.

***

It had been the custom in Charun, in ages past, not to bury the dead but rather to expose their bodies in high places, that the birds and the elements might strip them clean. The broad, flat roof of the College of Magicians, with its parapet and its golden tiles, had been one of those places, where the dead were laid out on platforms, between rows of ominous funeral statues. Though the custom had been long since abandoned and bodies were now decently buried under the earth, the bleached bones remained on the roof of the school for magicians, and so did the statues.

For Clyssus the necromancer, whose work was all of death, this aerial cemetery soon became a favourite retreat. When he was not down in the dark burial vaults under the building, he often took solitary walks among the iron angels and bat-winged deities of a vanished religion.

Several days after he arrived in the city, he was strolling there again, this time in company with two ancient sages named Halcyon and Iliaster.

"I had hoped," said Clyssus, "to find Morphea here in Alöepaticum, either in spirit or in body. Yet for all the multitude of unseen presences which seem to inhabit this building and the vaults below, he never comes at my calling."

"He died two days before you arrived here," said Iliaster.

243

The necromancer nodded his understanding. The first twenty-one days after death, a spirit lingered in the Halls of Judgment, and no magician, no matter how mighty, could conjure his shade during that time. Nor could the spirit return of his own will to any familiar place, no matter how fierce his longing to do so.

"We had almost hoped he would live to greet you. Except for the Princess Vitri, Morphea lasted much longer than anyone else. Indeed, many here were deeply moved by how long and how valiantly he fought to live." The sage stopped in the long, misshapen shadow of one of the winged statues. "Now that he is gone, we have abandoned all hope for the Princess."

Clyssus frowned. "To survive so long almost argues a natural immunity. But ... I understood that no one had survived this pest, this plague, when it first came to Charun thirty years ago."

He was something of an enigma to his companions, this Clyssus. A dark man with an even darker calling. Yet at the same time, he was filled with such energy, such intensity, as though, in the midst of death, he had somehow discovered the secret of increased life.

"No one did survive," said Iliaster. "And the pest never spread so far as Alöepaticum, though it took many lives in the smaller towns and villages just to the north. It is certain that Morphea was never infected, and as for the Princess Vitri, she was not born until many years later. But you are assuming that it is the same disease, which is by no means certain."

"I am assuming nothing," said Clyssus. "Yet I keep my mind open to all possibilities."

His restless movements brought him to the parapet. The great city lay stretched before him: Alöepaticum, city of granite, gold, and marble; city of temples, parks, mansions, and palaces ... and of course, city of a thousand wretched hovels, where the poor lived in filth and degradation. But the College of Magicians was located close to the King's palace, and from a high place like this one it was possible to observe the green lawns and the gorgeous formal gardens surrounding the palace. They made a far more pleasing prospect than the homes of poverty.

In a garden of orange trees and red roses, a bird sang sweetly, a girl in a scarlet gown played with a white monkey So *life continues*, thought Clyssus, *even in the midst of death and horror*. Then he gave a bitter laugh at his own expense, for thinking such banalities, and felt a momentary twinge of relief that he had not spoken the platitude out loud.

But the others saw him sneer and they heard him laugh. Not knowing the cause, they wondered what sort of man he was, to look out over the dying city and smile so cruelly.

"Tell us," said Halcyon hesitantly, "what spirits, demons, powers, and images you have already consulted, and which you mean to consult. We continue our own inquiries, and would not wish to duplicate your efforts." Like the bones on the roof, the two old men had been bleached white by the passage of many years, dried out like husks by the hot sun of Charun.

"You cannot duplicate what I do," said Clyssus, with that same dreadful smile. "That is, I no longer seek answers among the lesser imps and jinni. Many of them appear to know *something* but are unwilling or unable to speak. It is as though someone or something even more powerful prevents them. For that reason, I am determined to summon one of the greater powers, a very Prince of Demons, with whom I have had ... profitable dealings in the past."

And he spoke a name that struck at their hearts. It was the same name that Clyssus had heard muttered down in the streets, the one which had heralded his own approach. "It may be He who has forbidden the others to speak. His strength grows tremendously during times of pestilence and natural disaster."

Iliaster and Halcyon exchanged an uneasy glance. "We would not presume to teach you your own business," said Iliaster slowly "But it can be dangerous dealing with the

Lords of Chaos. As you know, once summoned they only depart with great reluctance. And while it is true that they cannot lie to the one who calls them, they are masters of deception, if only through misdirection."

"I know the dangers." Though Clyssus spoke softly, his dark face was eager. "But as you say, they cannot lie. And whether or not I will be misled will depend on what questions I ask."

***

That very same evening, Vitri died. Only the King noticed when she stopped breathing, and he said nothing, stubbornly refusing to acknowledge the truth. But when one of the Royal Physicians came into the room ... when he felt for her pulse and found none, put an ear to her chest and discovered that Vitri's heart, which had grown progressively weaker with every passing day, had finally ceased its wearisome toil ... when he solemnly announced that the Princess was gone ... then at last King Jesahach covered his face with his hands and wept bitterly. Grown surprisingly meek, he even allowed his servants to lead him out of the room and up to his own bedchamber, so that Vitri's women could prepare the body without interference.

Sometime during the process of laying the Princess out, somewhere between the washing and the dressing, somebody noticed that the youngest handmaiden was missing, along with the Princess's monkey. A search of the palace and its grounds followed, beginning with Vitri's private garden, growing increasingly urgent as little Emerald failed to appear.

At last they found the child down in the gardens, wandering in a delirium, and cradling in her arms the rigid body of the beloved monkey. No one had even guessed that the monkey was ill. That one small death sent a cruel shock through the entire court, simply because it was totally unexpected.

As for Emerald, she wept when they pulled the tiny beast out of her arms, and grew so wild and confused in her fevered state, they were forced to tie her down to a bed with silken sashes.

***

In a burial vault under the College of Magicians, a deep chamber lit only by a single brass lamp fuelled by the effluvium of decaying corpses, Clyssus prepared himself for the summoning.

In two days of intense study, he had reviewed every scroll, every tablet that he could find, every scrap of parchment or papyrus, which recorded the progress of the plague this year and thirty years past. From that mass of material he had formed a theory, a theory he meant to put to the test this very night.

By corpse-light, his dark face was solemn but no less arrogant than it had been before. He knew this was a serious, a dangerous business, yet Clyssus considered himself more than equal to the task before him. Was he not widely acknowledged as the greatest of necromancers? A man who had, through years of searching in dark, forgotten places, discovered the secret names of countless demons, jinni, and lesser deities, before whom the spirits of the dead quailed, and whom even the Lords of Chaos treated with a careful, almost punctilious respect?

But perhaps this would be the night when he learned the wages of arrogance, the price of vanity.

With great precision he drew his pentagram on the stone floor, and filled it with many symbols: a star, a triangle, a serpent, a cross, and seven concentric circles, Outside the points of the diagram, he sketched other signs in coloured chalk: an eagle, a man, a bull, a lion, a leopard. He donned a robe of the same coarse white linen that was used in the city for winding sheets, and threw a handful of acacia blossoms onto a smouldering

247

brazier at the center of the pentagram. Then he took up his gold-tipped wand and began his incantation.

There was a faint rattling disturbance among the bones of the dead, a breathless sigh from the rotting corpses, but Clyssus quieted them with a single harsh word spoken aside. Then he continued on with the spell of summoning.

"O Lord of Eternal Night, I call you. By all your many names I exhort you:
He Who Drives His Horses With Whips Of The Tongues of Adders. He Who Scourges His Enemies With Scorpions. Adzrahel. Beelzabaal ..." The list was long, and Clyssus felt his throat grow dry reciting it, his tongue cleave to the roof of his mouth.

The demon came like a whirlwind, he came like the voice of thunder, a presence too vast for the vault to contain. He was in the sepulchre, but he also penetrated the substance of the walls; was simultaneously above and below, within and without. Until Clyssus forced him into the pentagram, and he began to dwindle. Then he passed through a dizzying swift series of transformations—a wraith, a monster with gaping mouth and ivory claws, a victim of the plague—too many and too various for the mind of the man to compass them all. Finally, he took on a form that the necromancer knew well. The image of Clyssus himself.

"What do you require of me, Man of a Thousand Whispering Ambitions? What do you wish to learn of me, O Prince of Vanities?" The demon mocked him with his own smile.

For one brief moment, Clyssus hesitated. Those formless doubts that had threatened earlier now began to clamour in his brain. And yet, to summon the demon and attempt to send him away without first assigning him some task, asking some question, was a thing impossible.

With more confidence than he felt, with his heart leaping in his chest, the necromancer spoke his first question. "Why did Morphea bring the plague to Charun—and for what reason?"

248

The demon began to roar, and the animate hairs of his head flowed like a storm cloud around him. "O Clyssus, Clyssus," howled the Lord of Eternal Night, shaking with unseemly laughter. "That you of all men should ask me that question!"

***

Where black had been banished before, it now reigned supreme: black gowns, black veils, black beads, black gloves. And for Vitri's funeral, three days after her death, some of the women even painted their lips, eyebrows, and nails the same dusky hue as their gowns. But the Princess herself was dressed in white, and they heaped her bier with the pale silvery flowers that she loved best.

As for poor little Emerald, she had been left to die slowly in a remote region of the palace—where she was moved to keep the contagion from spreading—with only a single servant to attend her. The monkey was buried in Vitri's garden, and was slumbering far more peacefully under the earth, down among the roots of the Rose of Charun.

After they buried Vitri, after they burned their incense, made their sacrifices, and observed all the other ceremonies, King Jesahach and his court returned to the palace, where a meal awaited them: great joints soaked in spices, sweetmeats made bitter with vinegar and gall, and a dark purple wine laced with wormwood, which was know throughout Charun as Balm-Of-A-Broken-Heart ... all laid out on long tables between the gilded pillars of the central hall.

The feasting began but was shortly interrupted by an unexpected procession of magicians from the College, who entered the hall in robes of purple and scarlet, and masks of beaten gold. One of the mages unmasked, revealing a tawny face and burning dark eyes.

"By your leave," said the necromancer, bowing low before the King. "I have discovered the source and the cause of the plague."

249

Jesahach said nothing, gave no reaction, sat motionless on his cedarwood throne. Perhaps the drugged wine already dulled his senses; perhaps he was only weary and grief-stricken after his long vigil and the tragic outcome. But everyone else, the entire sable multitude gathered in that pillared hall, clamoured to hear more.

"It is a long story, not simply told," said Clyssus. "Yet I will try to do it justice.

"*Many years ago ...* " (began the necromancer) "*... there was a populous, prosperous kingdom. Indeed, in some ways the land was too fortunate, too prosperous. The cities were becoming overcrowded, and the common folk were breeding at such a tremendous rate that when a bad year came and the crops failed, there was widespread starvation. Now, the King of that country was a clever man, but he was not wise. Faced by this terrible problem, he did not open his vast granaries to feed the poor. His stores would only last them a single season, and if the next year was bad and the year after that ... well, he could easily see how a hundred thousand hungry people might eventually be tempted into mass insurrection. He thought it would be more expedient to reduce the population quickly rather than slowly— more merciful, too. His ideas of mercy and expedience, you will observe, were rather unusual.*

"*So this King went secretly to a magician that he knew, one as ruthless as the King was himself. But whereas the King was clever, wilful, and impatient, this man was curious, subtle, and brilliant. Well he knew his own brilliance, and his vanity was as immense as his knowledge.*

"*Long ago he had gained mastery over the Five Kingdoms of Matter: the material, mineral, vegetable, animal, and the fluid worlds. But in his manipulation of the animal and the vegetable kingdoms he had always excelled. He had already made a number of experiments in crossing species, by uniting the sperm of one with the seed of another: a lion and an eagle to create a griffon, a man and a mandrake to make a homunculus. And he dallied with spontaneous generation, as in the growth of worms out of dung, and grasshoppers and stinging*

250

insects out of the dust of the earth. But in his experiments with plants he had once come close to something that frightened even him, so that he abandoned those experiments for a time. Yet he was an arrogant man, especially proud of those things he had created, and it did not take much urging on the part of the King to make him reconsider. Besides, it suited his ambition, for he hoped in this way to become the King's advisor in all things, and so guide the affairs of Charun as it pleased him. So the mage began his experiments once more, and this time his efforts were rewarded with success.

"The year was dying, moving on toward winter, when the magician prepared to take a journey out of the city. Dressed as a peddler, he visited a number of small towns and villages where the poor and the starving were especially numerous. In each place that he stopped, the mage left something behind: a large brown seed with a prickly exterior, which he planted in secret near the village well or fountain.

"During the winter, the seed germinated and sent down roots, which quickly tapped into the waters below. When spring arrived, the people were surprised to discover a remarkable shoot growing in the centre of their village. For scarcely a month had passed before the shoot became a sapling, a sapling that rapidly turned to a budding tree shading their well. And when the buds opened, and the tree was decked in iron-coloured flowers, the sap began to run, infusing the Basilisk Tree (for so the magician had named it) and the waters that nourished the tree with a subtle poison which produced in its victims a sickness closely resembling the symptoms of plague."

The hall was very quiet while Clyssus spoke, everyone straining to hear what he said. Except for the King, who sat with his head down, while the colour came and went in his face as the blood beat under his skin, and his eyes were unnaturally bright. Every now and again, he moved his lips, as though he knew the story and was reciting it silently, along with the necromancer.

"This scheme was immensely successful ... " (Clyssus continued) " ... In fact, so many died during the summer that

251

followed, that the two conspirators became a little frightened. They decided to eradicate the menace as quickly as possible, before the trees could bear fruit and scatter the seeds, A King without subjects, they reasoned, is no King at all. And besides ... once the wind took the seeds it was impossible to predict who might die.

"So they sent men out secretly to every town where the Basilisk Trees were growing, to uproot the trees and to burn them at once. But one of these men met with an accident along the way, was injured, and was forced to recuperate several weeks in another village. Because the King and the magician had not trusted these agents with the truth, this man did not understand the urgency of his errand—so it never occurred to him that he ought to send somebody else on in his place.

"When he was finally able to travel, and when he arrived at his destination, he almost began to suspect the truth, because the village was empty, empty except for deserted houses, recent graves, and rotting corpses. But he pushed the idea back into some hidden corner of his mind, rather than confront the enormity of the King's wickedness. Relieved there was no one there to report his tardiness, he pulled up the tree and burned it roots, branches, leaves, and all, until nothing was left but silvery ashes.

"But something terrible had happened while he lay injured in that other village. The tree had produced a single fruit, and that fruit had burst open, flinging its seeds far and wide. It was fortunate, then, that the following year was a dry one, for most of the seeds fell on barren ground, where they baked in the heat of the sun and so died. But a single seed was carried far by the wind and it fell to earth, as fate would have it, in a shaded, untended portion of a small private orchard and garden, in the palace of the King.

"Many years passed. The seed, lying there in the cool, dry shade, neither died nor germinated, until a gardener came one spring and turned over the earth. Beneath the soil, the seed found just enough moisture to live and to grow. It never flourished there in the shade, so that instead of growing into a tree it was only a small shrub, nor did it blossom for many more years. Yet it was able to send its roots down and out, in a vast complex network, which eventually penetrated an underground spring that fed many of the wells and fountains in the city where the King and his daughter lived.

"Then came a year when the shrub was heavy with blossoms, though not the same startling, iron-coloured flowers of its hardier forebearers. These blossoms were delicate and silvery pale ... so beautiful, indeed, that the Princess when she first saw them was utterly enchanted. She made garlands of the flowers and wore them, carried sprays of the blossoms into the palace and kept them in vases.

"And when the sap began to run, when the shrub poisoned the waters of the city, when hundreds fell sick and began to die, the love that the Princess bore those silvery blossoms very nearly saved her life—as it may have saved her youngest handmaiden, as it almost saved her pet. From handling those flowers with their milder poison, the two young girls and the monkey had gained some slight immunity to the more powerful toxin that permeated the water. But the well-meaning efforts of the Royal Physicians, as they dosed her with herbs that were steeped in the poison, as they sweated her and bathed her in the deadly water, were eventually too much for the Princess. Like the magician Morphea she had lingered on, only to endure that much more suffering before death finally claimed her."

When the necromancer stopped speaking, Jesahach sat silent for a long time, with the hectic colour still in his face, and his shoulders bowed. When he finally spoke, his voice shook—though with anger or grief no one could tell.

"It makes an interesting fable, this story of yours. But tell me: How does it end? Did the King repent? Did he not have the Rose of— Did he not have the Basilisk Tree uprooted and burned, as soon as he knew it was growing there in his daughter's garden?"

"If he tried," said Clyssus sternly, "he accomplished nothing by it. The roots had gone so deep and spread so widely, it would have been impossible to dig every one of them up, not if he razed the palace and the entire city

253

surrounding it. And while the roots remained, the danger was not past, for the life of the tree continued, and any single root burrowing up to the surface might send out a shoot at any time, in a place where no one might find it."

Jesahach sighed deeply "Then this King that you speak of ... surely he commanded his gardeners to water the tree with the venom of adders, that it might eventually wither and die, right down to the roots."

"If he did," said Clyssus, dark and implacable, "that was the worst of all. The essence of the Basilisk Tree is poison, and venom could only nourish it. The tree would have thrived and the two poisons married, to make something more deadly, ten times more malignant."

Jesahach covered his eyes, and a tremor passed over him. "Was there nothing the King could do, then ... but watch his subjects die?" he whispered hoarsely.

"There was something," said Clyssus. "Something he alone might do, though it cost him everything." And he stepped forward, with a rustle of silken robes, and whispered something in Jesahach's ear. As he spoke, those who were watching saw the King's face grow progressively harder, paler, colder.

They saw that the magician had failed in his eloquence. There would be no repentance; there would be no cure. Even if they rushed from the hall and uprooted the tree, the pestilence would continue unchecked until the end of the summer. And even after it had run its course, there would remain the terrible knowledge that someday ... the next year, or the year after, or the year after that, a new shoot would push its way to the surface and the horror would all be repeated. Those who had wealth enough to leave Charun and begin again elsewhere would do so, while the poor would remain and wait for death. At last, Charun and the great city of Alöepaticum would be reduced to nothing more than a vast graveyard filled with decaying corpses.

But in the morning, the King was missing from his bedchamber. And those who went looking to find him eventually discovered his body, hanging by the neck from the branch of an orange tree in Vitri's garden. There was a wax tablet lying in the grass below his dangling feet, a letter addressed to Clyssus. The message was brief: *You will know what to do.*

And indeed, the necromancer did know: With the other magicians, he carried Jesahach's body off to the college, and there they worked many wonders. First, they drained off his blood and stored it in bottles made of stone. Of Jesahach's hair they wove strong ropes, and his bones they carved into curious shapes, which combined, made charms to hang on the doors of all the houses where the plague had entered. His skin they tanned and made into parchment, on which the doctors of the city wrote spells of healing. His internal organs, along with what remained of his flesh after they had finished rendering it, were burned to ashes, and the fat and the ashes they made into ointments to soothe the afflicted. As for those bottles of blood, Clyssus and Halcyon took them to the palace, after all these other things had been accomplished, and poured them out at the base of the Basilisk Tree. When the magicians were finished, there was not one bit of flesh, not one piece of bone, nail, or hair, not one drop of blood belonging to the King that had not been given for the good of his people.

And the small stunted tree with the silvery blossoms withered and died, right down to the very tips of its myriad roots ... the waters of Alöepaticum turned sweet and wholesome once more ... and those like Emerald, who lay at the brink of death, sighed and grew still, then sank into a deep, healing sleep.

Death Won't Be Cheated

Tales From Beyond the Veil

Coming Soon from Tickety Boo

Lightning Source UK Ltd.
Milton Keynes UK
UKOW04f0050221114

241996UK00001B/35/P